A
HABIT *FOR*
DEATH

FORTHCOMING BY CHUCK ZITO

Ice in His Veins

A NICKY D'AMICO MYSTERY

A
HABIT FOR
DEATH

CHUCK ZITO

MIDNIGHT INK
WOODBURY, MINNESOTA

First Edition
First Printing, 2006

Book design by Donna Burch
Cover design by Kevin R. Brown
Cover painting © 2005 by Larry Schwinger / Artworks

Midnight Ink, an imprint of Llewellyn Publications

Library of Congress Cataloging-in-Publication Data
Zito, Chuck.
    A habit for death : A Nicky D'Amico mystery / Chuck Zito.— 1st ed.
        p. cm.
    ISBN-13: 978-0-7387-0836-2
    ISBN-10: 0-7387-0836-4
    I. Title.

PS3626.I86H33 2006
813'.6--dc22   2005057684

Midnight Ink
Llewellyn Publications
2143 Wooddale Drive, Dept. 0-7387-0836-4
Woodbury, MN 55125-2989, U.S.A.
www.midnightinkbooks.com

Printed in the United States of America

For my father, Tony Zito

In memory of my mother, Joanne Zito

A
HABIT *FOR*
DEATH

THE CAST
(in order of appearance)

Nicky D'Amico .... Stage Manager for *Convent of Fear*

Benjamin (Benny) Singleton .... Artistic Director of St. Gilbert's
Summer Music Theater Festival

Patsy Malone......................... Assistant Stage Manager

Olivia Singleton............................. Chorus Member

Edward Rosoff............................... Musical Director

Sister Mary Corinne .... Wig Mistress

Joe Sobieski Jr. .... Actor, playing a police lieutenant

Marty Friedman .... Prop Master

Sister Sally .... Actress, playing Sister Klarissa

David Scott................................. Chorus Member

Stanley Sobieski .... Chief of Campus Security

Mary Frances Roberts .... Actress, playing Sister Klarissa

Ilana Mosca .... Costume Designer

Corporal Wallace Roberts ...... Pennsylvania State Police Corporal

Paolo Suarez .... A friend of Nicky, partner of Roger Parker

Roger Parker .... A friend of Nicky, partner of Paolo Suarez

Lee Dexter....................................... Set Designer

Harry Ott .... Security Guard

Phyllis East .... Reporter

Oscar Brocket .... Director of Public Relations for
St. Gilbert's College

Patricia Madison . . . . Legal Counsel for St. Gilbert's College

Rebecca Tipton . . . . Light Designer

Sister Grace . . . . President of St. Gilbert's College

Evelyn Dexter . . . . Wife of Lee Dexter

Members of the cast of *Convent of Fear*, police officers, members of the Friends of Decency and various nuns.

The action takes place in and around St. Gilbert's College in the town of Huber's Landing, Pennsylvania.

A Habit for Death is best read without intermission. Failing that, the author recommends taking it to the beach.

Please turn off your cell phones, pagers, and other electronic devices. The taking of pictures and the making of video or sound recordings is strictly prohibited.

Any resemblance of plot or character to anyone the author may have ever worked with is coincidence and due solely to the general benign insanity that infects all theaters, real and imaginary.

ONE

In the dormitory young Sister Klarissa glides from bed to bed. She tucks in a sheet and gathers in the arm of a child. She touches a forehead with a gentle stroke as she makes her way to the door, orphan by orphan. All the while she sings softly of love and devotion.

Across her face her decision is easily read: she knows her choice to leave is the right choice. She will miss the faces of the twelve innocents before her, but the decision is made. Her song soars into a rhapsody of unrestrained joy. As the last note dies in the still night, she reaches out to turn on the night light.

From the doorway she takes one last look along the row of sleeping children. She counts twelve little heads resting quietly on twelve little pillows; a nice, round, apostolic number. Each child snug under clean sheets and wool blankets, moonlight bathing their unlined brows.

There is a noise. A quiet rustle of a breath. She isn't certain what it is, but it is so close to her right ear, sending a shiver along her back. She gathers her black robe to her, hands straying unconsciously to finger the cross at the end of the plain wooden rosary that hangs about her slender waist.

She strains to hear the sound again, but nothing reaches her save the gentle breathing of the orphans.

Once again she reaches for the night light. Once again there is a sound to her right. She turns to face it. A shadow falls across her vision. The blow that knocks her to the ground is followed by a second and a third, leaving her senseless and dying on the dormitory floor.

Silence.

Except for the giggles coming from the orphan in bed six.

"All right. Stop. Hold it. What is going on up there?" The artistic director of St. Gilbert's Summer Theater Festival waddled his hefty self up the auditorium aisle to the edge of the stage. "You, in bed number six. Why are you laughing?"

Benjamin Singleton—Benny—oversaw the artistic operations of St. Gilbert's. He was also directing the season's opening musical. If artistic achievement is ten percent inspiration and ninety percent perspiration, Benny Singleton should have been well on the way to a smash hit. Despite the overworked air conditioning of the auditorium, he was soaked in summer humidity. He wore full, baggy commando-green rehearsal pants, sandals, and a light white cotton shirt. Still his clothing was plastered on wet. The bald spot in the center of his thinning blonde hair glinted with sweat.

"I don't know," answered the voice of an eight-year-old. Confronted with Benny Singleton's anger, laughter fast gave way to childhood terror.

"Shouldn't we do something?" That was my assistant, Patsy Malone, an aggressively competent college freshman with an unrelenting sense of duty.

"Like what? Personally, I'm rooting for the children," I said.

In fact, I was rooting for peace and quiet. It was Monday evening of the final days of rehearsals. We were almost exactly one week away from our first audience. Even though it would be a small first-preview house, an audience is an audience. They stand like a brick wall in front of you. If you smack into them without the right preparation, you get splattered. On the other hand, plan well, rehearse hard, and you can usually get through the first encounter without too many bruises. I was planning hard.

Unfortunately, the artistic director was not rehearsing so well. We'd scheduled the first technical run-through for Thursday. After four weeks of desultory rehearsal, the cast would meet the scenery and props for the first time. The light and set designers would argue with each other about whether or not anyone had ever mentioned that special green light. "Did you mean to make her look so *ill,* darling?" The costumes would produce their own private hell at another time.

"What do you suggest, Patsy?" I asked. "Shall I have him committed or just shoot him now?"

Patsy Malone thought about it for a moment. She hadn't been quite sure what to say to me since I arrived at her small college's summer theater program. All energy and enthusiasm wrapped up in five feet three inches of budding dykedom, she was immediately suspicious of my casual attitude. Patsy was far from casual. She ironed her T-shirts and covered them with vests. I'd won her over by our second week, when she realized that no matter what information she wanted to pass on to me, I already had a corresponding note on my pad. I was born with a stage manager's memory for detail. I knew where every prop went, when it moved, and who moved it. Impressed by my work, my assistant forgave my detachment.

"Shoot him, Nicky," Patsy said.

"Oh my God, you've made a joke at Benny's expense. I'm a bad influence, aren't I, Patsy? Go ahead, break it to me gently."

"I think he's going to hit that kid," she said.

Down front, Benny was shaking his fist at orphan number six.

I stood and stretched. "Everyone take ten," I announced.

I'm not a particularly tall man. The truth is, two-thirds of all the men I meet are taller than me, but sitting cramped into an auditorium seat at a plywood table will take its toll on anyone. Like any other self-respecting young New York City theater professional, I regularly attended the gym, though I wasn't exactly obsessed about it. Most of my efforts went into the treadmill or StairMaster. I wasn't setting any records for muscle mass, but I was fit. In the aisle I bent over, grabbed my toes, and stretched out my back, feeling my lumbars snap into place. At the rate my muscles were knotting, I'd be lucky to be walking by the week's end.

Singleton ordered the children out of their beds and into a line along the edge of the stage.

While the director and his child actors hashed out why it was important not to giggle while the young nun was being murdered, I contemplated taking a break myself. This wasn't an Equity production. There weren't any rules on break time. In fact, at St. Gilbert's Summer Theater Festival there seemed to be few, if any, of the normal procedures that operate in theaters. Certainly nothing was going to happen for at least the next ten minutes. Then again, watching Benny point his fist at orphan number six, I decided that it was probably immoral to leave him alone with a chorus of children. Instead of heading for an exit and leaving my assistant to watch the slaughter of the innocents, I strolled down to the front of the auditorium. Benny was not-so-patiently explaining some of the finer points of professionalism to his confused chorus, the average age of which was seven and one-half.

Olivia Singleton, the director's daughter, small in stature but, at twelve, older than the other children in the chorus, was not interested in any lecture.

"But Daddy, it's funny when she dies 'cause everyone can see she must have heard him coming. She'd have to be pretty stupid to get killed like that." Olivia unintentionally echoed one of the harsher criticisms leveled at *Convent of Fear* during its painfully brief Broadway run in the 1960s. "Pretty stupid" would just about sum up the general response.

Olivia was not a large child, but she had vocal power to spare under all that curly blonde hair and blue-eyed innocence. A precocious child, her adoration of Daddy was apparent in her miniaturized version of Benny's rehearsal outfit, complete with her own sandals, baggy green cotton pants, and white shirt. She was equally unrestrained in her dislike of his direction.

"She dies that way because that is the way I staged it, and that is the way it is going to be done," Benny said. "And I will not argue this with you, young lady. Now be a good helper and let's get back to work."

"But Daddy, everyone is going to laugh."

Benny turned away from his daughter in an effort to dismiss the entire affair.

"Olivia," I said, sensing that her father turning his back was not going to stop her, "would you please take the other children through their steps for the 'Bedtime Ballet'?"

"You're just trying to shut me up," she said.

"Of course I am. That's my job. Anyway, you like being dance captain, don't you?" I smiled sweetly at the child demon.

She considered my suggestion. I presented the opposite problem from Daddy: I could see she didn't like me, but she did love the way I worked.

"OK. But I don't like it. It's a stupid way to die. I'm sure Daddy will fix it."

I often wondered at the home life these two shared.

She led the children center stage and began the cloying circle dance that broke the dormitory scene in half, stopping the action dead. For that, and other theatrical atrocities, I planned to read *Anna Karenina* through most of the performances. If I was going to spend the summer hearing about broken vows, I preferred a grander treatment.

"Well, I'm glad that is settled. Olivia is usually such a sweet child. Perhaps now she'll behave herself," Benny said, snatching the illusion of victory from the reality of defeat. Father and daughter were dancing a duet of mutually misdirected praise. He turned and waddled back to his seat, casually commanding me to "Organize whatever is coming up next."

At first, it had seemed like a good idea: June, July, and August outside Manhattan in the clean air of the beautiful, tree-filled, sun-drenched western Pennsylvania countryside. There would only be three shows, the first and last musicals. I wanted a chance not to swelter in the August humidity of New York City, an escape from the grinding pace of making a living to pay for my tiny studio in the West Fifties. The trip was made more appealing by the idea of subletting my apartment at a small profit and paying off some back rent. And, yes, there was the question of getting away from a failed romance—the kind of affair where you know it's over but you still walk by his favorite restaurant or "unexpectedly" find yourself in front of his building. We'd met just before Thanksgiving. From November to April we passed quickly through infatuation (mutual) to infidelity (his) and on to inanity (mine). When I'd started thinking about trailing him at night as he went out for a drink, I knew I needed to get out of town. What can I say? I was still trying to master the dating thing. In the end, western Pennsylvania seemed barely far enough away.

St. Gilbert's College sat in the middle of Appalachian coal country, part of the town of Huber's Landing. Huber, whoever he was, was long gone, and so were the coal mines. The countryside was left to tiny farms and small towns that once thrived near industrial activity but now sat with indifference in the middle of a mountain range covered in pines, small creeks, and mid-sized lakes. St. Gilbert's itself was a private school with a student body of two thousand from which no one famous had ever graduated and no one infamous had ever dropped out. Its buildings, all red brick and vines, were a little gone to seed. It had no claim to fame, unless you counted the magnificent scenery.

That scenery was the only part of my ideal summer that didn't disappoint me. I learned one of those lessons they can't teach you at a theater conservatory: when someone promises you fulfillment, cash, and free time, run away fast.

Benny Singleton turned out to be an autocratic six-year-old disguised as a middle-aged man. It was a discouraging sight watching him hack his way through a play day after day.

That the play should be *Convent of Fear*, a musical thriller about a serial nun killer, only added to my disappointment.

The convent in question runs a school for orphan boys. Enemies plague the convent with trouble. A local developer wants the land. The church diocese, tired of losing money, wants to shut them down. It goes on from there, but the real fun starts with the murder of a young nun. There are singing police, frightened children, and dancing suspects. More nuns are murdered and more music slaughtered. In the end the murderer turns out to be the groundskeeper, whose only child drowned while on an outing from the school orphanage forty-five years earlier. How does a child with a father end up in an orphanage? Think amnesia. Think how you'd rather be watching a good movie.

The scene that orphan number six interrupted was the killing of young Sister Klarissa, love interest of the policeman. She had just finished singing about leaving the convent for her "true love." In the previous scene her true love had sung the show-stopping tune "Gonna Make a Habit of You." Does it matter that the Mother Superior is on the take?

As Benny retreated from his skirmish with Olivia, the musical director, a principal actor, and the prop master approached me simultaneously. I've never lost my childhood faith in first-come first-served, so I started with the musical director.

While actors at least have to give lip service to sharing the stage with someone else, musical directors often mistake themselves for God. Edward Rossoff was so confused he conducted everything around him. The best way to hold a conversation with Edward was at a distance safely out of reach of his extended hand gestures.

"I need more time in this schedule," he said. He waved one hand and poked with the other. "You have to get me more time. They all sound like shit. Like shit." Edward had a way with language completely at odds with his appearance: a man neatly attired in a dark suit and thick glasses, mostly bald and pushing sixty. He punctuated each "shit" with an ominous downbeat of his left hand. "I need time now. Today."

"Edward, I don't make the schedule," I said. "That's Benny's job. I just execute it."

"Well, you can just execute this music, because this schedule is shit. And that fat twit wouldn't know the difference." Edward was waving both hands in four-four time.

"Maybe you should ask him—"

A sudden cut. "You are not serious, are you, young man? Of course you are, you have never been in this pit of hell before. This shitting waste of space. Benny Singleton"—and here Edward raised his voice and both arms to crescendo—"wouldn't know how to schedule a six a.m. wake-up call. Well, I am not letting him embarrass me again. Bad enough I have to suffer with this shit of a score. I will not—do you hear me, Singleton?—I will not be embarrassed again. I will expect a new schedule by tomorrow. *Shit.*"

Edward turned on his heel and strode across the front of the house to the piano on the far side. This put him far away from me and far away from Benny Singleton, who was deeply involved in counting the number of pieces of fuzz on the seat in front of him. I guess he wasn't interested in sharing any rehearsal time today.

There was an audible sigh behind me. It came from Sister Mary Corinne, a nun who spent a lot of her free time watching rehearsals. Sister Mary Corinne was Edward's age. She had the harsh look that sometimes develops from too many years of self-effacement in the service of too many good causes. Her hair was gray and pulled back, framing a pair of wire-rimmed glasses that accentuated her sharp blue eyes. Like all the nuns of her order, she no longer wore a habit, but that didn't mean she looked relaxed in jeans and a white blouse.

"He really is a nice man." I assume she said it for my benefit. Despite her severe angular appearance, she was obviously not without some charitable views toward humanity. Edward Rossoff was an excellent musical director, but I was definitely immune to his personal charms.

"I'm sure he is, Sister," I said.

"Nicholas, it's bad luck to lie to a nun," she said without any trace of humor in her voice.

I turned to the next person in line. Joe Sobieski Jr. played the young cop who falls in love with Klarissa. He was a few years younger than me and looked even younger. He had the dark-hair, pale-eyes combination that dominated that part of the country. I might have considered him cute—I do like dark hair and pale eyes—but even when he was trying to be pleasant, Joe couldn't keep his entire face from frowning, eyebrows and mouth drooping downward into a scowl. As usual he was wearing nothing but dark clothing. For Joe the year was always 1984 and the location was always the Lower East Side. A year he no more than vaguely remembered, a location he'd never been.

"Will we get to my scene tonight?" he asked. "If we start over with these kids, I'm never going to get onstage." Joe put an emphasis on "kids" that turned it into a true four-letter word. He switched to a tone that hinted at his busy life outside the theater. "I just don't want to hang out here all night for no reason."

Now, I may, at times, be cranky and difficult, but when it comes to children, I figure seven-year-olds at least have an excuse to behave like seven-year-olds. With adults I am often not so patient. Nonetheless, I assured him that we weren't wasting his time and that we would be in serious need of him at any moment. Confidently assuring actors that time was not being wasted is one of the first tasks any good stage manager learns.

My internal clock was ticking urgently now, telling me that I needed to end this break. I took the prop master, Marty Friedman, by the arm and started toward my table.

"Walk and talk, Marty," I said, gently guiding him along the aisle. "What can I do for you?"

"I need petty cash."

That was another peculiarity of St. Gilbert's. Normally, as stage manager, I would be getting my petty cash supply for those handy incidentals—pens, paper, coffee, the occasional new novel for personal entertainment (yes, that could technically be considered stealing, but you take your perks where you can)—from the company manager just like everyone else. Or maybe the business manager. But at St. Gilbert's there was no business manager or company manager. So I dispensed cash and collected receipts and tried to keep an accurate count, though math was never my specialty.

"Receipts?" I asked.

"I don't have them on me, but I have to go shopping first thing tomorrow morning. I'm running out of time."

Marty Friedman was nervous. The type of guy whose first thought when the alarm goes off in the morning is "Oh my God, what's wrong now?" Marty was a former St. Gilbert's student who still returned summers to play at theater. In the off-season he taught high school English to children who are learning disabled. I have no idea how he ever managed to get through a day of such potentially anxiety-producing work. The oddest part of the entire package was his size. Marty Friedman was six feet three inches tall and nearly two hundred pounds. I literally looked up to him, always asking myself, "What could make this man so nervous?"

"Marty, you know I need receipts. Receipts in, cash out."

"I know, I know, Nicky. But I left all my paperwork at home. I've got to shop. We tech in three days and I'm not finished buying. And then I have to paint stuff. And then it has to dry, and the weather is way too humid, and you know how that is on paint. It will all dry tacky and have to be redone. I don't have time."

I had a choice. Lay out cash or listen to him for another five minutes.

"How much?" I asked.

"Another hundred."

That was twenty dollars a minute for the whining.

"OK, tell you what. Take a seat, and once this break is over we'll go to my office and do the cash."

"Oh, great. That's great. Thanks, Nicky. Really. Thanks."

The thank-yous alone could take yet another five minutes. I waved him away toward a back row.

It was time to start again. I chased two orphans from under my work table, where they were busy playing cavemen. The rest of the cast was scattered around the auditorium and stage. For a few seconds everything was peaceful. Then I noticed a bundle of black cloth heaped on stage left. I looked at it for several seconds to see if it would move. It didn't. I asked it to.

"Ah, Sister Sally. Sister? I think you can get up now."

For a moment there was no response. I was just beginning to think something was wrong when the bundle of cloth slowly unrolled itself into the shape of the young nun so recently bludgeoned to death in the orphans' dormitory.

"Oh, I knew we were done. I knew we were on break," she said. "I was just trying to get into character as a dead person. After all, I'm going to have to lie there for a long time." Sister Sally stood up and brushed dirt off her habit. Like all the nuns at the college, she'd abandoned the traditional black habit as everyday wear. The robes she was dressed in were actually produced by the St. Gilbert's costume shop.

"I am sorry that I got this nice new costume dirty, but the costume people wanted me to start working with it tonight. You know, we don't wear these things anymore. Anyway," she said, "I have to confess, I'm not feeling all that well. But I think resting there for a while helped."

In one of the few theatrically interesting twists of the summer, Benny convinced several nuns from the St. Gilbert's convent to perform as nuns in *Convent of Fear*. Not all the nuns of St. Gilbert's approved of the production, but the college administration thought the production would help liberalize the institution's image and increase its success rate at recruiting new students.

Sister Sally was one of the nuns who approved. She played young Sister Klarissa. Every theater group attached to a Catholic school has one nun like Sister Sally: young, energetic, perky-perky-perky. Sally genuinely loved the theater. She had a laugh like the sound of a helium balloon losing gas.

"I'm sorry you're not well, Sister," I said. "Do you need anything?"

"No. No. I'll be just fine. I believe in a positive attitude. Don't you?" All the while she was fingering the wooden cross at the end of the rosary that hung from her waist.

"Absolutely," I said. "Now remember, all you need to do is lie there. You don't really have to do any acting to play dead." Anything to cut down on the melodrama.

"Oh, I knew that too." Sister Sally laughed.

I winced.

"I just wanted to make my time in the theater as interesting as possible," she said. "I don't believe in wasting any of life's moments. Do you?" She laughed again. Very loudly.

I knew just where to start rehearsal.

"OK, everyone. Back onstage. Let's kill the nun one more time."

Once rehearsal was under way, the prop master and I headed for my office at the back of the house. I left Patsy to "sit book." This involved using the prompt book to cue the actors onstage if they should forget what to say or do next.

We were halfway up the aisle when *he* entered the auditorium. I know it's just begging for trouble for a stage manager to get involved with a cast member, but he was beautiful: about three inches taller than me, dark brown hair, light blue eyes, and muscles with just enough body fat to cushion them to the touch. He had a long torso but was wearing denim shorts slung low on his hips and ending just below the knees, which balanced him perfectly. A tight T-shirt clung to a V-shaped upper body that swept up from his waist with a natural, non-gymed, toned definition. His face and arms were smooth, suggesting only the lightest scattering of body hair. I am a big fan of the diversity of human genetics that can produce so beautiful a man. David Scott, member of the chorus and genetic delight, was the textbook answer to my broken heart. OK, maybe just a bandage on my wounded pride. All right, so it was lust. At least it seemed mutual.

Our eyes locked onto each other's with a decidedly reciprocal interest, anticipating smiles, nods, brushing lips, and late-night rendezvous. My imagination leapt several hours ahead to see the two of us sitting on a picnic table under a sliver of a moon and a field of stars. The sound of the lake lapping against outgrown tree roots mingled with violin music. We'd kiss, and then, as the score rumbled an incessant bass, we'd slowly lean back along the length of the table, the sweet, fresh, clean country air mingling with the now-raging scent of our bodies. And we'd scream and scream . . .

Scream?

Someone was screaming onstage.

I looked across the theater house to see the children's chorus huddled stage left. They encircled an object on the floor. The range of possible accidents in a working theater is strikingly large, from twisting ankles to being impaled with an unsafe prop to standing in the wrong place when something drops from the overhead light grid. As I checked for smoke or flames (neither was present), two kids fainted. Definitely an accident and definitely beyond the level of a twisted ankle.

I beat Benny and Sister Mary Corinne, but not Edward or Patsy, to the orphans. In the middle of their circle lay Sister Sally. Actually, she was doing just about everything but lying there. She was twitching, gasping for air, her arms flailing about uncontrollably. As she

14

thrashed, her black robes sponged up dust from the stage floor, giving her an ever-graying cast. Saliva dribbled from her mouth. She was moaning inarticulate spasms of pain.

Someone shouted, "Hold her down!" Then everyone rushed forward, trying to get a helping hand on Sally. More likely they were going to crush her than aid her. Holding a person down was one of the myths of seizure treatment. That and putting something between the teeth caused as much harm as anything else. Trying to prevent injury, I started prying people loose.

"Get back. Everyone just move back. Let's get something under her head to cushion it. Please, stay back." I was tugging at arms all the while I spoke. "Patsy, get the children to the other side of the stage, please."

With some effort we cleared a space around the nun. The seizure continued.

"Does anyone know if she's epileptic?" I asked.

"I've never heard her speak of it," Mary Corinne said. "Does she have a medical tag on?"

Good question, but difficult to answer just then.

The remaining adults—Marty, Joe, Benny, Edward, and Sister Mary Corinne—were still crowding in.

"Please stand back," I said. "Just move away anything that might hurt her if she hit it."

"Maybe we should put something in her mouth?" asked Marty.

"Asshole, that's exactly what you don't do for a seizure," Joe Sobieski said. I was gratified to know I wasn't the only one who knew what to do.

"Yes, it is," Marty said.

Patsy joined the debate. "Are you sure? I thought I read you shouldn't."

Olivia Singleton broke through the circle of adults. She rushed at Sister Sally, throwing herself on top of the prone figure. Sally bucked reflexively as Olivia clutched at her.

"Sally. No. Please," the child sobbed, burying her face and hands in the nun's habit.

"Olivia, honey." Benny stepped forward and gently pried his daughter free. He guided her across the stage, away from the rest of us.

"Is she going to die, Daddy?" Olivia asked.

He crouched down to speak to her. "Everything is going to be OK, Olivia." The other children gathered round.

"I don't think this is epileptic," Mary Corinne said. She was kneeling beside Sister Sally, whose moans were quieting. The thrashing slowed, but now more liquid was pouring out of her mouth. I agreed with her.

"Patsy . . . ," I said.

"911. Got it." She ran to the backstage phone.

"Sally? Can you hear me, Sally?" Mary Corinne bent over her prostrate friend, gently trying to wake her. "She's unconscious. But I think she's still breathing."

We waited in silence for the ambulance.

"I was in the emergency room last year. I saw something really disgusting. There was this woman who had a huge sore on her leg. It was red, and there was yellow stuff oozing out of it. And it was swollen so big that when they moved her, a nurse had to hold the lump. I bet she got tested for drugs. I got tested for drugs." Olivia was speaking to an enthralled children's chorus in the first row of the house.

One incredulous orphan spoke up. "Did not."

"Did too. They test everyone who comes into the emergency room."

Unfortunately, you just can't tell a group of preadolescents that rehearsal is done, go home. They need drivers. Patsy was working the phone in our office, trying to round up parents. I was sitting at my table in the middle of the auditorium, Benny on one side and Edward on the other. We were trying to decide what to rehearse next. Olivia, some fifteen rows away, was far more interesting.

"Well, we sure as shit cannot do her duet with Joe now, can we?" Edward said.

"No. That would be out," I said, trying to stay out of the range of his right hook.

"Who comes in next, and when?" Benny asked.

"I bet they cut her entire leg off," I heard Olivia say. There was an appreciative murmuring from the chorus.

"At eight-thirty the other nuns are due to rehearse the tea scene. That gives us forty-five minutes," I said.

"If my leg got cut off, I would want to keep it in a big plastic bag," Olivia was saying.

"Do you ever worry about the shitty emotional health of your child, Singleton?" Edward asked, not concerned if Olivia heard him. "Doesn't it bother you that one moment she's crying hysterically and the next she's . . . she's . . ." He jabbed his left hand toward the children.

"Children deal with things differently than you and I," Benny answered.

"Everyone deals with things differently than you," Edward snapped back at him.

Benny ignored him. "We can do the tea scene without Sister Sally. Patsy can read her lines."

"Or maybe make a backpack out of the leg," Olivia said. "That would be cool."

The task was to get as much work done without the nun as we possibly could. We didn't know the severity of Sally's medical problem, but if she was too ill to continue, we would have to replace her quickly. For that we needed the rest of the cast to be completely up to speed. There was no understudy waiting to go on. At St. Gilbert's all the actors were volunteers. They were giving up their evenings and weekends for the enjoyment of performing. They were, for the most part, a good-hearted and dedicated group, but you could only ask so much. To have requested one of them to spend time preparing for a role they might never play was definitely too much. No one brought up the possibility of replacing Sally.

"I read a mystery once about a guy who kidnapped women so he could skin them and make clothes out of them. It would be just like that with the backpack." Olivia's entranced audience oohed appreciatively. The child had stage presence. Too bad she was too young to replace Sally.

"And after the tea scene?" Benny asked. He was clearly inured to his daughter's outrageous fascinations.

"You were going to one-on-one with the gardener," I said.

"We can still do that. Patsy?" Benny looked past me to the house left aisle, where my assistant stood, staring at us with tear-filled eyes.

"Patsy," I said. "What is it?"

"Oh," she said. "Oh God. Oh Christ. She's dead. She's dead."

I walked to her, placing my hands on her shoulders and looking her straight in the eye.

"Look at me," I said. "Take a breath. That's right. Now, tell me what's happened."

"Mary Corinne just called," Patsy said. "Sister Sally died in the ER."

"And the best part is," Olivia concluded, "with a backpack of skin, nobody would ever take your stuff, because nobody would ever want to touch the bag."

TWO

I FELT MORE THAN a hint of guilt. I knew that my less-than-charitable thoughts about Sister Sally had nothing to do with her death, but I was appalled that I had more sympathy for a dead nun than a live one.

We canceled rehearsal for the remainder of the evening. Benny informed the parents who came to pick up their children of the "unfortunate incident." Ditto the actresses who showed up to rehearse at eight-thirty. We told everyone we would call them the next day to let them know what was to be done.

I was in my office, a generous term for what was, for most of the year, a storage room for old theater records and discarded props. Each summer, it was aired out for stage management to use. The cinder block walls were gray. The furniture—recycled scenery—was an assortment of chairs, file cabinets, and shelves that had seen about two decades too much use. The windowless room looked dreary on a good day. Today was not a good day.

Benny Singleton sat alone in a formerly overstuffed armchair. Marty Friedman and Joe Sobieski were pressed together on a small faux leather love seat. Olivia Singleton, who tagged along mostly because none of the adults thought to stop her, sat on the floor, her back to a bookcase containing boxes of rehearsal props, old scripts, office supplies, and a first aid kit. Edward Rossoff leaned against a battered filing cabinet. I sat at the desk, an overcrowded workspace given over mostly to an aging PC. Patsy sat next to me. Benny broke the silence. Sweating more than ever, his ashen look actually complemented the pea-green fabric of the chair.

"We need to rehearse someone to take the role," the director said. "Nicky, you are going to have to move fast. Bring someone up to speed by tomorrow evening. Use that girl, Mary Frances whatever. Call her in for tomorrow morning and get started. She'll do just fine."

"You are an appalling piece of shit for a human being," Edward said with the casualness of a man examining the bottom of his boot after a long walk in the mud.

Around the room there was a stir of discomfort. Marty seemed to shrink back even farther into the corner of the love seat. Joe shot him a look filled with contempt.

"Don't speak to Daddy that way," Olivia said from the floor.

"Livy, please. Maybe you should wait outside," Benny said.

"No. I'm staying with you."

Patsy began crying silently. "She was so sweet. She was always so nice to me."

I barely knew Sister Sally, and that laugh of hers drove me to the edge, but what Patsy said was true. No one ever had anything bad to say about the nun.

Patsy was the only one crying. No one else in the room—people who had known Patsy longer than I and were, I assumed, her friends—moved to comfort her. I put my arm around her shoulders.

"I can call Mary Frances tonight," I said, making a note on the pad on my desk, "but she won't be nearly ready for tomorrow's schedule."

Out of habit I began to plan. "And she will need time for the music," I said, making eye contact with Edward.

"Maybe we should postpone, or take a day off, or . . . hmmm?" Marty whispered.

Joe turned on the prop master with a smirk. "The show goes on, Marty. Don't you know anything about theater? Isn't that right, Benny? Nothing stops the theater."

"Sister Sally is barely gone from us. Now is not the time to fight," Benny said.

"Oh, very pious, Benny," Edward said. "You and I both know you don't give a shit about the nun. It's the box office that worries you. We couldn't afford a loss. Not even a postponement. Not now. We'd never recover. And this will fill any seat that's still empty."

Edward was right. The death of a nun in *Convent of Fear* was a guaranteed sellout. I could imagine the headlines: " 'Convent' Condemned by God!" or "Nun Struck Down for Blasphemy." Controversy, any controversy, always drew a crowd. It was true. We all knew it. What I didn't know was that St. Gilbert's Summer Theater Festival had money troubles.

"Edward, what do you mean, we'd never survive?" I asked. "How bad is it?"

"It is not bad at all," Benny said.

"Tell him the truth, Benny." Edward had both arms in motion now, as if to summon a chorus of accountants. "That's why you wanted to do this piece of shit in the first place. Controversy, Nicky. That's our fearless leader's idea of artistic choice. We need cash and we need it bad. The college's theater department is almost done with us. We're broke. We go over budget. We pull in mediocre crowds. It's just like when . . . well . . . shit."

Silence returned to my crowded office. This time it was about something other than Sister Sally. It was the silence of some shared history.

Suddenly, no one was looking anyone in the eye. These people knew something they didn't want to tell me. At one level I didn't object. I was not interested in the local gossip, but if it affected the production, it was my business.

"I am not following. Just like when *what*, Edward?" I asked.

"It doesn't matter," he said.

Joe Sobieski was openly grinning now. "Go on. Tell him. Someone will as soon as I leave the room. I'm surprised someone hasn't already."

"This isn't necessary, Joe," Benny said, a surprising tone of concern in his voice.

"No takers?" the actor said. "OK, let me. It seems, Nicky, that my dad, St. Gilbert's Summer Theater Festival's former business manager, was an embezzler. Took a lot of cash from the till until he was stopped. The financial situation now looks just like then."

I estimated the value of the furniture in my office. I considered the size of my paycheck. I began to think that Joe's dad was not so bright. Obviously, I was still not getting the entire picture, but at least I knew why I was the one dispensing the petty cash.

"Why don't you tell him the rest?" Marty asked, his voice quiet and soft.

"Why don't you go fuck yourself?" Joe stood up and walked out of the office. From my desk I watched him cross the lobby and exit the building.

Stunning as Joe's temper tantrum was, I wasn't about to let the topic of finances get away.

"I don't really want to know the rest. What I want to know is, are we on the edge, financially, or not? Benny?" I asked.

"We are not," Benny said. "Definitely not. We've had better times, and we'll have better times, but we are not on the brink of collapse. And I wish, Eddie, you would stop saying that."

"I will shitting well say whatever I want to say. And don't call me Eddie." Edward pointed a downbeat at Benny.

"Stop swearing in front of my child."

"Oh, Daddy," Olivia said.

I almost laughed at the thought of protecting Olivia from swear words, but it seemed an inappropriate time for mirth.

I come from a large Italian-American family. We've been known to fight on the odd occasion. Holidays generally included two or three outright brawls. Still, I have a real low tolerance for the bickering of others. Just now, all of the St. Gilbert's regulars were sounding like someone else's large, unhappy family.

"Well, if there is nothing else," I said, hoping to end the meeting.

"There certainly is something else," Edward said. "That girl, Mary Frances, doesn't have the voice for the role. If you had paid any attention at auditions, you would know that, Benny."

"I paid attention," Benny said. "She is a perfectly fine actress. And why don't you call me Benjamin, Eddie?"

Patsy started to cry again. "Stop it. Please just stop fighting."

I reached for a box of tissues.

"It's like a curse. A curse on nuns," Olivia said. "It's like a movie I saw. This mystery where the monks were all done in one by one by an ancient curse, except it wasn't a curse."

"Put a lid on the shit, kid," Edward said.

"Do not talk to my daughter that way," Benny said. "And Olivia, Sister Sally had a seizure. That is not a curse."

"Not yet." The demon child looked almost hopeful.

Benny stood up. "Let's go, Olivia."

Olivia looked wistfully around the room, like a drunk at last call. Her father dragged her away.

"I cannot stand that child," Edward said, directing his rage in a stiff-armed gesture toward the exiting Singletons.

"I don't think she likes you either," Patsy said, reaching for another tissue.

"And do you think I give a shit about that?" Edward glared at the three of us remaining in the room. We were not interesting enough to hold his attention. We didn't even rate a good-bye as he stalked out.

"I hate that man," Patsy said. I could see the tension ease out of her. The same was happening to me. Sobieski's off-handed viciousness on top of Benny and Edward in the same small room packed too much anxiety.

"Where the hell is Benny Singleton?"

The man in my doorway was large. Not wide like Benny, not as tall as Marty Friedman, but big in the way a six-foot man with a solid frame and too much energy—at that moment anger—can be in a confined space: large in the minds of others in the room. Large and, from his unsteady side-to-side sway, apparently drunk. I was glad for even the short distance between the door and my desk.

"Can I help you?" I asked.

"Yeah. You can tell me where Singleton is," the man said.

"He's not here," I said.

Marty's reaction to the man seemed almost reflexive. If you can snap to attention while still seated, that's what Marty did. He didn't look at the man, but he did jerk forward on the love seat, back straight, hands on his knees palms down.

"Where'd he go?" the man slurred his question.

I am not a natural at being polite to rude people, but he could have been someone important: major donor; the dean of whatever, responsible for signing off on the theater's budget; maybe even the guy who delivers the pizza during really long technical rehearsals. Even so, I couldn't resist being just a little difficult.

"I'll tell him you were looking for him," I said in my most professional tone.

24

"And what are you going to tell him? You don't know who I am," he shot back.

"That's true," I said, smiling.

Until then he'd been impatiently looking around, checking out my office, stepping back to look into the empty auditorium, then again into my office. Always standing half in shadows. Now he stepped forward into full light. I could see his face clearly. He was a bit fleshy under the eyes and chin and more than just a little flushed with whatever he'd been drinking. He had a moustache laced with gray and close-cropped, quickly graying hair. He wore light gray pants and a rumpled white shirt. There was a tie, but it was loose, and his collar was unbuttoned beneath it. Whenever his prime, it was just a memory now.

"You know who I am. And you know why I'm here," he said, pointing at Marty. "Tell Benny I heard about tonight. Remind him I warned him. I warned all of them. Blasphemous. I said my dead body, over my dead body. Now it's hers. A nun. This show's not going to open . . . blasphemy." He snapped out of his reverie and started shouting at me. "And remind that son of bitch that I am supposed to be kept informed of this shit. I want a full report tomorrow morning."

He left.

A full report?

I turned toward Marty, who, even though he was sitting upright, gave all the indications of being nearly catatonic.

"Who the hell was that?" I asked.

"Stanley Sobieski. Chief of campus security," he said. Now his eyes started to tear up.

"Sobieski? Is he related to Joe?" I asked.

"I think he's Joe's uncle," Patsy said.

"Yes," Marty added without moving.

So the chief of security didn't approve of *Convent of Fear*. At least he had taste in theater.

I just shook my head. "I take it he and Benny don't get along?" I asked.

"No," Patsy said.

Marty started to cry. He stood up. "I'm sorry. I'm sorry. She was so amazing." He wiped at his eyes with his hands. Patsy jumped up to give him a tissue. "I'm sorry. I'm sorry."

Patsy kept pushing tissues at him. "It's OK, Marty. Really."

First Olivia, now Marty. Did everyone love Sister Sally that much? I'd been in town four weeks and certainly I hadn't noticed that Marty felt so strongly about her. I was never very good at emotional outbursts. I did what came easily. I changed the topic.

"Patsy, what's with Benny and the security chief? Does he have a normal relationship with anyone?" I asked.

"Don't misjudge Benny. He may not be a great director, but he's a good-hearted guy."

Had she gone soft from grief?

"Last winter," she continued, "Olivia was rushed to the emergency room with severe food poisoning. Benny was totally ripped up over that. And he's been great to Joe since his father killed himself. Way better than his Uncle Stanley's been, anyway."

"Suicide?" I asked.

"Yup. And twenty years is a long time to go on acting like you care, so it must be real."

"Twenty years? This whole Sobieski thing took place twenty years ago? And there is still no business manager?" So call me selfish, but I hate dealing with petty cash. "What was he embezzling, anyway? This place is pretty poor."

"I don't know." Patsy rubbed her eyes. She looked terrible.

"OK. I've had enough of this," I said. "Why don't you two go. I'll finish up here."

"Great by me." Patsy stood.

Marty was still staring at the wall.

"Marty?" I asked. "How about it? Ready to call it quits here?"

He shifted his focus from the wall to my face.

"I still need money to shop for the props."

I left a message on Mary Frances Roberts's answering machine, then spent a half-hour on paperwork. Mostly this consisted of detailing the decisions made at rehearsal regarding props, costumes, and scenic or technical elements. Each night, I organized the information into a daily bulletin for the designers and technicians working on *Convent of Fear*. I tried to make it fun. I always included a quote of the day, some clever, witty bit of repartee said during the previous twenty-four hours by someone attached to the production. This time I skipped the quote.

Carrying my backpack and copies of the daily bulletin, I left my office at just past nine-thirty. The campus custodial staff locked McNally Hall each night, but it was my responsibility to see to it that the theater itself was shut tight. I locked my office door and then crossed the back of the auditorium, making certain the door to the light booth was locked.

Next I went down the right aisle onto the stage. An empty theater is an exceptionally quiet place. The carpeted aisles muffled the sound of my sneakers. Even onstage the emptiness completely swallowed the thump of rubber soles on the wood floor.

I did a quick inspection of both wings. Stage right is to the actor's right as he faces the audience, just the opposite of house right, which is to the audience members' right as they face the stage. If that's too confusing, just remember: wherever you are, that's the perspective that counts.

Stage left was a mess. Renovations to the loading dock located along the back wall had just been completed a few days earlier. We'd been trying to clean the stage, but trace amounts of fine construction dust clung to everything—rehearsal furniture, props, us. This was the material that coated Sister Sally's habit after her seizure. I could still see the pattern on the floor where she'd disturbed the fine powder. I found a push broom along the far wall and swept away the traces. No need for visual reminders. I made a mental note to double up the cleaning efforts.

As a result of the mess on the left, all the rehearsal furniture and props were stacked stage right. Along the back wall, two metal ladders anchored into concrete blocks provided access to the grid—a system of pipes hanging over the stage and auditorium for lighting instruments. I secured the loading dock and went in search of the "ghost light."

The theater world is full of superstitions. People will tell you not to whistle in dressing rooms and, if you do, send you outside to turn around three times, re-enter, and apologize. Some won't have peacock feathers onstage, others fresh-cut flowers. Even I call Shakespeare's great tragedy "The Scottish Play," not *Macbeth*, but that's because I can't bear to see the panic that grips otherwise intelligent people if I don't. The penalties for saying "Macbeth" in a theater are too long to list, but they start with hangnail and continue through regicide. I certainly don't believe in theater ghosts or the idea that you need to keep a theater lit at all times to chase the spirits away. But, since theaters are light-tight, without a ghost light onstage the next person to enter won't have an easy time finding a wall switch. The St. Gilbert's ghost light was a simple bulb on a bare stand. I dragged it center stage. After I turned off the overhead work lights, the "ghost" cast a pale glow across the stage and into the wings.

I exited by the stage left door and walked along the hallway, sliding bulletins under Edward's and Benny's office doors. This was a matter of form. Edward never read the daily notes, and Benny, though he did, would never admit it. After tacking a copy onto the drama department bulletin board, I took the stairs to the lower level.

The theater's production work was done on this floor. I took a quick pass through the costume, prop, scene, and light shops, leaving a copy of the daily notes for each designer.

Back upstairs, I pushed my way from the air-conditioned lobby through the glass double doors into a humid summer evening. I stood for a moment, giving my lungs a chance to kick into high gear so as to pump the nearly liquid air. The plaza fronting McNally Hall centered on a fountain with water flowing from the mouths of comedy and tragedy masks. Not bad for theater symbolism, but peculiar since the masks were held in the hands of a statue of St. Gilbert. Past the fountain the view stretched uninterrupted across a gently sloping grass quadrangle that bordered a lake. The campus chapel stood to the right, the library to the left. A pale, fast-fading sunset hovered above the water.

I saw someone staring back at me from the fountain. As my eyes adjusted to the dusk, not yet completely dominated by the lampposts dotting the quad, I realized it was David Scott. He wasn't staring. He was smiling. All five feet ten "what are you doing for breakfast tomorrow" inches of him was smiling. Yes, it was wrong—emotionally and professionally—but how often do the really cute ones toss themselves at you? More importantly, how often at *me*? Here was a turn of events I could learn to rationalize.

I started across the plaza, wearing my best "I thought we'd go for brunch" smile, when the shouting started to my right.

"There's one of the nun killers!"

And then the chanting of slogans.

"Repent."

29

"Satan loves the theater."

"Nun killer."

"Dead nuns can't love!" (My favorite, covering an ambiguous number of events.)

They were the Friends of Decency, out protesting *Convent of Fear.* Like the security chief, they considered the show blasphemy, particularly the plot line that involved the young Sister Klarissa, Sally's role, falling in love with the police officer who investigates the murders at the convent.

Apparently, someone had tipped them off about Sister Sally. They must have been circling the building looking for signs of life. There were two dozen or so of them and two security guards. The demonstrators looked like middle-aged escapees from a bowling league. Each one alone looked respectable in well-pressed, pastel-colored polyester summer casuals. Even the nuns among them, easily spotted in their sensible conservative skirts and blouses, looked reasonable. As a group, though, they were snarling and wild-eyed. They charged, waving signs and blowing whistles.

At first all I could think was, "Where's a drunken security chief when you need him?" Then I started to backpedal a step or two. I didn't expect help from the guards, who were retired, overweight local police keeping a slow pace behind the demonstration. For all I knew they were part of the mob. As I turned to run, the second nun of the day went down.

Flashing through my peripheral vision, I saw someone in a red wig wearing dark glasses and a yellow rain slicker. He was riding a bicycle at full speed and heading directly for the nuns. The charging protesters wavered, stopped, and began to scatter. One nun, probably as old as Sister Mary Corinne, was not fast enough. The cyclist ran her down. He was out of sight around the chapel before anyone could offer resistance. Several of the men followed, but they obviously weren't used to running.

I fought back my fear of religious fanatics long enough to go to the aid of the downed nun. Twice in one day was too much even for a lapsed Catholic like myself.

"Sister, are you all right?" I asked, crouching down next to her.

The security guards were on either side of me. Crowd control was a post-riot event for these guys. "That'll be enough there. Step away. Everyone clear back."

I was pulled back from the nun, who was now sitting up. She was scraped and dazed, but apparently not seriously injured. One guard radioed for an ambulance. The other looked at the protesters.

"Now, you see what you've done? You've just made things worse," he said. "Go home, why don't ya?"

The burst of violence seemed to satisfy something in them. They lowered their signs. Their faces sagged. No one met my gaze. They looked almost respectable. The nuns gathered around their fallen sister, comforting and soothing.

I turned away to see a man and a woman watching from the shadow of McNally Hall. After a moment he took her into his arms and led her away. Not an odd picture for a summer's night, except that the woman was Sister Mary Corinne and the man was Edward Rossoff, musical director.

Maybe the excitement was getting to me. I was hot. I was sweating. I was hungry. Maybe the divisions in the convent over the show were putting a strain on Mary Corinne. Certainly, it was none of my business.

I turned toward the edge of campus where my apartment was located, past the fountain, past the quad—

The fountain.

I looked for David.

Gone.

What was that about?

The light on my answering machine blinked a slow rhythm: one call. I wasn't interested. Then again, the evening being so difficult and all, maybe I was just afraid.

All the walls of the apartment were a pale and faded yellow. The furniture was a small step up from my office. Nothing was patched, but a few pieces were stained. The living area was a scratched coffee table and faux maple end tables, a couch, and mismatched armchairs. I ate at a white, Formica-topped dining table on metal chairs with red plastic cushions. The overall effect was late seventies garage sale. The only distinction was the bedroom. Not the way it was furnished or its size—just its existence. In New York City I had a studio. Here at least I had space, if not aesthetic satisfaction.

The air was motionless and hot. I turned on the fan. The wet air circulated. It was still hot.

I tossed my backpack onto a chair and poured myself a glass of water into a large plastic tumbler that had once been clear but was now scratched to opacity.

The day was definitely a record breaker: one dead nun, one attacked nun, no immediate prospect of sex, and miserable weather.

Of course, Sister Sally's was the greater tragedy, but I couldn't stop wondering if there wasn't some cosmic plan to keep me away from David Scott. My best friend in New York, Paolo Suarez, and his lover, Roger Parker, were always telling me I had bad dating karma. I couldn't really argue with that. My first boyfriend became a charismatic Catholic after our second year together. I was still getting Mass cards annually. That was at age seventeen. From then to twenty-four my dating choices were on the order of the guy who once called me to tell me he'd been thinking of asking me out a second time but wanted me to know that would never happen, unless I wanted to go for dessert right then, in which case I'd have to buy. Paolo said that it wasn't my fault. He thought I must have carried this over from some previous life. I just needed to clean up the mess this time around. Paolo was never specific on what this cleaning up entailed. I would have been happier with a case of bad breath; at least then I would know what to do.

I missed the boys. Paolo was a sculptor, independently wealthy thanks to Daddy's generosity. Roger was a computer consultant, originally from the Midwest. They were excitability balancing even temperament. The edgy, barely containable frenzy they sparked in each other—half sexual, half emotional—left their friends wondering how long before the bond between them would break. To date, the "affair," as Paolo always called it, had lasted four years.

My mind was wandering. I wanted dinner. First, I gathered my courage and pushed the play button on the answering machine. How bad could the message be? After all, when your leading lady dies on Monday, the rest of the week can only be an improvement.

"Nicky. It's Paolo. It's Monday afternoon. Lucky you, we're coming to visit. Tomorrow. We'll be there by late afternoon. Ciao."

This had to be one of those karma things.

THREE

I WAS BACK AT the theater by nine-thirty Tuesday morning. I like empty theaters—they hold promise. Audiences see theaters packed with scenery and productions, finished products varying only slightly from night to night. In a good rehearsal, I see a blank stage with actors and directors chasing down the best way to perform a scene, discarding one approach after another. Sometimes it works, sometimes it doesn't. I had a definite opinion about whether *Convent of Fear* was working, but I was keeping that to myself.

After turning on the work lights, I started the coffee. I swept the stage. More accurately, I evened out the ever-present coating of construction dust. In the process I erased the one slightly cleaner spot I'd created the night before, removing the last physical reminder of Sister Sally. I passed on mopping. The work crew was scheduled to return for yet one more "one last time" later in the afternoon. They'd been working in the loading dock for four weeks, in which time they'd remounted the access ladder at stage left, widened the doors, reset the floor, had two arguments with Benny, and eaten lunch twice on me (funny how that worked). Patsy and I swept and swept, but like sand at a beach house, the gray dust wasn't going away until we lost the ocean.

I positioned a few pieces of rehearsal furniture onstage to give Mary Frances Roberts something to work around. I read over the scenes we were going to rehearse. My intention was to work from ten until five with a one-hour break for lunch. I was not going to let anything disturb us. When Patsy arrived I sent her to work the phones, making certain the cast knew the updated rehearsal schedule. I was going to ignore the workmen, no matter how many veiled threats they made about working through opening night unless I fed them again. Yes, I had a plan. I should have had a plan to see Elvis: there was a greater chance of success, and in the end I would have been able to sell the book rights.

By ten a.m. the smell of freshly brewed mediocre coffee tainted the air. McNally Hall was ready, bursting to let loose the joy of creation, the thrill of drama. Unfortunately, all I had to offer the theater gods was one very nervous last-minute replacement.

In the common room of the convent, Sister Klarissa sits quietly as the Mother Superior speaks with the young policeman. Her eyes follow him with great interest, though the rest of her face betrays nothing of what her mind is thinking.

The Mother Superior leaves.

"I don't understand, Lieutenant," she says, rising from her chair and crossing to a nearby bookcase. Is she seeking comfort from familiar objects? Wandering aimlessly about the room? Who can answer such questions by merely looking at the suddenly lost nun?

"You say Sister Amilio was murdered, but you say you don't know how? How can you say that? How can you know and not know?" she asks.

"How does anyone ever know or not know?" the policeman responds.

"You're speaking in riddles," she says. "I would think a murder was enough riddle for one day." She takes a hesitant step toward him.

"I'm sorry. I seem to be all out of focus today." He rises and takes a step toward her.

"Out of focus? What an odd expression, Lieutenant. But I still want ... need ..." The nun moves to within easy touching distance of the policeman. "Need to know. Won't you ..." She speaks past just the hint of a pause. "Won't you tell me?"

"Sister Klarissa ... ," he says.

"Please, just Klarissa." There is a Chekovian moment of silence in the common room.

"Well, then. Klarissa. It's not that we don't know what killed her, it's how the murderer accomplished it. The delivery, if you will."

"I will," she says. "I mean, I see. It's all so clear now."

"Clear" is such a tricky word.

Mary Frances stood center stage, lost and very unclear. I stood on the apron, five feet away. I was trying to teach her the blocking for the first scene between Klarissa and the young lieutenant.

"That's fine, Mary Frances."

I will burn for the professional lies I must tell.

"Now cross to the telephone on that last line. Right. Except remember Joe will be there, so you need to get to the other side of the table."

"It's really not very well written, is it?" Mary Frances asked after making her notes on the scene.

Red flags started waving in my head. The prime directive of stage management is to always remain neutral on artistic matters. Any opinion expressed is a land mine waiting to blow at your feet. If the bit or scene works, everyone is happy, but if something goes wrong and you're on record with a positive comment, then it's "Well, Nicky liked it," or "This is the scene the stage manager wanted to do." At that moment you can hear your credibility with cast and designers rattle as it rolls off the stage into the orchestra pit and settles in the unlit, unused corner behind the guy who plays the triangle.

"I think you will find the material more memorable as you continue to work with it," I said.

Mary Frances had enough difficulties without having me trash the script. Not that she was at fault. Her situation would make any sane person nervous: she had no preparation, and she wasn't up to the part vocally, though she wasn't as bad as the musical director thought. As for acting ability, I had to give Benny credit on that one—she was good. In less than a week, Mary Frances would perform as well as Sister Sally after a full rehearsal schedule. Had she started four weeks earlier, she might even have been a better Klarissa. That bewildered look was perfect.

Mary Frances was a slender woman of twenty-two. She had long brown hair, which she did little to style. For rehearsal she wore a simple black skirt, a white blouse, and low heels, all very functional and nunlike. There was no hint of any underlying sexuality in anything Mary Frances did or said. The perfect novice nun. Getting her to make the transition to a lover so swept by passion she renounces her vows was going to be the difficult part.

We continued patiently through the morning. First we read a scene, then I showed her the setting and props, lastly walking her through the blocking. We repeated the blocking several times, each time adding more detail. I trod a narrow line between making the understudy's movements match Sister Sally's and leaving her with enough freedom to create a few bits of character on her own. We needed her to mesh with the rest of the company, but I didn't want to drive her crazy trying to imitate Sally's performance.

At noon we hit our first real obstacle. The costume designer, Ilana Mosca, thudded onto the stage like a piece of scenery dropped too fast from the flies. You can spot a costume designer across a crowded opening. Their outfits are always somewhat "kicky" but never quite chic. Ilana wore several layers of beige and pale green cotton gauze T-shirts, blouses, vests, and skirts, all riding carelessly atop brown boots. She'd been designing costumes and teaching at St. Gilbert's since *Convent of Fear* debuted on Broadway.

"Terrible tragedy, isn't it?" she said, interrupting our work. She whipped out a cloth tape measure. "You cannot of course wear a habit from dead nun. Very bad luck. Terrible. Now, stand still." She spoke with an accent seemingly unchanged since immigration—an accent that thickened under stress or with annoyance.

"Ilana, we're working," I said.

"Yes. It's good to work during time of tragedy. Let me measure."

"You have my measurements," Mary Frances said.

Ilana stepped back. She'd seen an uncountable number of young, eager actresses come to her obscure corner of Pennsylvania and go off to even more obscure futures.

"I am making you new habit. I would like to make it fit. You don't want it to fit? I don't mind. I am not going to wear it." She began to roll up the tape measure.

"No. No. Ilana, please—measure," I said. What was five minutes compared to the addition of an angry costume designer to our problems? "It won't take long, Mary Frances."

"OK. Stand still," Ilana said. She made a quick flip with her tape. "Have either of you seen the Straying Nun?" She wrote a number down on an index card she pulled from one of her many pockets.

"The what?" I asked.

"Sister Mary Corinne, the talentless. Every year I ask Benny to fire her. Every year he says no. But that is Benny. I am used to him. Arms out." Another flip of the tape, another number penciled in. "Maybe I shouldn't say anything to either of you. Who needs that trouble again?"

She made a quick circumnavigation of Mary Frances's head with the measuring tape. "When I was kid, nuns were respectable. They took vows of chastity."

Aside from watching rehearsals, Sister Mary Corinne styled wigs and hairpieces for the theater. I think she'd been doing that for the past fifteen years. She worked in a small room adjacent to the costume shop. Mary Corinne and all the room's contents and activities were under Ilana's jurisdiction. What, I wondered, wouldn't Ilana know about Mary Corinne after all that time and proximity? Certainly her clipped comments raised any number of tantalizing avenues for exploration. God help me, I went for the gutter.

"Chastity?" I asked.

"An old-fashioned word that you think would fit an old person," Ilana said. "Not this nun. And not for first time. Legs wide." Down the inseam.

"Oh, please," Mary Frances said. "Not those rumors."

"Rumors?" Ilana said. "No, I don't think so. Sobieski was no rumor."

"Mary Corinne and Joe Sobieski?" I was appalled.

"Breathe and relax." Bust and waist in rapid fire. "Why do the young only think of the young? The father. Her brother-in-law. It was a real scandal, Nicholas. A real scandal. She drove him to his death. I know. And now . . . but Benny insists. A heart like gold in that man. First the father, now the son. A heart like gold. Raising his children alone. Olivia is the youngest. A late child. The others are grown now, but Benny took care of them too. And still time for Joe Jr. If you see her, send her to me. She is late. And you"—she pointed a finger at Mary Frances—"have filled out very nicely since last year."

"I have not." Mary Frances began to show some passion.

"They never do, do they?" Ilana asked me. I declined to take a side. She let out one staccato laugh and said to Mary Frances, "Now that I've measured, lay off the snacks."

"Is that all, Ilana?" I said, thinking maybe I'd push her offstage.

"That's it for me," she said. "I'm out of here. Just pretend I was never here—never said word. But send the nun."

Ilana exited stage right.

For brisk efficiency, both in getting what she needed and dispensing gossip, Ilana was tops.

We took a five-minute break to regroup and then returned to work. Ilana hadn't put us that far back. We might still make it at least once through the tea scene by lunch break. In that scene the dashing young police lieutenant, disguised as a nun to better spy on the goings-on around the convent, has afternoon tea with the sisters. Of course, only the Mother Superior knows he is undercover. Of course, Klarissa recognizes him immediately. Of course, none of the other nuns do. Of course, he looks worse than Jack Lemmon in *Some Like It Hot.* Of course, it is completely unbelievable. Adding to the visual misery, Benny was insisting on elaborate tea-drinking business. Sister Klarissa was going to sip, slurp, gulp, and spit tea in response to the action onstage. And she wouldn't be alone in this. The entire scene was one long tea shtick.

"I'm really not certain how it is that she is the only one who recognizes him," Mary Frances said. Give her credit, she was trying to approach the text as if it made sense.

"That would actually be a question for the other actors to answer, wouldn't it?" I said, sidestepping nicely. "You recognize him, and that is all you need to worry about."

Mary Frances looked me straight in the eye. "You aren't going to give an inch on this play, are you?"

"I will give you all the help I can," I said with a smile.

Just then Marty Friedman appeared stage right with a shopping bag and began sorting through the props stored along the wall. He shook his head and mumbled.

"OK," Mary Frances said. "See me make a note? 'Not my problem.' " She smirked back at me. I was beginning to warm up to Mary Frances.

Offstage I heard Marty grumbling a bit more loudly.

"Marty," I called to him. "We're working here. A little quiet please."

"Oh, jeez, I'm sorry. Really. Jeez. Sorry." He turned his back to us and continued rooting around in the furniture.

"So the thing to remember here, Mary Frances, is that Klarissa is struggling against discovery, always trying to catch his eye, but never letting anyone else see what she is up to."

"OK," she said.

"Damn. Oh, I'm sorry. Jeez, Nicky, can I interrupt you?" Marty entered the stage proper. "I'm really sorry, but there is so little time left."

"Don't I know it," Mary Frances said.

It was quarter to one. I felt my schedule slipping away.

"Marty, can't this wait fifteen minutes?" I asked.

"Well, yeah. Sure. I mean, what's fifteen minutes? But it won't take long. It's just a quick question. I just need an answer on a prop—and some cash. I brought receipts. I am trying to save time, you know." Marty stood there sincerely believing he was helping.

Mary Frances started to laugh. "Go ahead. Answer his question. I brought my lunch. I'll just go sit in the front row and eat. I could use a long break anyway."

"OK. We'll break for an hour. Why don't you go outside and get some air?" If Mary Frances could be gracious, why shouldn't I?

"Out there? It's over ninety degrees. Who can breathe? I'll take the AC, thanks." Mary Frances jumped down from the apron. She picked up her blue-and-white-striped canvas bag and settled herself in the front row.

"Now, Marty, what is the problem?" I asked.

41

"I need a new nun's cross," Marty said.

By "nun's cross" he meant the boxy, dark wooden crosses we attached to polished wooden beads to create the oversized rosaries that the nuns wore about their waists. Technically, they should have been crucifixes, but on that point Benny had bowed to what he referred to as "local superstition."

"Did we lose one?" I asked.

"Well, last night I had enough," Marty said, "but today I'm short. I think it's the one Sally was wearing." He forced himself to speak her name with only the slightest hitch in his voice.

I closed my eyes and concentrated. "I remember her wearing it yesterday. I saw it in her hands," I said.

"Well, it's gone now. I can't find it. It wasn't downstairs with her costume, like it should be."

I opened my eyes and gave Marty the once-over. Don't get me wrong, I could see he was very upset about Sally's death—very. Still, I had a duty to perform. "Have you been talking with Ilana? This wouldn't have anything to do with the bad luck of a dead actor's props, would it?"

I'd never heard of this superstition, but if the costume was jinxed, who knew what pestilence hung about the props?

"Ilana did say it was bad luck to use a dead person's costumes, but she never mentioned props. Do you think that's a problem?" Marty was looking very pale.

"You are not serious?" I asked.

"I never heard that about props," he said. "Is it really bad or just so-so bad? Not that we *have* the cross, but there are the beads. Should I replace them too, do you think?"

Thus are traditions born.

"No. I don't think that. Trust me on this. Our leading actress is dead. You can't have worse luck." Then, seeing the look on his face, I realized I'd gone too far. "Marty, I'm sorry. I didn't . . . I mean, I didn't know you and Sally were so close."

"What? What are you saying?" Now he looked annoyed.

"I just . . . well, I can see you're upset."

"She's dead, isn't she? Isn't that reason enough?" He wasn't convincing me with this sudden burst of detachment, but I took the opening to get out of the conversation.

"I'm sorry. I didn't mean to suggest anything," I said.

"Well, there's nothing to suggest." Marty looked to be on the edge of sulking.

"Did you check with the ER to see if they had the cross?"

"I called. They said they'd turned everything over to the convent. I called the convent. They said there were no crosses. At least not our cross. I mean, it's a convent. They have lots of crosses. Even the one she wore around her neck—but not ours."

Was he lying? I had no way to know for certain. For all I knew, lying about a dead actor's props was good luck. Or maybe he took the thing as a keepsake. For some reason I found that depressing.

"I guess it got lost in transit," I said. "All right, we'll get another."

"OK. Here, look at these." Marty held out a trowel and a hand hoe. "They're for the gardener."

I inspected both for potential dangers, starting with the hoe. Stage managers called this "actorproofing." Every prop, piece of scenery, and costume is inspected for even the slightest possibility that it might prove a source of injury to an actor. The process is similar to plugging the electrical outlets when a three-year-old comes to visit. The hoe was useable, as its broad edge posed no threat, but the trowel was a definite no-go.

I touched the tip of the trowel. "This point is too sharp. You'll need to blunt it somehow."

"Maybe I should just get one of those little shovel things? Since I have to go out for the cross."

"How's your budget?" I asked.

"Oh, I'm fine." Marty tried to smile. The effect was fairly grim. He was not a happy man. "I always come in under budget. This will be six musicals in a row."

I couldn't argue with a record like that. In the end, budget counts as much—in some cases more—than content in the theater. I flashed back to an expensive musical production of *Titus Andronicus*. The singing children's heads in pie pans were not inexpensive. If a prop master can buy another cross and garden tool and still come in under budget, I say take what little triumphs a day offers.

A door banged open at the rear of the auditorium. Patsy Malone came running down the aisle toward us.

"Nicky. Nicky. My God, what are we going to do? This is terrible."

I crossed to the edge of the stage, Marty right behind me. Patsy slammed into the stage, out of breath. When she looked up at me, I could see the shock in her eyes.

Mary Frances left her first-row seat and placed an arm around Patsy. "You'd better sit down," she said. She guided Patsy to the front row. She gently placed Patsy in one of the blue plush seats, all the while making soothing "it's OK" sounds.

"Patsy," I said, sitting on the other side of her. "What is it?"

"Someone murdered Sister Sally."

Mary Frances rocked back in her seat. Her mouth opened. A quiet sound, something like "oh," seeped out.

"What?" That was Marty, still onstage. I turned to look at him. He was standing with his fists clenched at his side, his knuckles white. Before I could say anything, I heard Patsy start to sob.

I had to choose. I took Patsy's hand.

"Patsy, what are you talking about?" I asked. "She had a seizure. We all saw it."

"No. No. No. I have a friend at the hospital. She called me. Sister Sally tested positive for bug poison. A large amount. Now the police think someone poisoned her."

"Now, Patsy," I said, turning on the sympathetic voice I used for actors in distress. "No one would want to murder Sister Sally."

"But the drug test showed positive."

"Well, right, there's a problem. Who'd give a drug test to a nun?"

"Were you talking to Judy Winiski?" Mary Frances asked. "She's a fool." And for my benefit, she added more. "She's a volunteer. Last fall she let out that there was a typhoid case, very contagious. Can you believe that? I can't believe they didn't fire her."

"Nobody proved that was Judy." Patsy's words were defensive, but her face, as she focused on Mary Frances for the first time, softened its expression. "Anyway," Patsy continued. "It's true what Olivia said last night. They drug-test everyone now. They have to."

"Patsy, I know you're upset," I said, "but even if Sister Sally had insect poison in her, that doesn't mean murder. It was probably an accident."

"Judy said the police—"

"Exactly. Now, don't you think if the police really thought someone had murdered Sister Sally, they'd be here talking to us? Do you see any police?" I asked, waving my hands at the empty expanse of the theater house.

The back doors opened once more, this time to admit two uniformed policemen.

FOUR

"WHY DO YOU CALL it a murder scene?" Corporal Roberts asked.

"She collapsed right here, didn't she?" Mary Frances answered with a question.

Mary Frances, Patsy, and I sat in the front row. Corporal Roberts of the Pennsylvania State Police was leaning against the stage. He faced us, a slightly bored but pleasant man in a crisply pressed blue uniform. Behind him, a trooper methodically surveyed the wing space.

I'd tried giving the police a tour of the space, but the corporal had seemed reluctant to move, so I was left to stand and point to various aspects of the theater, including the spot where Sister Sally fell. He exerted himself when it came time to take statements from Patsy and me, separating us to get independent accounts of the previous evening. Afterward, he'd sent the trooper as his eyes to inspect the actual "scene" of the event.

As someone whose entire knowledge of police work came from watching hyperkinetic television shows, I was a bit disappointed by the lack of activity. I expected photographers and fingerprint dusting, or at least yellow crime scene tape. But, unless life is truly different in rural Pennsylvania, the police did not consider Sister Sally a murder victim.

"Mary Frances, just because Sister Sally died suddenly does not mean she was murdered. Understood?" the corporal said.

"OK, Dad. But it seems odd to me," Mary Frances said.

"No. It seems perversely exciting to you. That is not the same thing, is it?" he asked.

"You're her father?" I asked.

"Oh yes." He smiled.

"Is everyone related around here?" I asked.

The corporal laughed. "This is a small town."

"I'm not related to anyone here," Patsy said directly to Mary Frances. "I'm from Philadelphia."

"I take it you are not from around here, Mr. D'Amico?" the corporal asked.

"No. I just work here for the summer," I said.

"You know, I have cousins in Philly," Mary Frances said to Patsy.

"What part of Philly?" Patsy cozied, leaning slightly over the armrest she shared with Mary Frances.

"Where from?" Corporal Roberts asked me.

"New York City."

"Well, then I guess we do seem small to you," he said. I'm not certain that he noticed Patsy and Mary Frances warming up to each other, but then I'm not certain how he could have missed it.

"Now, everyone, I want to stop this murder rumor right here, with us. Understood?" he said.

"Of course. Anyway, we don't know where the poison was administered, do we?" I added.

"Poison? Murder?" Corporal Roberts spoke to his daughter. "If your mother were hearing this, you'd be out of this production."

"You're not getting me out of here, Dad."

"Just a joke, Mary Frances." The corporal turned to me. "All right, then. I see the news is here already. How did you hear about the poisoning?"

"Patsy told me," I said.

"Oh, thank you," Patsy said. She punched my right shoulder.

Corporal Roberts retrieved a notebook and pen from the breast pocket of his uniform. "And how, Ms. Malone, did you hear about poison?"

"Rumor?" Patsy said.

"Ah-huh." The corporal stared at Patsy. Roberts was a solid, if slightly paunchy, six feet. His good humor softened his imposing size, but his voice carried an unmistakable demand for information. He flipped through his notepad.

"Young lady, I have no reason to suspect this death was anything but accidental. However, and I stress this to all of you, that does not make this situation one for jokes. Now, I don't have a note on rumors." He eyed Patsy.

"I have a friend at the hospital," she said. "She mentioned bug poison, that's all."

"Friend's name?"

"Does it—"

"Judy Winiski." Mary Frances answered the question and, laughing, said, "She could never keep a secret."

"Leaking confidential medical information is not funny. Is that clear?" So Corporal Roberts was not all jolly-jolly.

Mary Frances stopped smiling. "Yes, sir."

"Sir," the trooper who stood behind Corporal Roberts said, "the entire stage area seems fairly well swept, but there is a fine dust coating most of the non-stage spaces."

48

"That's from the loading dock renovations," I said. "That dust is everywhere. We sweep before each rehearsal. Even then it never really goes away. That's why last night I decided to sweep an extra time after rehearsal as well."

There is a moment in every TV cop show when the guest star talks to the police without a lawyer present, when Peter Falk first squints at the murderer, when Angela Lansbury tilts her head to one side and lets her gaze drift upward. None of these compared with the moment of silence that followed my comment—the moment when I knew that Corporal Roberts wasn't in quite so good a mood anymore.

"You swept after rehearsal? After Sister Sally died? And that's unusual?" The corporal trained a gray-eyed stare on me.

"Yes, actually it is," I said.

"Ah-huh. And why did you sweep?"

There was no backing out now.

"When Sister Sally was having her seizure, she was thrashing around on the ground. It left marks in the dust. I wanted to remove the reminders. Just so no one would be upset."

"Ah-huh." He made a note in his pad. "But you would have swept this morning, correct?"

"Yes, I would have."

"So no one would have seen anything today except you?"

"Well, only if I were here first. Patsy sometimes gets here before me, or someone could have come in, or . . . well, it just seemed right."

"And by sweeping, you removed all markings of Sister Sally's seizure?"

"Yes, I guess I did."

"I see."

"Sir," the trooper said. He was now holding a brown paper bag open for the corporal's inspection. "You should look at this. This is the stuff all over the wing space. I've collected samples from several spots for testing, but . . ."

"I understand." The corporal nodded his head. "Mr. D'Amico, would you please show me where Sister Sally had her seizure? You two please wait here."

The corporal, suddenly all business and energy, and I climbed onto the stage. I felt like a sheep being separated from the flock. When we got to the spot stage left, he turned his back to Patsy and Mary Frances and began to whisper to me.

"As I understand it, as stage manager you are in authority here?"

"In many ways yes," I said. "I report directly to the artistic director. But this is not the military, and most everyone here volunteers, so 'authority' isn't really the best word."

"Understood, but you are the person most directly responsible for overseeing this space?" he asked.

"Certainly more than anyone else."

"So, if you had not swept the stage last night, it is unlikely anyone else would have?"

"Well, yes, but I thought you said there wasn't a murder. Why does this make a difference?" I asked.

"I'm not certain that it does, Mr. D'Amico. I'm just establishing what happened last night. Anything outside of the usual warrants a question."

The loading dock opened to admit four college workmen. They must have come from some other site. Just beneath a layer of fresh dirt, their work boots and jeans carried stains recording a history of repaired buildings. These guys were the opposite of the previous night's semiretired security guards: young, fit, and at least partially acquainted with the idea of working. They looked at the state troopers, then at me, and then at each other.

"Is this a bad time?" the crew head asked, dropping a bag of tools.

50

I could see him calculating an afternoon off.

"I don't . . . I don't know," I said. I turned to the corporal, who answered the question.

"Come in, gentlemen," he said. "I think you should be able to work, but first . . ." He called to his man. After a brief sotto voce conference, he said to the work crew, "There's been an incident here. If you would please take a seat in the auditorium, Trooper Avery has a few questions for you. It won't take long, and we would appreciate your cooperation. Thank you."

Trooper Avery was a smaller version of the corporal, not that much older than me. He led the crew to seats away from Patsy and Mary Frances.

"Now, Mr. D'Amico," the corporal said.

"You can call me Nicky."

"We do have a problem. Sister Sally was in fact poisoned by prolonged exposure to organo phosphates."

"Which is?" I asked.

"Bug poison. The problem is, it looks a great deal like this gray construction dust all over your theater."

"You mean there's more of it around?"

"Possibly. Though you've been so busy cleaning."

"But then why isn't anyone else sick?" I asked.

"That's why I say possibly. Her exposure could have taken place elsewhere. We're checking all possibilities. Perhaps she spent time yesterday at the convent garden."

"Then it could have been an accident?" I asked.

"Yes, of course."

"Then she wasn't murdered?"

"So you've changed your mind about that." He looked at me, eyes steady but slightly widened as if to solicit some response.

"No. I mean, I hadn't made up my mind."

51

"Even without murder, we have a duty to the public's safety. Why do you think it might have been murder?"

"I don't. I mean, I assumed."

"Why?" he asked.

Why had I? Was I just getting carried away with Mary Frances's enthusiasm for the idea?

"I don't know."

"Ah-huh."

"So how unsafe is it?" I rushed on, trying to divert more questions.

"Probably not at all. Like you said, if there were more here, someone else would be showing symptoms. But you need to really clean this place up. This kind of poisoning requires repeated and prolonged exposure to the skin. This sort of thing mostly happens when people use the stuff without gloves. They get it on their hands, touch their face—it ends up all over them. You have to keep your fingers on the source." He was giving me that look again.

Face. Hands. Fingers. What? I flashed onto Sally yesterday, laying on the floor, covered in dust. But that happened after she fell to the ground. Before that, in rehearsal, she didn't look any different than anyone else. I tugged at a memory of face, hands, and fingers. What was it? I pictured her standing in the dormitory scene, singing, then the sound behind her. She reaches for her cross.

"Oh God," I said.

"Do you want to tell me something, son?"

"Her cross. Sister Sally's cross. She had it at rehearsal, but it's gone now. She always rehearsed with it. And she played with it continually."

"You think someone poisoned her cross?" Roberts asked. He didn't have to say he thought I was watching too much TV.

"Well, it was just sitting on the prop table when she didn't use it. I mean someone could have. Anyone . . ." I faltered.

"Where is this cross?"

"Gone. The prop master—Marty Friedman—he was here earlier, just a little while ago. He reported it missing after last night's rehearsal." Where was Marty? He'd been next to me when Patsy came running in with her news. He took it very hard, then disappeared.

"So the cross and the prop guy have disappeared?"

"Well, no. The cross has disappeared. I assume Marty is around somewhere."

"But not with the cross? Which you think was poisoned?" The corporal sounded very much like a man who suspects he's being given the runaround.

"No. The cross is definitely gone."

"Ah-huh. Unfortunate. Mr. D'Amico, it is never smart to hold back information."

"I'm not holding anything back."

"All right. I need to speak with anyone else who was present last evening. We need to alert everyone who was in this theater about possible symptoms."

Patsy called to me from the orchestra pit. "Nicky, someone's here to see you."

Having never been involved in any sort of police investigation, I was a little vague on the etiquette of taking visitors while being questioned.

"Do you mind? Are we finished?" I asked.

"For now," Roberts said. "But I am going to need that list of the names with phone numbers and addresses as soon as possible, please."

"Easily done," I said as I walked toward Patsy and my guest, feeling the corporal's eyes focused on my back.

The dark-haired, olive-toned man standing next to Patsy motioned me to come close.

"Love the uniform, Nicky, but he seems a little old for you," Paolo Suarez whispered in my ear. Patsy giggled.

"You are undermining my authority in front of my staff," I said.

"I wasn't listening. Really." Patsy laughed again.

"Patsy, why don't you go to the office and get a contact list for Corporal Roberts? OK?"

"Is he going to question everyone?" she asked.

"More likely he's going to see if anyone else got sick yesterday."

"What is going on around here?" Paolo asked. "I thought I'd find you lazing away in sylvan splendor, but your assistant tells me there's been a murder. And that nut outside on the bicycle. How many times have I told you? It's not safe to leave Manhattan."

"No one has been murdered," I said.

"What nut on the bicycle?" Patsy asked.

"Some nut in a raincoat and a not very flattering wig—Early Lucy Red—just ran down a nun in the parking lot," Paolo said. "Clobbered her in a perfectly good parking space too. Thank God there was another spot not too far away."

"This is too weird. That's two nuns this guy's gotten so far. I saw him run one down last night," I said.

"Hmmm . . . two nuns down and one poisoned. You know, maybe this is my kind of town," Paolo said.

"I don't think that's funny," Patsy said. Making fun of me was all right, but making fun of wounded nuns offended her.

"And why is it so hot and humid? I thought it was supposed to be cooler in the country. All that grass and trees and nature. It's like August in Manhattan around here." Paolo wiped the back of his hand across his forehead. "Thank God they have electricity this far out."

"Patsy, please go get Corporal Roberts his contact list, OK?" I wanted her out of there before Paolo did irreparable damage. And Paolo could do damage faster than anyone I knew. He was definitely an acquired taste. Patsy huffed and headed for the office.

I sat on the edge of the stage. "This is not a good day."

"I'll say," Paolo said. "This place is not easy to find. We got lost twice. You-know-who can't navigate worth shit. But he's even worse at driving. How can you grow up in the Midwest and be a worse driver than me? I grew up in Manhattan."

"Paolo," I interrupted. "Not just now. I promise I will listen to all the complaints you've stored up since I left the city, but not just now."

Paolo stepped back. It was an unnecessary movement, but that was Paolo. He was an artist, sculptor by vocation, with a direct understanding of what happened around him. He could mask his perception, as he was doing now, with verbiage and theatrical show, but he rarely missed a nuance. He had black hair and deep brown eyes that could stare straight through a man. For all that, I think I liked Paolo when I first met him as much for the fact that he was no taller than me as for anything else. Just today, despite his protests, he also looked cooler than me with his brown baggy shorts and white muscle T stretched across his wiry body.

"Let me guess," he said. "This is not a rewarding artistic experience, you are not having fun, and—wait, it's coming to me . . ." He paused to raise his right hand to his forehead and closed his eyes. "You are not getting laid."

"Right, right, and right. Where's Roger?"

"*She* stopped to help the nun in distress, something my lapsed Catholicism forbids."

"*She*"? Oops. This I did not need. Paolo only gender-bends when he's really pissed.

"So, how is Roger?" I asked.

"We seem to have developed different definitions of fidelity."

"Oh, Paolo. What did you do?"

"Me? Why does it have to be me? Let me guess: artistic type, Latin heritage. Those are ugly stereotypes."

"So what's his name?" I asked.

"I can't believe you. You really don't think it's possible that the virgin of the cornfields could be cheating on me? Well, get it right. The techno-geek has been in one of those online cyberslut places chatting up every anonymous dick that comes by, thank you." Paolo's voice was filling the theater.

"Well, that's not really—"

"Don't even try to tell me it is not the same thing. I am warning you." Paolo took another step back. "And I am counting on you to take my side."

"Excuse me," Corporal Roberts said. He and his trooper had come down off the stage. They approached warily. I think Paolo was outside the realm of their usual experience.

"Do you have that list?" the corporal asked.

"I sent Patsy for it. She'll have it in a minute. Can I get you anything else?" I asked.

Roberts turned to Paolo. "And you are?"

"Paolo Suarez. Visiting from New York."

"Another one?" the corporal said.

"Another *what*, Sergeant?" Paolo said with instant dislike.

"Corporal. Corporal Roberts, Pennsylvania State Police. Visitor. Another visitor."

"And a good thing too," Paolo said. "The way the locals go after one another, you need tourists. I just saw someone run down a nun in a parking lot. Some nice town you've got here."

The corporal ignored Paolo's tone. "What nun? What parking lot?"

"I am sure I do not know the nun's name. But my lover will probably know when he gets here."

The trooper cleared his throat at the slight extra emphasis Paolo gave to the word "he." Corporal Roberts waited.

"As for the parking lot," Paolo said, "go out the front door, take a right, then another right. You'll come to it."

Roberts dispatched the trooper to "check it out" and turned to me. "Did you know about this?"

"Paolo just told me. But it sounds like the same guy from last night."

"Ah-huh. Last night?"

I gave him the details of my run-in with the Friends of Decency. For a moment it looked as if Paolo was going to cheer when I got to the part about the bicycle and the nun. He managed to control himself. I didn't mention Mary Corinne and Edward Rossoff or their embrace outside McNally Hall. It wasn't exactly a deliberate omission, but somehow it just seemed too private a moment to relate to anyone. What could it have to do with the bicyclist?

"Ah-huh. Why didn't you mention this?" The ah-huhing was beginning to get to me. Corporal Roberts looked like he thought I was trying to hide something.

"I didn't think of it?" Then again, maybe I did sound like I was trying to hide something.

The corporal dropped another ah-huh into what was fast becoming a tense situation. Relief was up to Patsy. How long did it take to find a contact sheet?

Paolo unloaded more of his bad mood. "Listen, Captain. I'm new here, but it seems to me that you have a problem. One murdered nun and two assaulted. Not a good sign."

"Corporal. I take it you are a homosexual, Mr. Suarez?"

I don't think anyone had ever actually asked Paolo that question. Some things are just assumed.

Paolo began, "And I take it you are—"

"Paolo. Please." I stopped him.

"I'll just wait over here," he said. "Nice to meet you, General." Paolo removed himself to the front row.

"Your boyfriend doesn't like me." Corporal Roberts turned "boyfriend" into a curse word. I reversed my opinion of the corporal.

57

How had this unpleasant man produced the above-averagely talented and rather interesting Mary Frances? She must have some mother.

"He is not my boyfriend. His boyfriend is parking the car."

"He doesn't seem to like nuns much either. Do you?"

"Like nuns? As in what, for breakfast? As in would I poison one?"

"Just a question, Mr. D'Amico."

Patsy arrived with the contact sheet.

"About time," I snapped.

"I had to make a copy, and the machine on this floor is out of toner. I went to the library. Corporal Roberts, did you know that another nun was run down?"

"He knows." I took the paper out of Patsy's hands and shoved it at the corporal. "Is there anything else, Corporal Roberts? Or may I get back to work?"

"Nothing else for now, thank you."

The corporal said good-bye to his daughter and headed for the lobby. On the way up the aisle, he met a tall, strawberry blonde man who turned his head to inspect the state police as they passed. Roger Parker continued along, joining Patsy and me.

"Love the uniform, Nicky, but isn't he a little old for you?" Roger asked.

Still in the front row, Mary Frances, hearing Roger refer to her father as a potential object of my affection, howled with laughter.

Paolo shot her a sour glance and said to his lover, "If you must arrive late, at least arrive with an original line. I already said that."

I was beginning to think bug poisoning preferable to this visit. It would certainly be quicker.

FIVE

EXCESS WAS A WAY of life at the D'Amico family table. Dinner included low grade beef, too much starch, overcooked vegetables, and plenty of social spice: laughter, shouting matches, the occasional food fight, one or two nonfamily guests, and the odd relative. Every night my large Italian-American family gathered around the kitchen table, adding two or three folding chairs to a matched permanent set of six. In that crowd I learned the invaluable social skill of conducting at least three conversations while snagging my share of food—pass the pasta, pass an opinion. Nothing since I left home had challenged my belief that I could make witty chitchat under the most adverse dining conditions. Then I had dinner with Paolo and Roger at Ernie's Family Restaurant.

Job responsibilities forced me to leave them on their own between the departure of the state police and our exit for food. Dead nuns, homophobic state police, and feuding best friends do not trump a first audience. Mary Frances and I got in another two hours of rehearsal while the boys wandered separately about the building. Absence did not make their hearts grow fonder. The pause was more like a break between rounds.

"Why are we eating at five o'clock? Civilized people do not eat at five o'clock," Paolo said. He stopped on the sidewalk, his silver-framed, oval-shaped sunglasses glinting in the afternoon sun.

"Civilized people do not rehearse from seven to eleven every night," I said.

"And where do we eat in Humbert Humbertville?" he asked.

"It's called Huber's Landing," Roger said. "It was on the sign as we drove in. You saw it."

"You are so literal, my love. That must be an asset with your on-line adventures."

"So," I said, "here's the Thing."

We were in the parking lot behind the auditorium. The 1974 Volkswagen Thing stood out among the late-model, smooth-lined compacts. The bright, lemon yellow, boxy-shaped car was Paolo's favorite, and only, adult toy. It was his answer to Roger's mass of electronic gadgetry: the iPod, the BlackBerry, the camcorder, the digital camera, the cell phone (with camera), the two laptops (one with software that lets you speak to your computer, both with more than enough processing power to fly a NASA shuttle), and the cappuccino/orange juice maker.

As we stood admiring the Thing, a van pulled into the lot. The door popped open, and out piled the assorted loonies who comprised the evening shift for the Friends of Decency. They eyed me warily across the asphalt.

"Who are those people?" Roger asked.

"The Friends of Decency. They're protesting *Convent of Fear*. Every night they picket in front of the theater. Last night they attacked me when they heard that Sister Sally was dead."

"Theater critics," Paolo said. "A good sign."

I quickly hustled us off campus. Time enough later to face the picket line. Anyway, the stifling heat was getting to me. I longed for the air-conditioned comfort of Ernie's, even with its rust-red leatherette banquets and shiny fake-wood-grained paneling. That sort of longing is the sign of a really hot day.

In its favor, the food at Ernie's was decent, the service friendly, and the price good. Actually, if you came from Manhattan, the price was a miracle. All of which was incidental, since Ernie's was the only restaurant in Huber's Landing, a very, very small town housing, aside from the college, a gas station, a post office/hardware store, a branch bank, two bars, and the restaurant. If you wanted to shop, see a movie, or indulge in any other common commercial comforts, you had to travel to a much larger small town about thirty miles to the south.

We settled into a booth. Paolo sat on one side. Roger trapped me against the window on the other. No one said a word as the waitress gave us water and menus. I tried to decide between a cheeseburger and the all-you-can-eat salad buffet as Roger detailed their trip from New York.

Unlike Paolo, or maybe because Paolo was so edgy, Roger was behaving as if all was right in their little world. I couldn't be certain if he was deliberately trying to irritate his lover or if he was incredibly happy to be out of the city for a few days. Either way, he sat in that booth being relentlessly cheerful.

"Of course, we were the only Thing on the road," he said. "We came south on the Jersey Turnpike. Past all those rest stops with funny names: Clara Barton, Eleanor Roosevelt, Mitzi Gaynor. I made that one up."

"And we just had to stop and press a penny in a machine at each and every one of those exciting little rendezvous," Paolo said.

"I enjoy myself when I travel. Is anything wrong with that?" Roger asked me.

"Well—"

"We came across PA on the turnpike," Roger went on. "Do you realize that there are only two roads west through this state? You either take the turnpike across the south, which is really old and not very good, or Interstate 80 across the north. There is nothing in the middle."

"I grew up—"

"Exactly. So on the PA Turnpike, we get to see some really beautiful scenery. You do have to say that. Going from the coastal plains up into these mountains. Lots of farms in the middle. I love pine trees. There were no pine trees where I grew up and, God knows, no mountains. We also saw cows. Plenty of cows. There were cows where I came from, so that's not so much as interesting to me as it might be for others. Like Paolo, who grew up without cows."

"Something I have suffered for ever since, I assure you," Paolo said.

"Of course, it's not like a real country road, so you only see these things from a distance, but just south of Harrisburg—"

"Stop this," Paolo said, laying down his menu. "Now, or I am going to drive back east without you. You can stay here with the nun killers or walk home."

"Hostility is not going to solve anything," Roger said.

"Not true. When we get home, I am going to act with great hostility toward your modem, and you will never be able to chat online again."

"That would be removing a symptom, not the cause." Roger was a very logical guy.

I was spared the cause. At that moment the waitress returned to take our orders. I chose the cheeseburger—rare. It seemed like a raw meat kind of night.

"How did you guys manage to drive all this way and not hurt each other?" I asked when we were alone again.

"Who said we didn't?" Paolo asked. "Anyway, the day isn't over yet, is it?"

Paolo started to flag down the waitress. "Do you think they could make a dry martini here?"

"Why don't you just ask for gin over ice?" Roger said, somewhere between helpful and hateful.

"Oh, recrimination. Never marry a man who doesn't drink, Nicky. They are forever clocking everyone else's consumption."

"Why are you two here?" I asked.

"I would think that would be obvious," Paolo said.

"Yeah," Roger added. "It's the only thing we've agreed on in three days."

"I'm missing it here, guys," I said.

"We came for your help," Paolo said.

I stared at him, trying to understand.

"So you can help us sort this out," he persisted.

Roger smiled at the idea as if it were not completely unhinged. "After all, you introduced us," he said.

Obviously, there was a logical progression here for the boys. I just wasn't getting it. I looked out the window at the sleepy side street, deserted or, more likely, never really used. I imagined walking down that street, shirtless, with David Scott strolling along next to me. Walking along on a sunny day, a day like this only less humid, brighter, and underscored by the light sound of an upbeat piano tune. We'd have Popsicles. I love Popsicles—cool, liquefying Popsicles. I'd take mine and stroke the beautiful cleft between his pecs, press my tongue against his chest and start slurping the sweet—

"You're daydreaming again," Paolo said, puncturing the image.

"No, I'm not," I lied. I didn't fool them. They knew me too well.

I had introduced them. That was true. I just hadn't realized that I was providing a warranty with the introduction. Four years earlier, fresh out of theater school and new in the city, I was temping at a law firm on Wall Street, where I befriended Roger Parker, newly minted systems operator. One night, I dragged him to an exhibition of sculpture by a friend of a friend. The friend's friend was Paolo. A stunningly mysterious courtship followed, and six months later they merged furniture and housewares. Paolo insisted it was because Roger was so "white."

"And I don't just mean visually," he'd said, "though God knows he is gloriously pale. No, just everything about him is so Midwestern, so washed out. He's like some bizarre triple-wrapped, extra-sealed surprise package. Down there somewhere is an entire emotional life, just waiting to pop out at odd moments."

Roger, of course, being so very "white" and so properly liberal, would never make any public comments on Paolo's ethnicity. For him it was all about "urban" and "exotic." All very heavily coded language that expressed exactly the same fascination.

I focused on their eager faces.

"You mean you drove out here so that I could play referee?" I asked.

"You make it sound so unpleasant," Paolo said.

Roger looked upset. "We thought you'd want to help."

"Guys, follow along with me, OK? I have one dead leading lady, one bad director, one miserable script, and an opening less than one week away. I am a little overextended just now."

"Not a problem," Paolo said. "We can help each other."

"How?" I asked.

"I am a sculptor. I know about design. And Roger can always fetch things."

"That was just mean, Paolo," Roger said.

"I have designers, and I have an assistant."

"I do not fetch. OK?" Roger insisted.

"Sorry, Rog. Look, guys. Really, I am very, very busy."

"Exactly what is happening around here anyway?" Paolo asked. "I expected to find you in your own private Walden, not awash in corpses."

"One corpse," I corrected him. I told them the story of Sister Sally's death.

"So was she murdered?" Roger asked.

"I doubt it, Rog," I said. "Who would want to murder a nun?"

"Well . . ." Paolo let the word hang over the table.

"Seriously," I said. "Everyone liked her. In fact, I think the prop master, Marty Friedman, was in love with her."

"Isn't that illegal?" Roger asked.

"Only if she's underage. Otherwise, you just get a nasty letter from the Pope," Paolo answered.

"It's a zoo around here." I shook my head. "The artistic director and the musical director are locked in some weird emotional death dance. They hate each other, but they keep working together year after year. I heard that three years back they both had heart attacks within a month of each other."

"It's too bad about the nun," Roger said, putting on his best sympathy face.

"Oh, please," Paolo said. "Mr. 'I Love a Mystery.' Do you know how many versions of *The Hound of the Baskervilles* I've had to watch in the past four years? Admit it, Roger—you wish the nun had been stabbed six times and then torched."

"Another mean comment, thank you." Roger looked ready to toss a vinegar cruet at his lover.

"Guys," I said. "I thought we were going to talk about me for a moment?"

"Of course we are, Nicky. Ignore him," Paolo said. "You were telling us about dead nuns and sick directors."

"I'm telling you, guys, it is so bad, I find the children a welcome break."

"That is bad," Paolo said.

"You hate working with children," Roger agreed.

"Yeah, and this group is a real set of winners, led by the artistic director's obsessively adoring twelve-year-old daughter."

"Therapy," they said in unison.

"Big time. But at least when the kids are angry at you they're straightforward about it and they don't resort to clever dialogue." I meant this comment as a reproach to both of them. They each assumed I meant the other and exchanged "I told you so" looks across the table.

Dinner arrived. My cheeseburger bled perfectly. Paolo attacked his roast chicken ("good, wholesome comfort food") with enough anger to kill the bird again. Roger picked at a caesar salad.

"You know, I think she was murdered," Roger said. "Maybe she was pregnant and someone wanted to hide it. Nuns aren't supposed to get pregnant, right?"

"She wasn't murdered," I said. "Anyway, killing her wouldn't hide a pregnancy. The autopsy would show it."

"Oh. Maybe she knew something she wasn't supposed to know?"

"Jesus, Roger," Paolo said. "Are you listening to him? She wasn't murdered. I'm going to find that drink." He went to the bar in search of gin.

"Roger . . . ," I started after Paolo was out of hearing range.

"I know, I know. It was a mistake. A big mistake, and I wish I could take it back."

"But how did he find out you were in a chat room doing . . . what do you do in chat rooms, anyway?"

"Chat. Talk. That is it, I swear. I was just making conversation. I was not looking for sex. I signed off, but I forgot to clear the screen.

He sat down to do his checkbook, and the window with everything I typed was still there."

"Not good." I managed to keep my laughter down to a smirk. Roger was a computer consultant, the kind of guy everyday people ridiculed a decade ago but who now act as high priests of info culture. I guess even high priests have bad days at the shrine.

"Oh, laugh. Even I can see the irony in this one. You know, he wasn't even going to let me bring my laptop along, but I wouldn't come without it."

"Why do you need a laptop computer with you?"

Roger looked at me as if I had suggested we strip down to our Calvin Kleins right there in Ernie's Family Restaurant, as if I intended to take a busboy on the Formica tabletop.

"Why do you ask questions like that?" he said.

"Questions like what?" Paolo stood next to the table, scowling at Roger. He held a martini glass in one hand. "What are you dodging now?"

"Suspicion is an ugly emotion," Roger said.

"Enough." I waved my fork. "If you're going to stay, you're going to behave. Sit, Paolo. Sit."

Paolo sat.

Just then David Scott entered the restaurant. He actually looked better with his hair plastered down with sweat. Oh, I had it bad. He asked for change at the cash register. David turned, saw us, and smiled.

"Beautiful," Paolo said.

"Who is he?" Roger asked.

"One of the actors," I said. "He's a senior here. Or was. Just graduated."

Change in hand, he came our way. Even the way he walked . . .

"Hello, Nicky."

"Hi, David. What's up?"

"Really sad about Sally. She was great. I always liked her. Of course, our parents were always fighting, so I really never got to spend much time with her when we were growing up."

I was speechless in the face of his damp T-shirt clinging to his torso.

"Hi," Paolo said. "We look like people, but actually Nicky ordered us with his burger." He turned toward me. "That's why he's not introducing us, isn't it?"

"Sorry. David, this is Paolo and Roger, friends of mine from New York."

"Nice to meet you."

"Please, sit." Paolo patted the empty space next to him.

"Thanks." David sat, oblivious to Roger's annoyance.

"So," Paolo said, "you grew up here with the poor dear thing?"

"We're cousins. But like I said, our parents—actually, our fathers—didn't get along."

That comment snapped me back to the conversation.

"You're cousins," I repeated.

"Oh, yeah. I've known her forever."

So far there was Benny and his daughter and Corporal Roberts and his daughter. Now Sister Sally and David Scott turn out to be cousins.

"What's so odd about that, Nicky?" Roger asked.

"Nothing, I guess. There just seem to be a lot of relatives around."

"This is a small town." David smiled at me. Who cared how small the town was?

"So, tell me, what's up with Marty Friedman and Sally?" I asked, pursuing the first topic of conversation that came to mind.

"Poor Marty. He's been in love with Sally since first grade. She was never interested, not like that. Always nice to him, though."

"But he remained devoted to her, did he?" Paolo asked.

"The longest running crush I ever heard of," David agreed.

"Amazing, isn't it?" Paolo asked no one in particular as he gazed out of the window. "How some people can remain faithful for decades."

"So, what happens next, Nicky?" David asked.

"Mary Frances Roberts is going to step in. We need to bring her up to speed."

"This is the worst caesar salad I've ever had," Roger said.

"Who orders caesar at a family restaurant in backwater Pennsylvania?" Paolo snapped. Then, to David, "Nothing personal, of course. Lovely place. Really."

"Oh, you didn't offend me. I can't wait to leave. I'm off to New York myself when the summer is over."

"Really?" I said.

"Yup. You know, Nicky, we should make sure and exchange—"

"Here you are. I thought you'd be home. I tried there first." Patsy Malone, with her newly minted, continuously shell-shocked look, appeared suddenly at my elbow. She was even missing her trademark vest.

"Hello, Patsy. You see, Roger? My assistant doesn't fetch. Her job is to follow me around town and deliver bad news. Now what?"

"Edward is missing, and so is Sister Mary Corinne." Patsy sat down, squeezing Paolo and David closer together on their side of the bench. She looked like a marathon runner at the finish line.

"What?"

"Don't you have to be missing forty-eight hours before you're officially missing?" Roger asked.

"Leave it to the inspector. Oh yes, hours and hours of PBS *Mystery!*" Paolo said.

Patsy looked confused. "What do you mean?"

"I should probably go. This looks like business," David said, working his way out of the booth. "I'll see you at the theater. Bye."

Before I could say much of anything else, he was out the door.

"Something wrong, Nicky?" Roger asked, looking at my expression.

"Nicky has a major crush on that guy," Patsy said.

"Please. Let's leave my emotional life out of this, OK?" I was begging. I did not want to be the object of Roger and Paolo's displaced anxiety. And when had Patsy noticed? Was I being that obvious?

"The answer to your question is that my darling Roger is mystery crazed," Paolo said to Patsy. Then, to me, "A crush, huh?"

"Oh," Patsy said to Roger. "You should meet Olivia Singleton. She loves mysteries."

"Who is she?" Roger asked. "Another nun?"

"No. She's the director's daughter," Patsy said.

"Ah, the twelve-year-old in need of therapy?" Paolo said. "You see, beloved, I am not the only one who looks at you and thinks of adolescence. But, this crush business."

"Patsy," I said, trying to gain control over the conversation, "what makes you think they're missing?"

Patsy blurted out the facts in one long breath. "I was trying to find Edward to talk about the schedule, but he wasn't at his afternoon session for summer students, so I called his house, but his housekeeper said he hadn't been home since yesterday, and then Ilana came looking for you to tell you that Sister Mary Corinne still hadn't shown up for work, but you weren't around, so I called the convent and they were worried because she didn't come home last night either."

"Did any of this surprise Ilana?" I asked.

"She didn't seem to be. Why?"

"Just a thought," I said. An annoying thought.

"Do you think they ran off together, Nicky? This nun and this music guy?" Roger asked.

"This town is better than *Valley of the Dolls*," Paolo added.

"I have no idea what to think," I said, "except that this is not going to make my evening any easier." I signaled for the check. "I'd better get back and call Benny."

"Who's Benny?" Roger asked.

"The artistic director," I answered. "He's going to have to make some choices about tonight. Never an easy thing for Benny."

The waitress laid our bill on the table with a cheery "Thank you."

"But what can we do without music?" Patsy asked.

"Well, since we need to rehearse Mary Frances, there is actually a lot to be done."

"Mary Frances, Mary Corinne, Patsy Malone . . . all so Catholic," Paolo said.

I stood up. "That's enough. Back to work."

"But, what are we supposed to do?" Roger asked me.

"I'll give you the keys to my apartment. You can go settle in."

Paolo vetoed the idea. "No. We came here so we could be with you. We will go to the theater together and face the dying and missing Wives of Jesus."

"That's Brides of Christ," Patsy said.

"A nun's a nun, darling. Did I ever tell you about the time Roger asked a nun for directions to a bathhouse?" Paolo peered at Patsy like a cat about to taste feathers.

"I have never asked a nun for directions to anything. You're hallucinating again," Roger said.

"Perhaps you're right." Paolo headed for the exit. "Why, just last week I was hallucinating I loved you," he shot back over his shoulder. Suddenly, Roger looked very worried. He hurried after his lover.

"So," Patsy said to me as we followed a discreet six feet back, "how long are your friends going to stay?"

SIX

As we approached the campus, I was depressed by the heavy, wet, immobile air. The humidity was brutal. I longed for a good summer storm, the kind where the thunder and rain rip across the hills, leaving everything drenched and cool.

Paolo and Roger walked ahead in silence, side by side. In the city they walked everywhere hand in hand. Roger told me that public affection had been difficult for him at first, but that Paolo had insisted. Paolo told me that Roger grabbed his hand on their first date and never let go. It was sad to see them separated by an invisible tension that might as well have been a solid wall.

Following behind, Patsy and I were also wordless. I didn't know what was on her mind, but I was trying to decide what we could rehearse without a musical director. Sure, I was curious about the connection between Mary Corinne and Edward Rossoff, although given Ilana Mosca's description of the nun and what I myself had seen of their embrace the night before, I didn't have to think too hard to come up with an answer. Well, why shouldn't they be happy together if that's what they wanted? It wasn't my business, except that it left me without a musical director and probably behind on wig production.

In the auditorium we found the children racing in the aisles and fighting in the rows. One was even climbing a ladder along the back-stage wall.

"It looks like a nursery," Paolo said.

"They're not even supposed to be here for another hour," Patsy said.

"Sometimes I think the parents drop them off early just to get rid of them." I pulled a ball cap out of the grip of one kid and restored it to the head of another. "Timmy, come down from the ladder. Now."

I led the way to the center of the house, where I found the cave-men back at play under my makeshift desk.

"OK. Cave's been flooded out. Everyone off to higher ground." I rattled the desk. The boys scampered away on all fours, giggling. "Patsy, make a note, we need to grease their tap shoes before each performance, OK?"

It's not that I don't like kids. I adore my nieces and nephews. It's that I don't like them in large numbers, unsupervised by their own parents.

"They don't tap," she said.

"Damn. OK, what's up first?"

Patsy sat next to me, and we began our evening prerehearsal ritual while Paolo and Roger, in deliberate and continued silence, sought out seats on opposite sides of my workspace.

Each night before rehearsal, Patsy and I checked the sequence of events, firmly setting the flow of cast members in our minds. The evening goes much more smoothly if we don't have to refer to the schedule to know when the nuns' chorus is supposed to be singing in Room 101A or onstage with the orphans, who have just come from Room 102B, where the choreographer has moved on to the duet between the young police lieutenant and Sister Klarissa, freeing up the Mother Superior for her costume fitting. Tonight we had to truncate the chorus work and replace it with rehearsal of the larger scenes. By the time Benny arrived, we'd worked out a plan that utilized everyone who was on call for the evening.

Naturally, Benny fussed. He complained as if I personally had shoved Edward into Mary Corinne's omnivorous embrace. He griped about the heat, which looked as if it was about to do him in. He was dressed in a baggy white linen shorts-and-shirt outfit. Instead of looking cool, the white accented the violent red flush of his face. As he stood in front of me, sweating and panting, I thought about his heart attack. Surely the theater gods would not be that cruel? Not even to *Convent of Fear.* When he began to whimper about the children, I reminded him that one of the lovelies was his own daughter. He ignored that comment. Instead, he whined that he could not possibly produce good theater under these conditions. I agreed that his chances of producing good theater were slight. Patsy giggled and Paolo raised an eyebrow, but Benny soldiered on. Finally, with just two minor changes, he announced that he had solved the scheduling problems.

Then he turned to Paolo.

"So Nicky's friends are going to see theater magic in the making. Ooohhh. Fun, huh?"

Paolo stared at him silently until Benny turned and walked away.

We had thirty minutes to set up. Backstage was in reasonable shape. Aside from final cleanup, it looked as if the college work crew had finished their renovation of the loading dock. They were two weeks behind schedule but still on time for opening. I started sweeping. I always left the prop setup to Patsy. During performance I'd be sitting in a booth at the back of the auditorium. Patsy would be the one actually on "deck" supervising the scene crews.

First up would be the tea scene that Mary Frances and I had spent so much time rehearsing that afternoon. I should have stayed with her, doing my best concerned stage manager's routine with the understudy, but I needed the break that dinner hadn't provided. Anyway, Patsy was only too eager to prompt Mary Frances through her dialogue and blocking. So, instead of standing around onstage, script in hand, helping Mary Frances weave her way through an afternoon at the convent with the girls, I headed downstairs to make the "rounds."

The rounds. For one blessed half-hour each evening, I was free of Benny, free of having to watch *Convent of Fear*, and mostly free of screaming children. I strolled from designer to designer, noting their questions, answering previous inquiries, and offering them a glimpse of what was happening in rehearsal. I was St. Gilbert's own version of the information superhighway. The goal was to keep all members of the production team in sync.

I always stopped first in the costume shop.

"I've always thought nuns were bad luck, but you don't say that thing in place like this," Ilana said the moment I appeared in her doorway.

Ilana stood, hands on hips, speaking through three pins that stuck out of her mouth. She was working on a nun's habit draped over the costume dummy in front of her. Her primary crew, a seamstress and one guy who was a whiz with cutting and fitting, were busy at the machines and table.

"Not that I don't slip up and let it out," she said. "But they think you joke." What exactly Ilana's staff and students thought of her varied over the years. Just then rumor was current that her first job in America had been as a female professional wrestler. I never believed it.

Ilana Mosca was my favorite designer. I enjoyed her blunt, outspoken style. She, in turn, enjoyed having a fresh ear and telling me her favorite stories, long since worn out on the permanent staff. I think she even laid the accent on extra thick when we were alone. I admired the entire performance.

The costume shop was the most cluttered of the shops. The walls were lined with shelves and drawers containing bolts of cloth, buttons, snaps, zippers—every type of metallic or plastic fastener. There was half a wall devoted just to ribbons of varying size, color, and tint. Running through the center of the room was a long cutting table flanked by two sewing machines. Ironing boards stood along the far wall. This close to performance, there were also racks of costumes in varying degrees of near-completion filling half the room. The air was leavened with a hefty dose of pine-scented air freshener.

"So? Why are you here?" she asked.

"Just to see your lovely self. I'm making the rounds," I said, waving my clipboard.

"Then you can tell Benny Singleton that without the Straying Nun, wigs will not be done in time."

In some people crisis brings on a sense of elation. Ilana was one of those people. She was absolutely exhilarated at the thought of impending wig failure.

"Not done in time, Ilana, or just that much more difficult to finish?" I smiled. I knew she'd have every piece of hair ready for opening. Ilana would never permit a loose end. What's more, she knew I knew. We were engaged in a burlesque that every designer and stage manager performs by rote.

"Done, yes, but not done so well. All hurry not good. You see when times come." I swear her accent thickened so much that her lower lip began to droop from the weight. The woman at the sewing machine started to grin.

"Ilana," I said, "now tell me, exactly how bad is it? Can we do anything from our end to help?"

This was Designer Stroking 101. Get the designer talking and soon enough, if they're any good, they'll find a solution. You get credit for listening and being so very supportive. Ilana went over her options, some out loud and some in a mumble, until she was satisfied that she could, with a bit of effort here and there and considerable sacrifice of her already overburdened self, bring wigs and costumes in on time.

"But I don't like." She was scowling happily.

"And neither do I. But what am I going to do? While you're fighting hair, I'm missing a musical director. But maybe you heard?" I was fishing. Not for a moment did I suppose that Ilana didn't know that Edward was also gone missing. In fact, if anyone knew the certain truth about the connection between the musical director and the nun, I was betting on Ilana.

"You want to know something, ask. Don't make noise at me." Ilana jabbed a pin into the nun's habit. "And don't make puppy face at me." She turned and jabbed a pin in my direction. "We're neither of us stupid, Nicky. And at least one of us is busy. So get to point."

"OK, OK, Ilana. Aim that thing at someone else. So, what can you tell me abut the two of them? Am I going to get my musical director back, or do I send Patsy to whistle in the orchestra pit on opening?"

There was a metal stool next to the table where the whiz kid was working. I plunked myself down. As funny as the idea of Patsy whistling the score of *Convent of Fear* was, there just weren't many options.

"Do not look so unhappy, Nicky. I do not know where they go, but I bet he will be back soon. Edward Rossoff is man who will not walk out on his job. He will see they get back."

Her implication was clear.

"*He?*" I repeated back to her.

"Yes. He. In her, I have no faith. That one breaks vows like I break wind."

"Oh, please," the whiz kid moaned from his end of the table.

"Well, is true. She broke vow to God, and she broke promise to Sobieski, and she will kill Edward too."

"Kill him? Are you saying Mary Corinne killed Joe's father?" I didn't believe it. Neither did the whiz kid nor the seamstress, both of whom just shook their heads and kept working.

"She was having affair with him, she stopped, he killed self. You tell me?" Now she was ripping pins out of the costume and re-sticking them with double the energy. I began to cast a cautious eye around the shop for votive candles, incense, or other signs of ritual. I didn't see any, but still, I was glad it was Mary Corinne and not me that Ilana was thinking of as she gleefully pushed pins into the dummy.

"I thought he killed himself over the money?"

"Look around, Nicky. There was never much money. Broken heart. No one speaks of money till after he is dead. Then Benny brings out records. Big scandal, but Sobieski already gone." She emphasized the last word with one more pin and reached for her scissors.

"You're telling me no one said anything about embezzlement until after the guy was dead?"

"Yes. And some blame Benny for smearing the man's memory. But what should he do? Let everyone think he had stolen money himself? He had to protect his children. He was alone with his children. He did everything for them. I was there. Always there. But only so much can you help." She started cutting away at the fabric. "And more, the boy is born between her ending the affair and him killing self. Shameless."

Two children came running into the costume shop laughing, racing to hide among the costume racks. When they saw me, they stopped, turned, and ran the other way. I barely noticed them. When you have a children's chorus running everywhere, they become like background noise. It was the costume racks that drew my attention away from Ilana's story. There was a row of nun's habits, each with a cross hanging from its waist.

"Ilana, aren't those nun's crosses supposed to be props?" I asked, sniffing carefully for a territorial battle between design departments.

"Props, costumes. Does it matter this close? Marty brought them to me so I could see how they look on habits."

"Good. Did he get the replacement?" I asked.

"What replacement?"

"For the missing cross."

Ilana thought for a moment. "There is no missing cross. I have cross for every habit, even this one. I counted just an hour ago."

"Really? Well, I guess he found it. I hope Edward turns up so easily."

"Yes. I think he will. I think they will be back. You will get your musical director. I will get pain from that nun. Now get out. I have work. My work. Her work. Everyone's work."

I left her mumbling gleefully at the dummy.

The prop shop was just opposite the costume shop. As I stepped out of Ilana's preserve, wondering at the match between Mary Corinne, fallen nun, and Edward Rossoff, foul-mouthed petty tyrant, I heard shouting.

"Tonight, damn it! I need it tonight." Joe Sobieski was laying into someone.

I looked into the prop room. Joe was standing in the center of the room, that is to say in the middle of four tables whose square figure formed the primary workspace, glaring at Marty Friedman. The prop master was standing outside the tables at a vise clamp, working on what looked to be the garden tools. Marty, whose six-foot frame was shirtless under a pair of paint-splattered bib overalls, looked like a terrified professional wrestler, unwilling to enter the ring. In his case it wasn't an act.

"You're shouting," Marty said, trying to calm Joe.

"Is there a problem, Joe?" I asked. "Do you need a specific prop tonight?" I didn't think needing a prop from the prop department was such a bad guess. From the look on Joe's face, you'd think I was the biggest fool on earth.

"This has nothing to do with you, Nicky. OK? It's not about the show. It's personal between Marty and me, so leave it alone."

I reminded myself that this was a guy whose father committed suicide when he wasn't even a year old. I tried to create some simple, immediate excuse for his outburst: car trouble, girl trouble, bad hair day. I grappled with sympathy. I lost. Maybe I'm just not as imaginative as I thought.

"Well, then I'm sorry to interrupt, but I'm here on business."

"Oh, that's fine." Marty looked relieved to be interrupted.

"Fine," Joe said. "I'm out of here, but we are not done. Got it?" He pushed past me and down the hall. Every exit that guy made was like bad film noir.

I turned back to Marty, who immediately went back to work.

"I'm trying to dull this thing, like you asked," he said as he scraped a metal file along the point of the garden tool.

The prop room was not as large as the costume shop. Nor as tidy. Where Ilana ran a thoroughly well-organized, well-inventoried stock of supplies, Marty oversaw something more resembling the garage workshop your uncle might putter around in. I couldn't make out any sense of order in the room. Not that I'm at all adept at the building or painting end of theater, but organization is my specialty. Disorganization looks the same wherever you find it. There were stacks of loose materials and open, overstuffed drawers. The floors and counters were never completely swept clean. The only thing the prop room had over the costume shop was the smell. It smelled like a theater. Ilana believed in air freshener, lots and lots of pine-scented air freshener. The prop room was all glue and paint.

"So, everything OK down here?" I asked.

"Yeah, sure. Oh, you mean with Joe. Don't worry about that. It's nothing."

"OK." I just stood there.

"We go way back. I mean, we grew up together. We're cousins, you know."

No. I didn't.

"Cousins? God, everyone in this town really is related. So, are you related to Sister Mary Corinne?" I asked.

"No. Joe's dad and my mom were brother and sister. Mary Corinne is Joe's mother's sister."

I shook my head. Fathers and daughters, fathers and sons, aunts and uncles, cousins: this theater really was one large, unhappy family.

"Well, anyway," Marty said. "Don't worry about Joe. He gets stressed, but it's OK. Really it is. OK?"

"OK, Marty, sure. I'm just making rounds here," I said.

"Oh, right. Yeah. Well, then." He indicated the garden tools laid out in front of him. "These will be done soon. I'll just bring them up-stairs for you and Benny to look at."

"That's fine," I said, thinking that Benny was never one to waste too much energy checking out the props.

"And I found another cross to match the ones we have," he said.

"You know, I was just in the costume shop, and there was a cross for every costume."

"No." He shook his head. "I haven't put the new one there. There's one missing."

"I don't know, Marty. I was just there and I saw them, and Ilana said none are missing."

"Really? But I looked, really I did, Nicky. Honestly. I couldn't find it—"

We heard a loud crash from the scene shop next door. I tried the door that connected the two shops, but it was jammed shut. We ran for the hallway. As I approached the scene shop door, I decided that I would never leave the peace and quiet of New York City again.

Lee Dexter, set designer, was a very strange man. He might have been the nicest guy at St. Gilbert's. He had a warm affability and a great sense of humor. I'd heard that he'd married his high school sweetheart in a completely cinematic love story. Unfortunately, if there was ever a candidate for pharmacological help, it was Lee Dexter. Living right alongside "Nice Dexter" was "Crazy Dexter." You just never knew when all that pleasantry would be replaced with sputtering rage, threats, and shouting. So when Marty and I came rushing into the scene shop, I wasn't surprised to see him threatening to spray-paint someone.

Lee, a short, powerfully built bear of a man, had backed his opponent into several flats. The sound we'd heard was the crash of scenery tumbling off to the side.

"Get out of my shop," Lee was shouting.

"You're blocking the goddamn door," Paolo Suarez shouted back at him.

There they stood, Lee armed with an apparatus that looked like a fire extinguisher but was designed for spraying paint in textured patterns on scenery, and Paolo—thoroughly outgunned—holding a can of spray paint as if it were mace.

I tried to contain my laughter. I didn't want to set Lee off any worse than he was.

"OK, gentlemen. Let's just put down our weapons and no one will need paint thinner. All right?"

"I am not putting down this sprayer until that son of a bitch drops his spray can," Lee said.

"Good luck, asshole." Paolo held his ground.

"Oh, man," Marty said. "This is bad. This is really bad." He was starting to shake. "I'm going for help."

I didn't think we needed help, but Marty was gone. Then again, I wasn't all that certain he'd ever be back. I wouldn't want to have to count on him during a real fight. I did not consider two guys armed with spray paint a real fight. A fashion disaster in the making, but not a fight.

"Anyone want to tell me what is going on here? Paolo?"

"You know him?" Lee shifted his eyes briefly in my direction.

"Oh yes. He's a friend of mine."

"Well, I found your *friend* trying to repaint my scenery."

"I was not," Paolo said. "I would never have repainted without your permission, Nicky. Though God knows, this palette needs mouth-to-mouth. He's using chartreuse."

"It's sea foam, you son of a bitch!" Lee was shouting again.

"Enough already." I stepped between them. Once false move and I'd be piebald, though probably nicely textured: they were both good artists. "Paolo, the color palette is not for you, or me, to question. It's up to Lee and Benny. Now, unless you intend to spray me, put down the can."

The three of us stood motionless for a moment. Paolo stepped aside and placed the spray paint, which I could now see was a deep blue, on a table next to the flats.

"I was merely going to suggest something a little more subtle," he said.

"Get out." Lee pushed the nozzle of his sprayer past me and took aim at Paolo's face. I risked gently pushing it aside.

"You would attack an unarmed man?" Paolo said.

"Paolo, please go back upstairs and watch rehearsal," I tried, guiding him toward the door.

"Sure, make me suffer." He started to stroll with a mannered casualness toward the exit. "Stick to chartreuse. What do I care? But wait till the light hits all that yellow. I'm not going to be looking at it every night." He was gone without looking back.

"Who the hell is that asshole?" Lee dumped the sprayer along the wall. He began to breathe more evenly. The splotchy red marks on his face were subsiding.

"Oh, just a friend visiting me from New York. He won't bother you anymore. Swear. What happened?"

"I found that asshole in here in front of the garden flat, shaking a spray can and going, 'Oh no, no . . . this won't do.' " Lee had started lisping. Normally, I don't put up with straight folk doing the fake-lisping routine, but he looked so pathetic: a mincing, bearlike caricature of the graceful Suarez. Anyway, it was my friend who'd made him so angry. I figured I owed him a little.

"If I hadn't stopped him," Lee said, "he would have painted the entire piece cerulean, and then I would have had to mottle the walls and redo the borders in stippled washes. I don't have time to rebuild."

What could I possibly say to that? "I promise this will not happen again."

"Well, just keep him out of here."

The frightening thing about Lee was the sudden on/off quality. In a moment he was ready to settle down and do business. There were notes from yesterday's rehearsal that I wanted to review, to be certain that Benny's new blocking wasn't going to run—literally or figuratively—into problems with the scenery. By the time we were both satisfied that no actors were likely to be walking through walls, there was absolutely no trace of his prior mood.

"Look. I'm sorry," he said. "About that outburst. I'm just under a lot of stress trying to get this done."

"No apologies necessary, Lee," I said, not meaning it but figuring I could collect a few points for being gracious. "Everyone is under a lot of pressure right now."

"Yeah. After last night. I had to leave when Ilana came back down and told me."

"Ilana? What did Ilana tell you?" My mind was drifting. I'd been in and out of scene shops for years, and I still wasn't certain what that piece of equipment in the far corner was for. The one with the serrated edges, the two pulleys, and—

"What do you mean *what*? About Sally." Lee's tone snagged my attention back to the moment.

"Of course. Stress, see? We're all a little whacked." I tried to cover my lapse in attentiveness. "So when did Ilana tell you this?"

"When she came back down from the stage last night. She said that Sally was being taken away in an ambulance."

I conjured up a picture of everyone who had been onstage when Sally collapsed. There were children huddled off to one side. Around the prostrate figure of the nun were Benny, Mary Corinne, Patsy, Edward, Marty Friedman, and myself. No Ilana.

"Ilana wasn't onstage," I said.

"Well, she went that way. She came in here and said she was going upstairs to take a thermos of soup to Benny and did I want anything. A lot of good taking soup to that asshole is going to do her."

"She never made it," I said, while I thought about why anyone would want soup in this weather. As for the rest of it, from the moment I'd arrived at St. Gilbert's the animosity between Lee Dexter and Benny Singleton was only barely overshadowed by that between Benny and Edward Rossoff. How these people ever got a production before an audience was a mystery.

"Well, she must have seen something. Came back down here and told me that an ambulance was coming. That poor Sally was writhing on the floor . . ." Here his eyes started to tear up.

"I'm sorry, Lee. I didn't realize you were that close to Sally." Impulsively, I asked, "You weren't related, were you?"

He forced the tears back with several rapid blinks. His eyes lost the soft cast they'd taken on. A sharpness entered them as he stared at me.

"No. And what the hell business of yours is it how well I knew her?" He stood up.

"I'm sorry. I didn't mean anything by it."

"I'm going to get coffee." He left without another word.

I put the entire episode down as another Crazy Dexter moment. Anyway, I was just being polite. I didn't really want to know anything about his relationship to Sally. I was more concerned about Ilana. She must have arrived in the wings just about the time Sally had collapsed, yet she had stayed completely out of the action. Some people just don't deal well with medical emergencies.

This set of rounds had been way too eventful. I took advantage of the empty scene shop to steal a quiet moment from the night.

I am always amazed that I can feel so at home in a shop. I was surrounded by wood and the tools for reshaping it in the form of any place or time on earth or in imagination. Like I said, I was no good at the building/painting thing myself, but this was a theater scene shop, not a "real" shop. I'd studied "real" shop in high school. After six weeks in metal shop, I'd produced the handle of a hammer. After eight weeks in wood shop, two legs of a three-legged lamp. That sort of relationship to traditional boyhood schooling made theater the perfect refuge for a quirky, anxiety-ridden teenage homo waiting to grow up and leave home. I'd spent many late evenings painting, pasting, and rehearsing. In the year after high school, long evenings turned into long nights at the local community theater.

So there I sat, inhaling the most comforting scent in my life: the slightly burnt smell of cut wood laced with resin and paint. Breathing deeply, I closed my eyes. The tension in my neck and shoulders began to release.

I tried to think about *Convent of Fear*, but mostly I kept coming back to the story Ilana had told me about Sister Mary Corinne and Joe Sobieski Sr. It was all so melodramatic: affairs, embezzlement, suicide. I tried to imagine Sister Mary Corinne twenty years younger. Was she really capable of feeling that kind of passion or of arousing it in someone else? Today she seemed so solid, so stable. But twenty years ago she was breaking her vows for a man who would eventually kill himself in despair over losing her. And now it looked like she was doing it again. It was all beside the point. I had a show to do.

I took another deep breath.

"Hey there."

I jumped, startled. And there he was. Alone. Just us.

David Scott smiled at me as he entered the shop.

"I'm sorry. Am I interrupting?"

"Ah. No." Snappy comeback. I tried to recover. "Actually, I was deep in thought about the state of American theater, but I can get back to it." Much better: witty, suave, inviting.

He crossed the room, looking like breakfast, lunch, and dinner all in one.

"Come to any big decisions?" he asked.

He was wearing his trademark tight T-shirt and baggy knee-length shorts. For some reason (lust?) I couldn't stop noticing what great legs he had.

"Only that it is easier if the people involved don't keep disappearing. Shouldn't you be onstage?" I asked.

"Not yet. Benny is restaging the tea scene." He stopped just one step short of standing on the bottom rung of the stool.

"Restaging? I guess I'd better get back up there and see what he's doing." I didn't move.

"Yeah. Patsy looked a little stressed."

Then he leaned forward and kissed me. Just like that. No preliminaries, no more small talk, just lips to lips followed very soon thereafter by tongue to tongue. I reached out and placed my hands on his arms. I could feel the bump of his triceps beneath his shirt. He pulled himself in closer to my chest, straddling my legs. We stayed that way, him standing over me and running his hands along my back while I laced my fingers across his waist. All St. Gilbert's troubles were suspended for the long moment of that kiss.

"Excuse me. Child present."

David leapt from standing over me and landed on his heels almost a foot away. I snapped my head toward the door.

Olivia Singleton stood there, trying to look shocked but only managing to smirk and sneer at the same time.

"You're needed onstage, David. Daddy's looking for you. Now." She tried to rearrange her expression into total childlike innocence. She failed.

"Thank you, Olivia," David said as he headed directly for the door. He was certainly a cool player. "I'll see you upstairs, Nicky."

"OK, see you there," I said as he brushed past Olivia.

The child and I were alone for a moment of silence.

"So," she said before turning to leave, "how *is* the state of the American theater?"

I watched her disappear through the door. She'd been watching us the entire time.

SEVEN

SISTER KLARISSA ENTERS THE day room of the convent. She loves this room. You can see it in her face. Her eyes settle affectionately on the mantle, where several trophies from the orphanage's softball team are proudly displayed. The deep cushioned chairs and couches, the polished but slightly battered coffee table, and even the somewhat worn area rugs all speak to her of comfort and home. Sister Klarissa loves the convent.

She particularly loves afternoon tea, the hour when the nuns gather for a simple cup and plain conversation. There are fewer nuns in these unbelieving times. The dwindling numbers make Klarissa's calling that much more significant. She is certain of this. How precious, then, these few minutes together when she can learn from the older ones the wisdom of service and sacrifice.

As the youngest member of the convent, Klarissa sits farthest from the fireplace. She does not mind. Today, as always, with small steps and reverentially bowed head, she makes her humble way to the footstool in front of a bookcase filled with leatherette-bound volumes. From here she will be able to hear every word the Mother Superior says. Already, as

Klarissa settles onto the damask cushion, the room is filling. Her eyes move across the assembled nuns: Sister James, small and fragile of body but strong of will, still attached to her old-fashioned name; Sister Apollonia, plump and pleasant looking but ill tempered and prickly; Sister Willomina, gaunt and financially minded.

Klarissa gasps as the Mother Superior enters with two visiting nuns. Sisters Lucretia and Hedwig are introduced to each member of the convent. As Klarissa curtseys, her eyes meet Lucretia's in a searing moment of recognition. The strong jaw and sturdy build of the older nun, the cherubic, soft face of the younger—they could only mean one thing. Why is it that no one else sees, when to Klarissa it is all so obvious: Sister Lucretia is the lieutenant and Sister Hedwig his assistant. They have gone undercover.

Klarissa is stunned by the lieutenant's presence, stunned by her response. Why does she begin to tremble? Why is it suddenly so hot? She reaches up to loosen her collar. The lieutenant smiles at her. Immediately, as if a pin has pricked her, Klarissa gasps and begins to rise. A stern look from the Mother Superior, as well as a pleading glance from the handsome lieutenant and his equally charming assistant, keep her in her seat.

Tea is passed. Cups are filled and handed round in an elaborate and time-consuming ritual. Still no one speaks. The moment drags on. And on. All motion stops.

"Where the hell is the gardener?" someone onstage shouted.

I was watching rehearsal from the rear of the house. Patsy leaned on the edge of the apron, looking intently at Mary Frances. I wished I could believe it was her dedication to the task of helping our new Klarissa, but I was more and more willing to think that someone else was contemplating crossing the professional line with a cast member. I consoled myself with the rationalization that at least my infatuation was not a leading player, just shallow lust for a man I'd barely spoken to. You'd have to be me to find that thought comforting.

Benny stood on the edge of the stage, his arms folded, head sunk on his chest. He was hatless tonight, and the wispy remnants of his blond hair could not cover his shiny bald spot. As the pause onstage lengthened, the spot grew more and more red.

In a bit of melodramatic pantomime that Benny had worked into the scene, the gardener was supposed to appear at the window and brandish a pointy garden trowel. Klarissa was to spot him, gasp, and again be silenced by the Mother Superior, who still thinks that Klarissa is about to give away the policemen's presence. The gardener once more glares at Klarissa and shakes the trowel. She teeters as if fainting, regaining her composure at the last moment. The gardener disappears. Only Klarissa has seen him. Not too surprising in a room full of nuns who can't spot two guys in drag at three feet. After the gardener vanishes, the dialogue is to continue as written. The entire interruption takes about one minute, makes no sense, leaves five nuns onstage with nothing to do but try to look busy, and adds nothing to the plot. Except now there was no gardener, yet everyone sat completely still as if expecting him any moment.

As far as I could see, the only redeeming part of the tea scene was that David was onstage. And he looked great onstage even in his "civilian" clothes. Actually, given he'd be in a nun's habit for this scene, he looked better than he would in costume. Then I realized that I had no idea what he thought of *Convent of Fear*. In fact, we'd barely communicated, except in what I preferred to think of as the Shakespearean mode of romantic eye-to-eye contact, more contemporarily known as cruising. What if he liked *Convent of Fear*? Could I have even a brief fling with someone whose taste was that dreadful? I guess I wouldn't know till I tried.

Benny's blaring voice cut into my reverie.

"Line!" he screamed at Patsy.

"After that sort of surprise, how could I possibly sleep in my own bed?" Patsy read the cue out clearly. Still no one spoke.

Finally, Joe, the only person in costume since he was going to spend so much time in drag and wanted to get used to it, screamed at Patsy.

"Where the hell is the gardener?"

"I cut the gardener from this scene," Benny shouted back at him.

And hadn't told anyone except the gardener.

I made my way down the aisle toward Patsy, who was taking far too much heat. Along the way I passed Olivia and Roger in animated conversation.

"But the best part is when the monk guy tries to look innocent and holy, but you know he knows who did it," Olivia said to Roger as I approached them.

"That's the penny-drop," Roger said. "That's the moment when the detective figures it out. You can see it in his face. I love that moment."

"Oh, wow. Did you see the one where the French baker deep-fries the actress and the cops catch him because he'd spent all this money on rare spices?" Olivia asked.

"Are you sure that was PBS?"

I kept moving. Onstage, Benny and Joe were in a tense face-off.

"Hi. How're we doing?" I said as I leaned on the stage next to Patsy.

"How does it look?" she answered.

"It looks like no one here knows what they are doing. Where have you been, Nicky?" Benny glared down at us.

"Let me see that book." I slid the prompt book in front of me and, while looking through the scene, answered Benny. "I was making rounds, Benny. Visiting all the little gnomes who work in the basement. No, it's still here."

"What is?" he asked.

"The blocking for the gardener. Neither Patsy nor I have erased it. Benny, did you tell anyone other than the gardener that he was cut from the scene?" I finally looked up, though not at Benny. I swept my glance across the stage, taking in all the actors.

"Of course I did. I cannot believe that you have all forgotten." Benny turned his back on me and addressed the cast. "I realize we have all been traumatized by recent events, but we need to focus, people. I need you to pay attention. Is that clear?"

"It's clear you can't do your job," Joe said, coming forward.

"Oh Christ. Here we go." The Mother Superior sat down on one of the many folding chairs that was standing in for the real furniture. She let out an elaborate sigh. "Is this necessary?"

Joe continued, "If he knew what he was doing, we—"

"I know exactly what I am doing, thank you very much."

"Then why is this play such a mess?" Joe demanded.

"This is not the time, Joseph."

"You are not my father. Do not give me that fucking attitude," Joe was shouting.

I wasn't interested in where this conversation was going.

"Gentlemen," I said. "I think we should focus on the task at hand."

Joe turned on me. "You don't know. You have no idea what the 'task at hand' is, Nicky. But everyone is going to find out soon enough. And some are going to get hurt more than others."

Obviously, I was missing something. I noticed that Benny's color shifted from angry red to pale white in a moment. Fear? Maybe. Maybe he was about to keel over with heart failure.

"Joe, you're holding up rehearsal," Benny said. "Please get back to your place." His voice had quickly lost its power and volume.

"Me? I'm not the problem here. I've never been the problem here. You've had a—"

I heard Roger calling out: "No. No. Come back here."

In my peripheral vision I saw someone leaping onstage, a blur of motion. Then Olivia was trying to tackle Joe. She hit him at a full gallop directly in the midsection. She wasn't big enough to do more than knock him back a step or two. She probably wouldn't have been able to do even that, except she'd caught him off-guard.

"Leave him alone. Don't say that." She began punching Joe.

Everyone was too amazed to react. We watched the child pummel the adult to no effect.

Finally, Benny rushed forward and dragged Olivia away. She kicked and screamed the entire length of the stage as he hauled her into the wings.

"This looks like a good time for a break," I said to Patsy. "Everyone take ten!"

The actors dispersed, some to smoke, some in search of coffee or soda. Joe and Mary Frances both came directly for me. I greeted them with a neutral expression.

"Is it always like this?" Mary Frances asked before Joe could start complaining.

"No," he answered on my behalf. "Sometimes it's worse. Sometimes people die. But that's Benny. When that prick is involved, no one is safe."

"That is not funny, Joe," Patsy said. "You shouldn't make fun of Sister Sally's death. And you owe Benny a lot more than that. He's been good to you."

"Owe him? Anything he ever did for me, he owed me."

His ranting was beginning to take it out of Patsy. Her eyes started to tear.

"Now look what you've done, you dumb shit. Apologize," Mary Frances said. She took on an extremely protective stance. I thought she was going to hit him. I considered applauding.

"Oh, cut me a fucking break. What are we going to do, Nicky?" Joe asked, simply ignoring her.

"We are going to finish our break—you have eight minutes left. And then we're going to continue rehearsal. With any luck, none of you will actually hit or otherwise injure each other, but I'm not betting on that anymore." I said it with as much indifference as I could manage. It put Joe off long enough to let Mary Frances jump back in.

"Come on, Pats. Let's get some air." She reached out and took Patsy's arm, hauling her onto the stage. Together they headed for an exit, bonding complete. Worse things could happen than an affair between my assistant and a leading actress. And at St. Gilbert's they already had and probably would again. At least the two of them looked good together.

When they were almost out of earshot, Joe let loose with a single, not-so-whispered "Dykes." Mary Frances froze in mid-step. She turned. A thin, tight smile showed beneath one of the coldest looks I'd ever seen.

"Because I've known you for a very long time, you get away with that. But only once." She held his gaze for a long, theatrical count of three. Then she and Patsy left the stage. I was impressed. So was Joe. He changed tactics immediately.

"We are not going to get enough done tonight," he said to me.

"I'm on break too," I said, taking the prompt book and heading for my table.

I took a deep breath. Something was seriously wrong. Oh sure, one actress was dead and the script and staging were a disaster, but beyond that I had the feeling there was even more going on. I was certain Joe was on the verge of making some serious accusations about Benny when Olivia tackled him. Benny definitely looked like he was expecting the worst. Yet another layer in the history that tied these people together. I'd been told that Benny was the very essence of kindness to

Joe Jr. all his life. Obviously, Joe had a different definition of gratitude than most. I had very little hope that after break we'd get much accomplished.

The house was empty. Everyone, including Roger, had fled when I'd called for a break. I couldn't blame them. That's when I realized that I hadn't seen Paolo in the auditorium. I only hoped he wasn't wandering around the building rewiring lights or sewing new costumes.

What we really needed was for fate to cut us a break and provide a little peace and quiet in rehearsal so we could get some work done. Bad timing, however, is every bit as consequential as good. At just the moment when the cast and Benny were beginning to re-enter the theater, Marty Friedman strolled onstage, and the gods of comedy dragged our little tragedy in the making once more toward farce.

"Hey, Nicky," he called to me. "I finished the garden tools. You can use them in the tea scene if you want."

Mary Frances jumped on Marty's announcement. "Maybe we could use them to bury the animosity."

Patsy giggled. Far too appreciatively, it seemed to me, since the joke wasn't that funny. Some of the nun actresses picked up on the effort to lighten the mood. They laughed out loud.

"Very clever, Mary Frances," Benny said. "But I'm sure our problems are just the heat-of-the-moment variety. No one is taking any of this personally, are they, Joe?" He was cloyingly jovial.

Joe had already taken his place off stage left, waiting to enter. He poked his head into view.

"You're right," Joe said. "And let me apologize. I said if you knew what you were doing, we wouldn't be in this mess. I take it back." He withdrew into the wing.

Benny accepted that rather lame apology. "Excellent. In a few days we'll be opened, and everyone can have a good laugh at the cast party.

Nicky, can we get started, please?" He couldn't quite keep all hint of desperation out of his voice.

"Of course," I said. "Marty, we've cut the gardener from this scene and won't need those props just now. Everyone, places, please—top of the tea scene."

The cast regrouped themselves outside the doorway in order of appearance. Marty Friedman stood center stage looking at me.

"You mean you don't need these at all?" he asked.

"We don't need them now, Marty. We'll still need them for Act 2, Scene 4, in the garden," I answered. When he didn't move I added, "We're going to start now." That cleared him out.

We began. Patsy again moved to the edge of the apron with her script to help prompt Mary Frances. I stayed at the manager's table, keeping an eye on the entire scene. Mary Frances re-entered, followed by the nuns, Joe, and David.

The first nun to speak called for a line.

"So there I was trying to steal a swig of Scotch from her bottle," Patsy cued.

The pace picked up from there, though never by much. When we finished the tea scene, we were a full hour behind schedule. This meant an extra hour for the children to just wander around bored. If a chorus of bored children doesn't frighten you, you are much braver than I.

Most of the cast, including the incredibly unpleasant Joe Jr., left after the tea scene. The children, Benny, Mary Frances, the Mother Superior, Patsy, and I remained to work. I noticed David hanging out down front. Maybe I would redeem something from the evening.

It took about fifteen minutes to find all of the children. Three of them had wandered off to explore the shops downstairs. We located them sitting at the long table in the costume shop, happily and quite pointlessly applying sequins to scraps of fabric.

"I'm grandmother, Nicky," Ilana said, turning over the children. "I know all about keeping little ones busy."

She assured them that their "costumes" would be waiting for them the next time they visited.

By the time we got everyone onstage to run through the "field trip to the river" scene, the kids were hyper with too much candy from the machines in the lobby. Twelve kids speeding from excess sugar consumption is never pretty. Put them in a scene where they need to be solemn and you might as well be doing a Monty Python sketch. "Surreal" only gets you through the first five minutes.

The Mother Superior leads her charges down to the river. She has made this walk so many times she barely notices the twists and turns in the path, following from memory. Once, this walk was joyous. At this time of the year, when the trees would begin to turn green and the flowers to sprout, the Mother Superior would delight in the stroll along the riverbank. But that was before. Now her brow is furrowed, as it so often is these days, her gaze distracted as she listens to the rushing water, her head cocked to one side.

The children, young, innocent, and full of the vitality of youth, skip and hop along the path. They are oblivious to the shadows that haunt the Mother Superior. The shadow of death hangs over her. The death of a child not unlike them. It was an accident and all so long ago, yet the past reaches out to stain her heart and burden her mind. How can an incident so long ago still weigh so harshly on the world? She shakes her head.

Sister Klarissa walks beside her. "Mother, why do you look so worried?" she asks.

The Mother Superior smiles at the young nun. "Klarissa, there are heartaches you need not know. Events that shouldn't trouble you. But child, do as I told you and watch the children. We don't want any to fall into the water. No. Not again." And the Mother Superior quietly weeps to herself as Sister Klarissa withdraws to follow the line of children, her mind now also troubled.

But not for long. Never the primacy of the sad thought for Klarissa. She need only look at the smiling children, frolicking in the spring sun, to feel her spirits lift. The joy of spring, the joy of youth—the sensation of music wells within her, and once again she bursts into song, glorious strains of praise to the handiwork of God. But the Mother Superior's dark mood has infected her, and soon her song turns sorrowful, recounting the loss that must first precede the spring. The dying that gives way to rebirth. The children listen, and then, carried along, they too sing of death and rebirth of nature. The song is solemn and mournful. Not quite a dirge, but more than a lament, not quite . . .

I always stopped listening at this point. The problem with the field trip to the river, or at least the main problem, was the song "I'll Never Spring for Love." The composers intended a thoughtful meditation on the nature of Nature. It wasn't just the inappropriateness of a thoughtful meditation on anything in the middle of a musical comedy about a serial nun killer: the tune didn't match the rest of the score, which was straightforward book musical pieces easily identifiable as "show tune." "I'll Never Spring for Love" owed its soul to the blues. It had no home in *Convent of Fear*.

In full production the field trip to the river would be staged with lights and a nearly sheer backdrop called a scrim. The acting was going to do the work of conveying a sense of location to the audience. This left the burden of the scenic effect on the shoulders of the children's chorus, the Mother Superior, and Mary Frances. They were nearly breaking under the weight. They needed at least three or four more run-throughs before they would be effective. They weren't going to get them.

The schedule called for Lee Dexter and his crew to begin loading scenery onto the stage after we finished for the evening. Tomorrow, technical considerations would begin to impose themselves onto rehearsal with ever-increasing urgency. This was our final shot at acting work only.

Benny moved through the scene line by line, working against the odds. The late hour, the large amounts of candy bars and soda, and the general inability of children to truly rationalize nonsense all worked to shorten their attention span. Adult actors, out of self-interest or self-preservation, can and will pretend or convince themselves that something inane is making sense. Children often lack this facility. The orphans of *Convent of Fear* didn't know exactly what was wrong, but they understood instinctively that the trip to the river was not making sense. Benny explained, entreated, parabolized, and finally screamed at them.

I sat in the middle of the auditorium, wondering what my life would have been like if I'd stayed in New York and been arrested for stalking. Making it worse, I could see David sitting in the front row. He was keeping a respectable working-environment distance, which I appreciated in a respectable working kind of way, but no other. As I sighed over wasted opportunity, Lee Dexter sat down next to me. He brought the scent of the scene shop with him in the sawdust that clung to his stained T-shirt and jeans.

"How's it going?" he asked.

"The children don't like this scene. They're tired. They've had way too much sugar."

"Ugly."

"Not even close, Lee. Not even close. How's about you?"

"I'm set. As soon as you clear out, I'll start loading in." He referred to a clipboard in his hand. "Tonight I figure about three hours, then back here tomorrow afternoon." He tossed the clipboard on my table and scratched at his beard. "I know you guys are hurting without music tonight, but it actually makes my job easier. I can pretty much guarantee we'll be ready for you at six tomorrow night. It won't be complete, but we'll have all the movable parts."

Lee wasn't at fault for Edward Rossoff and Mary Corinne running off, but his attitude seemed a little casual to me.

"Well, I'm glad someone is getting something out of this," I said.

"Sorry, but it's the truth. I am not responsible for what that woman does with her life or how she does it." He settled back in the matted blue fabric of the seat and stopped talking.

I watched the action in front of me. Looking at the stage from this distance during a work-through rehearsal was something akin to watching a silent movie. I imagined them as an emotionally twisted version of the Von Trapps, marching their way across the Alps. The Mother Superior replaced the captain. Maria urged her charges to climb that mountain, lift that barge, tote that bale. Sing out, kids. Concentrate. Concentrate.

Now, Benny was shouting at the children to concentrate, concentrate and be dignified. For Benny, *dignified* passed as an action verb.

We went through another forty-five minutes of one variation or another of rehearsing the scene: Benny and the kids, Benny and the Mother Superior, the Mother Superior and Mary Frances, the actresses and the children. All the while David sat quietly down front and Patsy took every opportunity she could find to whisper something in Mary Frances's ear.

Finally, we called a halt to the evening. Parents arrived to take the children away. The remaining adults relaxed noticeably. My part of the workday was almost done. Lee, Benny, Marty, Patsy, and I needed to sit down to make certain we were squared away for tomorrow's first technical run-through. I noticed that Mary Frances joined David, who still did not look like he was in any hurry to rush home. Maybe, just maybe.

The next day would be the first time we integrated the props and sets into the show. It would be a start-and-stop affair as we worked out the bugs on changing scenery. The props are less trouble, but even so, there are always a handful that somehow do not end up where you expected them to be. Add to that the actors' sometimes legitimate, sometimes not, complaints about the hand props, and the night can get very long. I once knew an actor who insisted that the rubber ball part of his paddle-and-ball toy was not the right size. He could not possibly make the thing work. Since the goal is to make the actor comfortable, it doesn't matter if he's right or wrong. If there really isn't a problem with the prop, you pretend. I took the paddle ball away, waited a day, and brought it back, claiming it was a brand-new version that worked perfectly. He was delighted.

"What about the construction?" Benny asked.

The five of us were seated at my table, yawning, blinking, stumbling toward opening night.

"Jerry says that they're almost done. Basically little more than cleanup," Lee answered.

"Who is Jerry?" Marty asked.

"He's the foreman. I've known him for a while. He's a straight shooter. If he says they're almost done, they're almost done."

"OK," I said. "Construction is a check. How about load-in?"

"Starts in half an hour. We actually have a lot of stuff stacked on the right. I expect to have everything here by six p.m."

"Marty?" I asked.

"I'm practically done as it is. I just need to lay out the prop tables and find a spot for everything to live." By this Marty meant that he was going to place a long table in either wing, cover them with brown butcher paper, and label a space for each and every prop. Using this system, the crew would quickly know if a prop was missing before a performance started.

There were other details. We reviewed the placement of scenery for scene-change purposes: what went right, what went left. I wanted to be certain that the backstage area would be wired with headsets. I needed to communicate with Patsy, who, starting tomorrow night, would be backstage during the remainder of rehearsal and all performances. Of course, headsets don't work if you don't wear them. I could only imagine the struggle it was going to be to keep her plugged in instead of wandering after Mary Frances. We did not discuss that.

We did cover the question of staffing. Benny and I were concerned that there be enough hands backstage to move everything quickly. Slow scene changes will consign even the best production to low-quality status.

"I have a good crew, *and*," Lee said, obviously pleased with this news, "David Scott has volunteered to do some of the scene changes. He said he's not on that often. Since he's been in rehearsal the whole time, he'll be a big help in keeping everything straight as we load in."

Definitely a good news/bad news moment: good for the scene changes, bad for me. David was not waiting patiently through an extra hour and a half of *Convent of Fear* in order to sweep me away for a night of wild, uninhibited sex. He was waiting to load in scenery. At least I'd get a good night's rest before first tech.

When the meeting ended I picked up my book. After every rehearsal I take my prompt book someplace "safe." At St. Gilbert's this meant carrying the script the thirty yards from the makeshift desk to my office. This is not because I think someone is going to steal the thing. It isn't even because the notes inside are so essential for running the show. If I had to, I could, with a little effort, recreate enough of what was on record to get through a performance. No, the truth is I carefully secured my prompt book in the bottom right-hand drawer of my office desk each evening because then I slept better. Some would call this a theatrical superstition. I prefer to think of it as a sane precaution.

I found Roger sitting at my desk trying to hack his way into a locked file on my rundown, barely-one-step-above-scrap computer. Paolo was flopped in the armchair reading an outdated copy of *Architectural Digest* he'd dug up from one of the cluttered shelves.

"There's a locked file on here," Roger said when I entered the room.

"Isn't there some sort of computer consultant's code of ethics that says you shouldn't be poking around in other people's hard drives without permission?" I asked.

"You're asking him about ethics?" Paolo did not look out from behind his magazine.

"Please," I said. "It's late. Move." I pushed Roger to one side and deposited the script in its drawer.

"Aren't you at all curious?" Roger asked.

"No. I am tired and horny. Move."

Roger was clicking away at something on the screen. "Well, someone has locked some financial record on your computer. I'd be curious."

I ignored his comment.

"Would you let me sit down, please, so I can finish my notes? I don't care about someone's checkbook."

He did not get up.

"I don't think this is a checkbook, Nicky. This is QuickBooks. It's for small businesses. Record-keeping things: balance sheets, cash flow, red ink/black ink. You know, where the money goes."

"Who would care where the money goes around here?" Paolo asked, shifting his legs over one arm of the chair without looking up. He'd meant to be sarcastic, but his comment brought me back to my conversation with Ilana Mosca earlier in the evening. Why was it always coming back to the money? Maybe a little curiosity would not be too out of line.

"Rog, is there some way you can open that file?" I asked.

"This is not good," Paolo said from within his magazine.

"What happened to 'computer ethics'?" Roger asked.

"I'm your host. Don't quote me back to myself. It's rude."

"I'd need a back door. Some way around the password protection. I'd have to send away for it. But, yes, eventually—a day or two—and we'd be in."

"How do you send away for a 'back door'?" I asked.

"Well, you do it via e-mail to a company I know in Seattle called DataFree. Fortunately, I just happen to have brought my laptop with me, so I can do it from your apartment tonight." Roger was speaking to me, but tossed the word "laptop" at Paolo like a brick.

"I can hear you, beloved," Paolo said. "No need to shout." Finally, he looked up from his magazine. "If you two must play boy detectives, I can't stop you. But I'm on the record right now—this is a bad idea."

"I'm not afraid of a bad idea," Roger said.

"No, you never have been." Paolo went back to reading.

EIGHT

My office was a wreck. There were papers scattered across the floor, the furniture, the desktop—every level surface. The shelves of rehearsal props were tipped over. Chairs lay on their sides. The drawers of the filing cabinets hung open, their contents spilled onto the floor next to them. This wasn't burglary; it was vandalism. Whoever ripped through my office the night before had been very angry. It's one thing to search a filing cabinet. It's quite another to empty it and then kick a dent in the side.

A security guard, one of the near- or just-past-retirement-age types the college employed, stood in the middle of the confusion, talking baseball with Marty Friedman.

"You trade Martin, you got no one at third, and what do you get for it? Dauber? Greco? See, what I'm saying is, why, if you got nothing but holes in the infield, do you want holes in the outfield? That's what I'm saying, see?" I could tell the guard was making what he thought was a serious point by the way he screwed the wrinkles in his face into a tight clench.

"Excuse me? Hello."

"Here he is," Marty said, adding, for the security guard's benefit, "It's his office."

"Oh, it's your office? Too bad about that. Who are you?" the guard asked.

"I'm Nicky D'Amico. What happened?"

"So you work here? I don't see theater that much. My wife wants to go, and then we go. But she doesn't want to go much."

"Really? Well. And exactly what happened here?" I repeated the question.

"You were here last night? Doing what it is you do here?" he asked.

"Yes. I'm the stage manager. We had rehearsal."

Marty upended the armchair. Brushing some magazines aside, he sat sideways with his legs hanging over one arm of the chair. With someone else, it might have looked casual, but Marty kept darting his eyes back and forth around the room as if he were searching for escape routes. In his hand, he clutched a wad of small slips of white and off-yellow paper.

"They wrote on your wall too," the guard said, pointing to graffiti just above my desk. The office wrecker had defaced the gray walls with a bright blue marker.

" 'My spirit is broken, my days are extinct. Job'?" I read aloud. "Great. Now I'm getting work critiques from thugs."

"Ah. Jeez, Nicky," Marty said. "I think that's not 'job' like in the office, but Job like in the Bible."

So I was a little shook up and not thinking clearly. Or maybe I just didn't know all that much about the Bible. As far as I could figure, that didn't matter. What did matter was that someone would take a food processor to my office, then scrawl Bible verses on the wall. To me it screamed Friends of Decency.

"So, what's a stage manager do?" the security guard asked.

107

I longed for the suspicious but organized Corporal Roberts.

"I work for Benny Singleton. Think of me as his assistant." Those words cost me, but I really didn't want to get into a protracted job description, which non-theater people rarely understand. I hate explaining not being in charge but still being responsible.

"Oh, I'd say you were more than Benny's assistant, Nicky. Not that there is anything wrong with that." Marty quickly added the second thought as if Benny might have the room bugged.

"A real gentleman, Mr. Singleton. A real fine gentleman," the guard said.

It was almost ten a.m. After the last evening's rehearsal, Roger, Paolo, and I had returned to my small and now-crowded apartment. I went to bed and left the boys to fend for themselves in the living room. For the better part of two hours, all I could hear was a low grumbling of conversation as they continued to thrash out the finer points of on-line infidelity. In the morning I found Roger asleep on the floor and Paolo asleep on the couch. Neither looked comfortable. I wrote out a note with instructions on where to find coffee, then snuck out. After a night and morning like that, I just didn't have the diplomatic patience for navigating a conversation with the guard and Marty.

"Someone broke in here, right?" I said.

"You could say that. But not technically. Someone entered and ripped the place apart, all right," the guard answered. He had a clipboard with a form on top, apparently some sort of "entered and ripped apart" report. When I'd given him my name, he'd carefully and painstakingly written it down.

"Technically?" I asked.

"There's no sign of forced entry," the guard said. "Did you lock the door last night when you left?"

"Yes."

"Well, now, that's a problem. Not that you locked it. That's the right thing to do. Always lock the door. But the door wasn't forced, was it, Marty? No. Are you absolutely certain you locked the door?"

"Yes, I'm certain."

"It was unlocked this morning," Marty said. "I came by to bring you my receipts, and I found the door open and this." He gestured to the disorder around him. "I called security."

"But there's no telling when this happened. No witnesses. No one saw it," the guard said, and he looked about. "But I'd say it took time to do this much damage. A lot of time. Why anyone would spend their time ruining other people's offices, I don't know. Do you?" Here he looked directly at me. It took me a moment to realize that the question was not rhetorical.

"No. I don't," I finally answered.

"No. You don't. Do you, Marty? No. No, you wouldn't either. Why would you? You two wouldn't do something like this."

"And it couldn't have been very quiet," Marty said.

"Nope. It probably wasn't. Probably done during the night, when no one was around. When did you leave here, Mr. Dimico?" the guard asked.

"That's D'Amico." I spelled it for him again as I pushed my way through to my desk. The drawers hung open. The intruder had rifled the contents of each, emptying them onto the desktop. I immediately searched for my prompt book. It was apparently untouched in the bottom right-hand drawer, just where I'd left it. Not so the metal lockbox with petty cash. That stood forced open on my desk. I looked at the computer. The bulky, aging, off-white PC looked solid and secure amidst the riot of paper and office supplies.

"Damn," I said. "They took the petty cash."

"How much?" the guard asked.

"I think maybe $120, but I'll have to sort through these papers for the receipts and total it all up."

"Too bad about that. Just don't understand. No, sir. And you left when?"

"I—my friends and I—left here just a little after ten o'clock. But the technical director and his crew were still here."

"That's Mr. Dexter, right? Oh yes, Mr. Dexter is one hard worker. People think theater is easy, but I know it isn't. I see. Mr. Dexter is one hard worker."

"Oh yes," I agreed. "I don't know when they left," I added, figuring at least one of us should care about the timing of events.

"That's important, when they left," he said. "Unless he did it." The guard laughed at his own joke. "Unless he did it." He repeated his punch line twice more. "That's a good one."

I started to sit at the desk, then hesitated. "Any objection?"

"No, go right ahead. Time like this, it's good to be comfortable," the guard said, getting himself under control. "Now, I need you to make a list of everything that might be missing. I know it's not fun, but the list is important. Real important."

"I make lists for a living," I said, turning on the computer.

"OK. Now I know what a stage manager does. Or some. You probably do more than that, don't you? You wouldn't need an office just to make lists, would you?"

"No, I wouldn't," I said as the computer began booting up.

I looked up at the guard and at Marty sitting next to him. The guard looked like he could be someone's grandfather. Too lightly colored in his hair and eyes to be mine, but someone's kindly old pap-pap. He was dressed in a not-too-well-pressed drab blue-gray, button-down shirt and darker blue pants. The outward signs of his authority were his clipboard and a hard plastic nametag on his shirt that read, "H. Ott, Security." Marty was looking lost, as always. But that was the problem in

110

Huber's Landing. Everyone looked so innocent and guileless, squeaky clean in a Middle America sort of way. You'd never think that people were embezzling and committing suicide over it, or that nuns were having affairs with married men or being run down by some lunatic on a bicycle. Probably a religious lunatic related to the nut who wrote on my wall.

"Oh shit," I said.

"What? Is something missing?" The guard raised his pen in anticipation.

"No. I mean, I don't know. But the guy on the bicycle. The one in the yellow raincoat and red wig. Do you know about him?"

"Oh yeah. Couple of years ago it was skateboarders using the campus roadways. What did that girl on TV used to say? 'It's always something.' "

"Well, he ran down another nun today. I saw it on my way over here. I was going to report it when I got here, but . . ." I just waved my hand at the papers in front of me.

"Oh. Again? That'll be a different report. So where did this happen?" The guard was flipping through the forms on his clipboard. There must have been a specific one for nuns in distress.

"In front of the gym. He hit two nuns and knocked them both down. He kept going and headed around the other side of the building. I chased after him."

"You did? Did you catch him?" Marty asked.

"No, Marty. He was on a bicycle. But I was hoping to see which direction he headed."

"Tough to catch a guy on a bicycle when you don't have one yourself. And which direction was that?" the guard asked. Having found the correct form, he scribbled notes on his clipboard.

"Well, I don't know. When I rounded the building, he was gone."

"Too bad. You know what I think?" the guard asked both Marty and me.

"No," I said, guessing exactly what he thought. "What do you think?"

"I think it's this play you're doing. Nuns run down, Sister Sally murdered, the theater vandalized. Someone hates this play you're doing. Me, I don't go to the theater much. I don't get excited over this stuff. Some do, I guess."

The color drained from Marty's face.

"She was not murdered," I said. "And I don't think you should be spreading that rumor." I was angry that the guard was probably right about someone targeting *Convent of Fear*. He was wrong about Sally, but I couldn't ignore that Bible verse on the wall.

"Well, if that's it. Make a list of anything that might be missing, Mr. Dimico, and let us know. But I bet nothing else is gone. They just don't like your play. No. They don't like it at all. Me, I don't go to the theater. Not much. Don't see why anyone would get so excited." He put his pen in his pocket.

Well, I didn't like the show either, but you didn't see me going around knocking over furniture.

"What about my computer? What about that?" I asked.

"I don't know much about computers. Never had reason to use one. What about it?" he asked.

"Well, who do I see if it's damaged?"

"I don't know. I guess whoever gave it to you. The department? Maybe Mr. Singleton?"

I just shook my head. Swiveling in my chair, I reached out and clicked open the word-processing program. Everything seemed to be working.

"What have you been doing, Nicky?"

Benny Singleton maneuvered his ample self through the doorway. He was dressed coolly in safari wear—khaki shorts, button-down beige shirt, khaki canvas sneakers—but looked very overheated. The overwhelming physicality of his bulk pushed the room over its occupancy level. The dingy gray walls, bright clean spots showing where cabinets and shelves had been knocked aside, seemed to close in tightly. I was always feeling more crowded in Huber's Landing than I ever had in New York City. With Roger and Paolo in my living room and four of us trying to navigate my disrupted office, I thought maybe I should rent a motel room along the highway just for a little time alone.

"Hello, Benny. I think the Friends of Decency are getting a little more aggressive. I believe it's from the Bible." I pointed to the writing on the wall.

"My spirit is broken, my days are extinct," Benny read in a whisper. His face was blank as he continued in an even quieter tone, "Job, chapter 17, verse 1."

"You know it?" I was amazed.

Benny recovered himself quickly.

"Of course. You will find, Nicky, that a knowledge of the great works of Western literature is an invaluable aid. An artist cannot create in a vacuum. Of course, this is a disgusting use of scripture. I'm going to send down a work order immediately to have this place repainted. You'll need to get it cleaned up for that, you know."

"Guess I can go now." Marty popped up from his seat. "Here. Here are my receipts."

He shoved the wad of paper in his hands at me.

"Thanks," I said without much enthusiasm. I wasn't exactly being fair. Marty couldn't be held responsible for finally doing the right thing by his paperwork on the one day I would be least prepared.

"You don't need me for anything else, do you, Nicky?"

"No, Marty. I don't need you. Thanks."

Marty squeezed around Benny, who made no concession to passing traffic. Benny settled into the armchair. He kicked a stack of papers to one side and stretched out his legs.

"Harry," he said to the security guard. "Nicky and I have a meeting to attend now. Can you spare us?"

The guard got a kick out of this. His face broke wide open with a grin.

"Me, spare you? Now that's funny, Mr. Singleton. That's a good one. OK. Mr. Dimico, you just make a list and let us know if anything else is missing. I'll go now, Mr. Singleton. Can I spare you? That's good." Like the best audiences, Harry left laughing.

"What's he mean, anything else?"

"They got the petty cash," I answered.

"You should have locked it up."

"I did. What meeting, Benny? I don't have anything on my schedule. Not that I can find my schedule at the moment."

"Last minute, Nicky. I just heard about it myself. The public relations people want to see us."

"Why? And stop kicking paper around, will you? This place is enough of a mess."

He looked at his right foot, which he'd been idly swinging back and forth, scattering several folders full of old theater records.

"Oh," he said, as if he hadn't noticed. "They want to talk about Sister Sally."

"Can't you go without me? I need to clean this mess up."

The phone rang. I reached for the far right corner of my desk, but the phone wasn't there. The ringing came from my left. I pushed aside a month's worth of sign-in sheets and lifted the receiver.

"Stage management," I answered.

"Good morning. Nicholas D'Amico, please."

"Speaking."

"Ah, good. Good morning, Mr. D'Amico. My name is Phyllis East."

"Good morning."

"Mr. D'Amico, I'm sorry to call at a time like this, what with Sister Sally so recently departed."

"That's OK, Ms. East. I understand. What can I do for you?" I tried graciously hurrying her to a point.

"I'm calling about publicity photos for the show, but I guess that might be difficult. I mean, you haven't had a chance to reshoot since the nun was stabbed, have you?"

"There was no stabbing here." The Huber's Landing rumor machine must have been in high gear.

"Oh, I'm so glad to hear that. She was so loved, wasn't she?"

"Universally. But you wanted publicity shots, is that right?" Again, to the point. Whatever local editor Phyllis East represented must have had quite a job keeping her on track. I looked at the cabinet where the photos had been stored. It was empty now. The pictures were probably on the floor nearby.

"Oh yes, please. That is, assuming you are going to continue with the show. You will be opening as scheduled, despite the terrible accident?"

When I mentioned publicity, Benny became agitated. He was waving both hands in a "Stop—go no further" motion.

I put one hand over the receiver and, sotto voce, tried to get him to elaborate. In my ear, Phyllis East, whose voice was the aural equivalent of honey sliding down your throat, was asking if "poor Sally had a chance to say a good-bye before tragedy struck her, poor thing."

"No press," Benny was saying. "Do not talk to the press."

"All she wants is pictures," I said to him. "What's that?" I said into the phone.

"I was just thinking how sudden it must have been, wasn't it? The poor dear probably didn't get a chance to say anything."

"Say anything to who?" I asked.

Benny was on his feet.

"Hang up. Hang up the phone," he was shouting.

"Yes. Did she say anything before she died?" Phyllis East repeated her question.

"What paper are you with?" I asked.

"*The Allegheny Sentinel*," she said. "I'm sorry, I should have said that up front."

"*The Allegheny Sentinel*?" I looked at Benny as I said the name.

"Folded three years ago," he snapped back at me.

I was caught off-guard by his comment. If I'd been a little more crafty, I might have gotten more information out of the honey-toned Ms. East. Instead, I muffed the chance by involuntarily repeating his comment into the mouthpiece. My reward was the click of a disconnected line.

"What the hell was that?" I asked, hanging up the receiver.

"That is no doubt why we are going to Old Main," Benny responded. His agitation was causing him to go red in the face.

"I don't really have the time for any of this," I said.

"They specifically asked for both of us. You can clean up later. Let's go. Sometimes, Nicholas, we must do certain tasks we do not want in order to get along in life."

"List is longer now," Ilana Mosca said.

We both turned to the door. Ilana, draped in three layers of varying shades of purple, the outer one a gauzy, semitransparent fabric revealing six pockets in the layer beneath, stood scowling at the mess in my office.

"You too," she said.

"Me too what?" Benny asked.

"Not you. Him. Vandals. Costume shop is heap of trash."

My list of "certain tasks" just kept growing.

I was just one of many stage managers passing through over the years, my presence touching the theater only lightly. Ilana, however, had occupied the costume shop for almost two decades. Her sense of order was deeply imprinted in the organization of every object and bit of cloth. This difference between us heightened the visual impact of the destruction. Where my office looked vandalized, the costume shop was chaos beneath the heavily pine-scented air. Neatly sorted and carefully labeled drawers of buttons, fasteners, zippers, and ribbons were each emptied, their contents tossed onto the floor. Bolts of fabric lay tumbled onto their sides. The ironing boards and irons, the sewing machines, the dress dummies—nothing but the center work table was left standing upright.

"Devastation. Devastation." Ilana moved to the middle of the room. This was a blow severe enough to overwhelm even her natural urge to greet disaster with glee. She bent over and started scooping up handfuls of buttons.

"Ilana, have you called security?" I asked.

"Why? Will they clean?" she replied, absently beginning to sort the buttons by type and color.

Benny and I stood just inside the shop, next to the overturned racks of costumes for *Convent of Fear*.

"Nonetheless, Ilana, we need to report this," Benny said. "And I suppose have the entire building looked at."

Of course, the entire building. If my office and the costume shop were in this shape, what would we find in the scene and prop shops? Or on the stage?

"No, this is it. I am first this morning. My door is open, but everything else is locked. I check before I come upstairs." Now she was making little piles of colored ribbon on her central work table.

"I'll just double-check and then call." I was turning to leave when she started to pound on the table.

"Damn. Damn. Damn. It is enough. Enough." She started in anger and trailed off to a whimper. She hunched over the table, leaning on her hands. Her shoulders started to shake.

Benny went to her. "Ilana, please." He put his arms around her and began to whisper something I couldn't quite make out.

Suddenly, I was the absolute outsider. The guy who came in for three months this summer, replacing the guy who came in for three months last summer, both to be followed by some new stage manager next summer. It was one of those moments when you just have to look somewhere else. In this case, at the trashed costumes for *Convent of Fear*. Looking down at the mound of nuns' habits and orphans' clothing, I couldn't tell if the damage extended beyond the need to launder everything. I bent over, bracing myself to see slashed fabric and ripped seams. After poking through a few pieces, it was obvious that, other than being tipped over, the costumes had not been damaged.

"Ilana, look," I said from my position crouched on the floor. "The costumes aren't really damaged at all. Just a bit dirty."

She cast one horrified look in my direction. I assumed she was embarrassed to realize that I had witnessed her breakdown. She erased that expression with one of resignation.

"Yes," she said, agitation overwhelming syntax, "it should not be as bad as that?" Then she began to cry into Benny's arms once more. I thought I heard her say, "No more," but her words were lost beneath tears.

"Wow." Olivia Singleton was in the shop and sprinting to the far side of the room. She grabbed a piece of fake fur and wrapped it around her neck. "This looks just like that movie where the drug guy had his gang rip up the beauty parlor because the lady who owned it wouldn't pay him money. Can I have this?" She was modeling the fur in a partially shattered mirror.

"Olivia, now is not the time," her father said.

"But I look good in it. You're not going to use fur for nuns, are you?" She made a face at the mirror, blowing herself kisses.

"Get out. Get out," Ilana started shouting.

Olivia froze mid-pose, one hand on her hip, the other miming holding a cigarette. A cheap theatrical pose she'd no doubt seen numerous times on the stage at St. Gilbert's. Her eyes locked in the mirror with Ilana's. There was nothing but hatred in that look.

"I said *out*." Ilana stepped forward, but the child was faster. She slipped to her left, putting the work table between herself and the designer as she headed for the exit.

"Ilana, really," Benny started.

"Out. Out of my shop. Everyone." Ilana turned on all three of us. "I will clean myself. Get out." She was screaming and shaking and crying all at once.

Olivia was already in the hallway, still wearing the fur. Benny mumbled an ineffectual "Of course" and shuffled toward the door. I wasn't so certain about leaving her alone. Olivia's antics, out of control as usual, had pushed too far.

As if she knew my impulse, Ilana looked directly at me and said, "Go, Nicky. I will be OK."

She bent over to pick up more buttons. I left.

"She didn't take that very well."

Benny and I were walking toward Old Main, the administrative building. I assumed he meant Ilana's reaction to the break-in, not Olivia's behavior. Criticizing Olivia was not high on Benny's list.

"It's going to take a lot of time and effort to put that place back in order," I said. "I'll check on her when this meeting is over."

The afternoon heat broiled us. Rain? I wished. Barely a yard outside the air-conditioned auditorium, I sagged under the weight of the leaden air. Benny, dressed for tropical weather, did no better. The farther we walked, the slower we walked. My consolation was the view. The buildings of St. Gilbert's might be on the slightly shabby side of genteel, but the landscaping was lovely. We wove our way through dense green quads trimmed with well-tended trees. Flowerbeds lined the sidewalks. The campus always looked like a garden to my nature-starved New York City eyes.

A handful of people joined us in creeping across campus to appointments that couldn't be broken. That view provided some consolation as well. After all, what's summer without a handsome undergrad sauntering by shirtless? All that heat. All that sweat. I thought of David out and about on a day like this. The T-shirt would be off. The hair on his chest just slightly damp. A breeze would play through the hair on his head as a piccolo played a spritely air. The long, hip-hugging shorts would slide down to reveal just a hint of waistband, or maybe even—

Benny was speaking to me. "You don't agree, do you, Nicky? You think I did the wrong thing?"

"Of course not," I said. I had no idea what he was talking about, but I figured I couldn't go wrong with Benny by telling him he did the right thing.

"They were blaming me. But I wasn't the one. I was doing my best, but who could keep things in the black with your own business manager siphoning off funds? I couldn't."

"Who could?"

"I owed it to the theater, Nicholas. I owed it to my children. The truth, Nicholas. The truth is what matters. In art. In life."

"Truth. Yes. Truth." Don't get me wrong, I'm all for truth. I am just not certain I believed in Benny's truth or Benny's ability to get to the truth or that Benny would know the truth if it dropped from a nearby deciduous tree and cracked him on the head. Anyway, I still had no idea what we were talking about.

"It wasn't easy. Joe was a good friend. But what could I do?" Benny gave this last line a real world-weary reading, like some sophisticate trying to avoid a charge of tenderness. "Embezzlement is a crime."

Ah, embezzlement. I remembered Ilana telling me that it was Benny who'd produced the proof of embezzlement after Joe Sr.'s suicide. How typical of my life in Huber's Landing that every conversation should be about crime. This never happened in New York City either.

"So after Joe's death you showed everyone the books?" I tried to pick up the direction of the conversation.

"Yes. I just said that. I couldn't let everyone think I was mismanaging the theater, could I? Aren't you listening, Nicky?"

I was listening. What I couldn't figure out was why he was talking. Why tell me any of this?

"Of course, I didn't care that he and Mary Corinne were having an affair. That was none of my business. I am not the type to rush into other people's lives. No, no. I do not get involved in other people's business, Nicholas. It's never wise. You're young, but it's a lesson we all must learn." He actually wagged his finger at me.

Turning a corner, we came to the entrance to Old Main. The building was the oldest structure on campus. Originally, it held classrooms and offices, but the course work was now done elsewhere, and only the administrative functions remained. Two newly planted weeping willows flanked the main entrance. Even though they barely reached the red bricks of the third story, their slightly yellowing leaves cast more than enough shade for anyone who might want refuge from the heat.

There were two people taking advantage of that cool, comforting space: Patsy Malone and Mary Frances Roberts, all in white, their sandals cast aside, curled neatly into the base of one willow, slurping orange frozen drinks and laughing. They waved to us, then dissolved into renewed laughter. I waved back. What I wouldn't give right then to snuggle under a weeping willow with an orange slurpy drink and a certain secondary player.

Benny breezed past them with barely any acknowledgment.

"I do not approve of staff-cast romantic entanglements, Nicholas. I do not approve at all."

So much for other people's business.

The interior of Old Main reminded me of how badly most theater facilities are treated. The designers, Benny, and I toiled in small workspaces and smaller, often windowless offices, surrounded by walls in serious need of paint. The second floor of the administration building presented a paper pusher's paradise: each office separated by an expanse of glass panels framed in rich, red-toned woods. The offices were spacious, the views lovely. Did I imagine that the air was sweeter? Benny led us down a newly carpeted hallway (you could still feel the plushy cushion of the undermatting) through a glass door labeled Public Relations. A receptionist/secretary looked up from a desk larger than mine. Beyond her, through a door marked Director, we saw two men prowling the largest of the glassed-in enclosures. A woman sat quietly, watching them argue.

The receptionist/secretary asked us to take a seat, "as the director of public relations is momentarily tied up." She did not offer refreshments. As soon as we sat down, I grabbed the nearest reading material, a copy of St. Gilbert's summer catalogue, and, to all appearances, became entranced by the offerings of the foreign languages department. It kept Benny at a distance. After fifteen minutes of considering my options for learning Greek or Latin, the receptionist/secretary opened a portal in the glass and admitted us to the director's office.

One of the men, the director of public relations, took a seat behind a sleek desk whose surface space was lacking all signs of work. He was thin, the kind of fellow who slicks back his slightly balding hair and hopes no one will notice. Behind his glasses, his eyes blinked in a rapid staccato. In the air-conditioned comfort of Old Main, he seemed happily at ease in full suit and tie.

"Benny. Benny. Always good to see you. Always a delight. I am so glad you could join us. You and your young friend here. Hello. Oscar Brockett, director of public relations."

"Hi. I'm Nicky D'Amico, stage manager."

I shook hands all around. The other man I'd already met. Stanley Sobieski, chief of campus security, was sober today, and his clothes were more tidy than when he'd paid his late-night visit to my office after Sally's death. Still, he gave off the impression of a man not quite together. The woman seated calmly next to the desk was Patricia Madison, legal counsel. Benny, of course, knew everyone.

"So, Stanley," I said, in the effort to start off friendly, "you must be looking forward to seeing Joe onstage?"

"Don't bet on it," he answered.

In the silence that followed that comment, Benny and I seated ourselves in matching Danish modern armchairs, the type that look comfy but feel awful. Somehow that seemed right for this meeting.

"Let me get to the point, Benny," the director said. "There are . . . concerns. Of course, not with the quality of the production. We are never, any of us here in Old Main, concerned with the quality of the work at your theater, Benny. Always the highest, highest standards. No. Our . . . *concerns* relate more to the incidents, say perceptions, that seem to be accumulating around your current production. And be assured, Benny, be completely assured that we are behind you one hundred percent in your efforts to produce only the best theater, and we support, completely support, your prerogative to choose your own material. Here at St. Gilbert's we value—always have and I hope, speaking for each of us, always will—a spirited dialogue, wherever such a dialogue appears on the questions facing contemporary society. Of course, all due deference is owing—and we can, I think, that is to say, I am certain, agree on this. We assure you that no one, myself least of all, would ever attempt otherwise."

"The point, Oscar. The point," Patricia Madison said, smiling sweetly at the director. That smile softened the not-so-gentle verbal push. Obviously, her looks were deceiving. Her hair, shagged and frosted at the tips; her makeup, bright colors applied with a deft, delicate touch; and her clothes, unnecessarily voluminous over a slight frame, all conspired to give her a soft look. Oscar jumped.

"Of course, Patricia, the point. You see, gentlemen, we cannot be too hasty in dismissing the concerns of all parties. If the protests are such that they can be diffused with a simple elision of those elements involved which are perhaps most distasteful, and now with this unfortunate incident of Sister Sally's rather hasty death, they might preserve the main thrust while still somehow addressing those issues. All very simple, don't you think?"

I was lost.

"I see. Of course," Benny said. "And of course, we will cooperate fully."

"There. You see? I told you Benny Singleton was not an unreasonable man." The director beamed as if he had accomplished a miracle. He looked directly at the security chief, challenging him to disagree.

"Tell me, Oscar, how is your family?" Benny asked.

"Oh, just fine, Benny. You know, Marta will be starting first grade this fall."

"It goes so quickly, doesn't it?" Benny said.

The director nodded his head in agreement.

"Well, I don't think it's so simple," Stanley said. "And I hate to interrupt this little catch-up session, but don't you think we need to address a few security problems here? Patricia?"

Patricia smiled that megawatt smile.

"Of course, Stan. Oscar was just laying the groundwork, weren't you, Oscar? There's no point in getting ahead of ourselves. But we do need a little clarity. Like a good spring day. Now, Benny, you do understand that there will have to be adjustments?"

Benny looked at her, then at Oscar. Stanley remained on his feet, his moustached, well-fleshed body leaning against the plate glass. The only sound he made was something like a growl in the back of his throat. Benny ignored him, focusing instead on Oscar.

Then I understood. As long as the director of public relations was in charge of this meeting, as long as his obscure, impenetrable ramblings were the only official college pronouncement, then for just so long could Benny Singleton pretend to understand whatever suited his convenience. Benny had no interest in any clarity that Patricia Madison might provide.

"I'm sorry, Oscar. Could you explain these adjustments?" Benny asked.

"I doubt it," Stanley said.

"Stan, don't be difficult." Patricia again. This time, no smile. "We have a great deal to resolve here."

Oscar folded his hands. "Benny, let me be blunt. We are concerned. That is, the administration has concerns that there are issues confronting us that may not be in line with the typical problems we occasionally face when the theater, which we all know is a provocative medium—and I have no trouble with that—proves to be a strong stimulus to public reaction, which you know is my specialty and particular concern. Are you with me?"

"Absolutely." Benny took on a look of grave concern.

"Good. Now, what we want to do here is to prevent any further actions which might give rise to consequences that, when taken as a whole, could possibly prove to be the type of experiences that none of us wants to be embroiled in. Avoidance, Benny. I am a believer in avoidance."

"I completely agree," I said, in total good faith.

Stanley was prowling the room. "This is ridiculous. Patricia?" he asked. Now I was certain he was growling. I wondered if he hadn't worked his way down to his current job from some more lucrative and challenging career.

"Benny," Patricia said, "what Oscar is trying to say is that the protests have got to stop. The rumors about Sister Sally have got to stop. In short, Benny, no more noise from your production except the always expected glowing reviews." She punctuated this comment with another smile, but now her teeth looked a little more feral to me. "And of course, Mr. D'Amico, as the principal manager of the actors and crew, we'd expect your full cooperation as well."

Benny matched her tooth for tooth. "Now, Patricia, if you know how to stop religious fanatics from protesting, please, I'd love to hear it."

"Now, now, Benny. Like I always say, one doesn't get into a pissing contest with a skunk. We need to be subtle with these people."

That was a tough call. Was Benny the skunk? Was she the skunk? Were the Friends of Decency skunks? All I knew was that I wasn't going to say another word in this room.

"If this gets any more subtle, I'm going to snore off," Stanley said. "Look, Singleton, the deal is your production is angering people, and after Sister Sally's death and the state troopers sniffing around, we have more mess than we can handle. You need to fix this."

"Fix?" Benny's face was a mask of bewilderment.

"Yeah, fix. Change the show. Cut something. Add something. Whatever you do," Stanley said.

"What I do, Stanley, is direct theater. What I do not do is pander to lunatics."

"Who are you calling a lunatic?"

"Your opinion is hardly objective," Benny snapped back at him. "You've been against this production from the word go. You've let your beliefs cloud your judgment."

"At least I believe in something. I know what's right and wrong. I know blasphemy when I see it."

I could see a bad ending to this conversation. I could see several, and they all resolved themselves in me being unemployed after the college shut us down.

"Gentlemen. Gentlemen." Oscar held his hands up. "Please. We are all one team here looking to build synergy, not sow division. We need a coherent approach to the problems at hand that will allow us to funnel our energy in a productive fashion. Can we agree on that much?"

I was the only one who nodded.

"Benny," Patricia asked, "wouldn't you consider something, some minor change as a sign of good will? A simple gesture?"

"I will not alter my production to appease anyone. My job is not pleasing the masses." Benny struck a pose, head up, chin out. "Are you threatening to shut me down, Oscar?"

"Oh, no. Certainly not. Never," Oscar answered, completely craven in the face of a direct challenge.

Stanley let out another low growling sound. Even Patricia was annoyed enough to show it, her eyes narrowing in anger. The obsequious Oscar's assurances of continued unqualified support were obviously not part of her plan.

"We just want to be certain . . ."

Benny was done. He apparently no longer needed Oscar. Or this meeting. He stood.

"I am seventy-two hours from preview. Much as I love seeing you all, I need to get back to work. So, unless you have more to add . . . ? I assure you, I will do nothing which I consider deliberately provocative." Now there was a promise you could drive all of Huber's Landing through.

"Of course, Benny. No one was suggesting that you were being deliberately provocative." Patricia was smiling again. "But at a minimum I must insist that any further inquiries regarding Sister Sally or the play be referred to this office. We've been receiving phone calls. I do not want any of you talking to any reporters."

I stopped her and told her about the phone call from the supposed Phyllis East.

"You see, gentlemen? Now, why should you have to deal with that? As you say, Benny, you have only seventy-two hours till you open. Mustn't waste it, must you?" Patricia positively beamed at him in her fury.

"Of course, Patricia. That makes great sense. Nicholas, make a note of that. Good afternoon, everyone."

Benny headed for the exit. I jumped to follow him. Then I realized we hadn't mentioned the break-ins. I turned back to the chief of security.

"Ah, Stanley, you'll probably want to know that someone broke into my office and the costume shop last night and ransacked them."

"Oh great." He looked at me as if I'd done it myself. "This just doesn't stop, does it? Did you report it? Or is this one of those theater things the rest of us should just stay out of?"

"I did report it. I haven't had a chance to look around, so I don't know if they took anything besides the petty cash. But they wrote some Bible quote on my wall. I think it was the Friends of Decency."

"Of course. Blame it on the people who care about their religion."

"Stanley." Patricia's low, smooth tone carried a distinct warning.

"Nicholas, we haven't got all day," Benny said. He was standing just outside the office door. I don't think he was very happy with me.

"What was the quote?" Stanley asked, putting aside his animosity long enough to do his job.

"Something from Job. About broken spirits and extinct days," I answered.

"Broken spirit?" Stanley stared at me, appearing to reappraise my presence. I was certain I saw recognition in his eyes.

"Do you know that quote?" I asked.

"No," he said, "I don't. But I will have a look at the report."

I left then with Benny. We walked past the receptionist/secretary, heading back toward the main staircase.

"Benny, what just happened in there? Are we going to have to close?" I asked.

"Not now. They may have wanted that, but now that Oscar's committed himself he's stuck on his own ego. It would take at least three days to get him to admit he made a mistake, probably longer."

And we opened in two. Nothing would derail *Convent of Fear* now.

"You know, I think Stanley was lying," I said. "I think he knew the quote from Job."

"Nicholas, you're too suspicious. Nobody knows the big bad quote." Then Benny went silent.

Maybe I was getting better at understanding him, or maybe Benny was just that transparent. In either case I left Old Main convinced that both Benny and Stanley Sobieski were hiding something.

NINE

"Fifteen minutes. Fifteen minutes, please."

The "God mike" carried my voice into the dressing rooms, backstage, onstage, and the house. I sat in the center of the auditorium, leaning back in my chair, eye on the clock. From all sides, voices floated toward me, the whispered sounds of preparations swirling in the dark. Behind me the light designer and master electrician were programming the computerized light system. To my right the costume designer and director argued over wig production. In front the cast members, some in costume, lounged, waiting to begin.

We were fifteen minutes from beginning. Fifteen minutes means nothing in the theater, a chunk of time that no one notices. At five minutes the complaining would start.

I was enjoying the quiet preceding what promised to be a messy rehearsal. Since Benny hadn't been able to make up his mind about what he wanted to accomplish, the evening would be a bastard mixing of technical and nontechnical elements. We were going to add a few costume pieces and most of the props, but the real challenge would be overhead. Lights would be shifting in what would look like random patterns as Rebecca Tipton, the light designer, tested her setup. The idea was to make the next day's full technical rehearsal run more smoothly. I was all for that. Putting all the components of the production together for the first time was a grueling process that could last up to ten hours at a stretch.

Lee and his crew had stayed at the theater until two a.m., then returned at one in the afternoon. None of them had seen or heard anything related to the break-in. They had delivered on Lee's promise to get all the scenery onstage, movable parts operating by six o'clock.

I sat alone. Patsy was backstage. We were ready. We'd swept, mopped, and swept again. We'd taped a copy of the order of scenes in both wings, checked the headsets, pushed Marty along, and let the master electrician know that under no circumstances would the follow spot operators function on their own. I insisted that everyone involved on the technical side have a headset. That way, I could keep track of the entire performance. The drawback was the extra theater criticism I'd have to listen to from the techs. Who, I wondered, would be more irritating, those who liked *Convent of Fear* or those who didn't?

In all, it was a relief to be back at work. I'd been completely diverted from the production since the end of rehearsal the night before. The vandals and the meeting at Old Main forced me to sacrifice valuable rehearsal time with Mary Frances. Ilana rebuffed my offer to assist in the costume shop. She'd already called in her crew by the time I'd returned from the public relations office. In the end that still didn't leave me much time. I'd needed most of the afternoon to put my office back together. After carefully checking through the papers, files, and stored props, the only item that I could definitely say was missing was the petty cash.

When Roger and Paolo turned up for dinner (still complaining about eating so early), order was being restored on all fronts. The boys, Patsy, and I returned to Ernie's. Once we'd settled into a booth—Paolo and Roger on opposite sides again—I filled them in on my meeting.

"So the head of campus security and Joe's dad are brothers? Or is that 'were,' since one of them is dead?" Roger asked.

"I don't think the dead one cares," Paolo said.

"Probably not," Roger said. "If Joe and Marty are cousins, then is this guy Marty's uncle or dad?" He was very humorless in his detective mode.

"Uncle," I said. "Joe's dad and Marty's mother and the security chief are brothers and sister."

"So Mary Corinne is related to the security guy . . . how?" Roger seemed mesmerized by the family connections.

"She isn't really. Her sister married Stanley Sobieski's brother, Joe Sr." By now the waitress was serving our food. Tonight everyone was eating burgers.

"And how long has this town been inbreeding?" Paolo asked.

"I still don't see how any of this fits in," Roger said.

"Fits into what, Rog?" I asked.

"Who killed Sally," Roger said.

"I thought you said it was an accident," Patsy said.

"It was," I said. I was tiring of Roger Parker, Boy Detective.

"No, wait. I have it," Roger said. He slammed his hand down, drawing startled looks from the people at the next table. "The security chief."

"The security chief?" I asked. I wondered, if we all stopped listening, would Roger stop making sound?

"He did it. You said yourself the office didn't appear to be broken into. He has passkeys. He knew the Bible quote. He's probably part of the Friends of Decency. You said he was a religious nut. That's why they get away with so much. They have someone on the inside."

" 'Didn't appear to be broken into'?" Paolo rolled the phrase around in his mouth as if he'd bitten into a bad peanut. "Who speaks like that? When we get home I'm disconnecting the cable. No more English mystery movies for you."

"Roger, that makes no sense," I said. "Why would the chief of security want to trash my office? And anyway, I didn't say he was a religious nut. Just that he was religious."

"Intimidation. You said he was pushing to shut you down. So he knocks off Sally, sics his fundy goons on the theater, and trashes your office and the costume shop. He's probably the guy on the bicycle."

"I'm lost." Now it was Patsy. "What are fundy goons?" she asked.

"Fundamentalists," Roger said. He shook his head at her obtuseness.

"That is enough," I said. "Sister Sally was not murdered. It was an accident. No more. New topic. Moving on. I want dirt from the city and I want it now. OK?" I said.

Roger looked sulky and shoved a French fry in his mouth.

"You want dirt? I know dirt," Paolo said, and then he smiled at Patsy. "Did you know that Nicky once dated an honest-to-God axe murderer?"

"I did not mean dirt on me."

"You dated an axe murderer?" Patsy hung halfway between awe and disbelief.

"I did not. We had coffee. Once. And he wasn't an axe murderer then."

"It was more than an hour, wasn't it?" Roger asked.

"So what?" I wished I could tip my soda over on him, but I'd already finished it.

"If it's more than an hour, it's a date."

"Everyone knows that," Paolo said.

"I don't know that," I protested.

Patsy was laughing. "God, Nicky, even I know that," she said. "So, did he have body parts in the freezer or what?"

"He was not an axe murderer. Don't listen to these two."

"Not yet an axe murderer," Paolo said. "Two years later he had a freezer full of body parts. You have to understand, Patsy, Nicky is not the best at choosing dates. We try to fix him up with suitable people, but nothing helps. It's all very sad. We're thinking of holding a memorial service for his love life." Paolo's martini arrived just then. He detoured from my lack of a love life long enough to wonder aloud why anyone would make a martini in a juice glass. "I'm sure he's told you all about the man he left behind when he fled west?"

"I did not flee west. Will you stop?"

"I hope not," Patsy said. She was warming up to Paolo as Paolo warmed up to his topic.

By the time he and Roger were done detailing my dating history, including an unfortunate encounter with a guy who turned out be a male strippergram (who knew?), Patsy was laughing so hard she couldn't even eat. So was I. Strung together, the stories were funny in an emotionally gruesome way.

"Five minutes. Five minutes, please."

"Nicky? Nicky, could you pick up your headset, please?" This from the rear of the house.

"Yes, Rebecca," I said, flipping my headset mike into position.

"Nicky, I really need another fifteen minutes to make this worthwhile tonight." Rebecca's voice, like the rest of her, had a light, pleasant quality. I heard it now in my right ear. I could picture her focusing on her diagrams and cue sheets, eyebrows scrunched together, giving me only a fraction of her attention.

"I can give you five," I said.

"Five? What can I do with five? I need at least ten."

"OK, but I want house lights and run lights now so I can get the cast in place."

"Easily done. Let there be light." The lights in the auditorium came up halfway. Onstage, I could see blue lights winking to life along the back wall. During performance, these "run lights" would be masked from the audience.

"A pleasure doing business with you, Rebecca. You have ten plus the five I just called."

Marty Friedman's voice came floating through my earphone. "Nicky? Hello? Hello? Is anyone on here? Hello?"

"Marty, I'm here, but hold on." I reached for the microphone again.

"Ladies and gentlemen, we will be holding an additional ten minutes. We are now again at fifteen. Fifteen minutes, please. Thank you." Back to the headset. "What is it, Marty?"

Benny was standing next to me, saying, "Nicky."

"Give me a moment, Benny," I said. "Repeat that, Marty?"

"I can't find the tea set."

"How can you lose an entire tea set, Marty?" I asked.

"It was here an hour ago, and now it's gone."

"OK, OK. Keep looking. If you can't find it by the time we get to the scene, use the rehearsal one. I'm not stopping for a tea set. Patsy, are you on?"

"Right here," came her reply.

"Will you please help Marty find his tea set? Just get back on a headset in ten minutes, OK?"

"OK, Chief."

Chief? Ah, what had love done to my once somber Patsy?

Benny was in a foul mood. "What is going on? Why are we holding? Why wasn't I consulted?" He stood squeezed between two rows of seats, hands gripping the chairs on either side of him.

"Benny, I—"

135

"I am the director. I am the one who makes the decisions around here. Is that clear, Nicholas? Is that clear?"

"Of course, Benny, I just—"

"And I will be consulted. Is that clear?"

"Yes, Benny."

"Fine. Let me know when we're ready." He stomped back to his seat. Let him know when we're ready? Funny definition of consulting.

"What is with him tonight?" It was Rebecca, back on her headset.

"Who knows. I just hope it's not going to be like this all evening," I answered.

"Me too. Good luck, Nicky."

"Thank you. Can you give me some general light onstage, please?"

"Done. Call me if you need me."

Onstage, light poured down on an exterior setting of the convent.

"Psssst." I turned around. Roger was leaning toward me from one row back.

"Hey, Rog," I said.

"Nicky. I have it. I know who did it," he said.

"What?" I asked. "Took the tea set?"

"What tea set? No. I know who killed Sister Sally. It's blackmail, plain and simple."

Was there ever anything plain or simple about blackmail? Surely nothing as simple as Roger seemed to be at that moment.

"Roger, please. Please, listen very very carefully: Sister Sally was not murdered. It was an accident. Not unlike the accident you may face if you don't sit down and shut up." Into the microphone: "Places, please. Places for Act 1. Thank you."

Patsy checked in from backstage. "Nicky, I'm on."

"Find it?" I asked.

"Not yet."

136

Roger was insistently tapping me on the shoulder. "But Nicky, I'm telling you, I have the answer. It was Mary Corinne. That's why she ran away."

"Mary Corinne ran away because she is fucking the musical director. Would you please be quiet?" I was practically shouting.

"Nice way to talk about a nun. I'm ready anytime," Rebecca said into my ear. I could hear Patsy laughing. I turned my headset off.

"Roger, I'm working here. This is my job. I do not have time for this conversation. OK?"

"All right. All right. But what am I supposed to do?" he asked.

"Did you know our lights are computerized?"

"So?"

"So, the board is right in the back. You should go check it out."

"Not a bad idea. Better than watching this thing again." He zipped off. Rebecca would probably never forgive me. I turned my headset back on.

"Patsy. Are we ready?"

"Yes," she answered.

I spoke into the God mike. "Quiet, please."

The house fell silent. I switched the mike off. I paused a moment.

"House out," I said into the headset.

The auditorium went dark.

"Light cue one—go."

The stage lights faded up to scene level.

The first nun appeared.

"Well, what choice did I have? The bishop was standing right there with nothing on but his cassock . . ."

And so we continued to the tea scene.

Sister Klarissa sits quietly, her eyes never moving from Sister Lucretia's face. Only it isn't Sister Lucretia sipping tea so daintily from a small china cup. It is actually the police lieutenant. Klarissa marvels that even in the habit of a nun he still looks so masculine. Her brow furrows as she ponders this thought further. Should she even think such things? Is she not soon to take a vow of earthly chastity as she declares her eternal love for her creator? If she could only be as certain as the other nuns.

She sees them sitting about the day room. Their faces betray no sense of confusion. Sister Apollonia is devouring a sandwich with a gusto that seems almost gluttonous. Sister James sits with her teacup delicately placed on her lap. The others are talking, their tea getting cold. They are trying to get the measure of the visiting nuns. Company is so rare. Yet each seems content. Even the lieutenant's assistant, who is struggling with his robes, looks to be more at peace to Klarissa than she herself. She sighs aloud.

The Mother Superior asks her if something is troubling her. What can she say? Nothing? Everything? She pulls at her collar, feeling flushed. Has it gotten suddenly hot in the room? She could use a strong cup of tea to revive her. She beckons to Sister James, stretches out her arm, and faints. The lights go out.

"Hold, please. Everyone just stay put. Thank you," I called out over the microphone. "Rebecca, what's happening?" I said into the headset.

Running through the first act, the lights had dipped and varied, giving the convent the look of a building in a brownout. But up to that moment, Rebecca had kept enough light onstage for the actors to continue working. Random blackouts were not only annoying, they were unsafe.

"Rebecca? Speak to me, darling," I said.

"Hey, Nicky. Sorry about that. I wrote a blackout into the wrong cue. Give me a second and we'll have you back up and running." I heard her speaking to her electrician.

"We'll have the lights back in a moment, folks," I announced. "Just hold tight, please. Thank you."

"Nicky?" Benny was calling out of the darkness. "Nicky, since we're stopped, I need to change something here."

Light returned to the stage. Benny was walking up the right aisle, calling for attention.

"Oh God. I'm sorry, Nicky," Rebecca said.

If we hadn't gone to black, Benny would not have interrupted the action. We were behind as it was. It had taken an hour to fight our way to the tea scene. Once there, the interruptions that Mary Frances and I had suffered the day before began to take their toll. She wasn't sufficiently prepared. Already we'd spent over half an hour on the fifteen-minute scene. Not only was she having line trouble, I noticed that she'd given up even trying to get the tea-drinking business in. While Joe was guzzling the stuff, Mary Frances hadn't taken a sip.

"It happens," I said into the headset. "Patsy, how're you doing back there? I see you found the tea service." I could see the rose pattern on the white china teapot perched on the center table of the day room set.

"Yeah, well, that story is not nearly finished," she replied.

"What story? What happened?"

Marty Friedman walked onstage from the left. "Are we on break? Is this a break? Nicky, I need to speak to you." He came down from the stage. He did not look happy.

"Patsy," I said, "is there something I should know? Talk fast."

"We found the tea set with Paolo."

Great.

"Nicky." Marty was standing in front of my table. He was dressed in his "blacks": black shoes, black jeans, black turtleneck. Everyone on the run crew dressed like this. The idea was to be less conspicuous backstage. In the auditorium, with only the light from my work table shining on him, it appeared as if Marty's head were floating disembodied in front of me.

"I have a complaint to register," he said.

Well, at least he wasn't trying to spray-paint Paolo.

"Patsy, is Paolo backstage?" I asked.

"Oh yes." I swear I could hear her grinning.

"Would you please ask him to step out here? Thank you." I turned my headset off. No point in broadcasting this one.

"Look, Nicky," Marty said. "I don't want to make trouble. You know me. But I really have to tell you, this is not good. This is actually pretty bad, Nicky. You know what I mean?"

"I know, Marty."

"You wanted to see me, Nicky?" Paolo joined us. Being a civilian, he was all in summer pastels. He projected an air of complete innocence. If you didn't know him, you'd never know how much time he spent practicing that look.

"So, what happened?" I asked, but, oh, how I didn't want to know.

"Well, Nicky," Marty said, "I had the tea set on the table stage right, ready to go on for this scene. I remember putting it there specifically because I'd actually run out of room on the main table and I'd gotten Lee to help me move up one of the little workbenches from his shop. You know, the ones that he keeps—"

"Tea set?" I interrupted him.

Paolo jumped in. "The tea set is ugly. My grandmother was the queen of kitsch, and even she had better-looking china."

"That tea set is my grandmother's." I thought Marty was going to cry as he said this.

"Guys, please. Paolo, I asked you yesterday to lay off, didn't I?"

"I wasn't doing anything," he said.

"We found him with the tea set in a classroom across the hall," Marty said.

"No, you found me *and* the tea set in a classroom across the hall. It was not *with* me. It was there when I got there. I swear, Nicky, I wasn't doing anything. I was just passing an idle hour sketching in chalk on the blackboard. Though God knows, one afternoon and a good paint job wouldn't be wasted on those things."

"Well, then how did it get from the prop table to the classroom? Huh?" Marty asked.

"How the hell should I know why you can't keep track of your props?"

"That's enough," I said. "We aren't getting anywhere."

"I agree with that," Paolo said. "I'll be in your office in case anyone wants to get a rubber hose and beat more information out of me." He started to walk away.

"Yeah, well . . . ," Marty started. "Well, I bet you'd like that."

Paolo stopped. We both stared at Marty. Not that the comment was much of a comeback, but from Marty Friedman?

"Listen, you with all your taste in your mouth," Paolo said. "There are only two people in this 'we eat earlier than anyone on earth' in-bred little town who can make that kind of joke with me. Him"—he pointed at me—"and that prick I'm married to. One of them is angry at me, and I am angry at the other. Neither of them is you. Understand?"

"Well."

"Good." Paolo finished his interrupted exit.

"Jeez, Nicky. I didn't mean to offend him," Marty said.

I was trying not to laugh. Poor Marty. "Well, Marty, I'm sure it will be OK. And I will talk to him about the tea service. Nothing was broken, right?"

"No. I just don't want people playing with the props."

It was a reasonable request. Props break all the time in performance. No need to add extra wear. I assured Marty that I would be very definite with Paolo. Satisfied, he returned to the wings.

"Patsy?"

"I'm here, Nicky," she said into my ear.

"What's going on up there?" I could see that Benny was still on-stage talking to the actors.

"Benny and Joe are arguing over what Mary Frances should be doing."

I like many things about stage managing. Organizing people, material, and information appeals to me. I also enjoy being part of creating a good working environment. That means mediating between artists, helping them find ways to work together. And though it sounds corny, I always get a thrill at the downbeat of the overture in front of the opening-night audience. Unfortunately, I can't have any of the things I like without the things I don't: temper tantrums, egos, the untalented.

I put down my headset, stretched, and strolled toward the stage, where Benny Singleton and Joe Sobieski were frittering away the last run-through before technical rehearsal. The rest of the cast sat unhappily resigned to the continuing feud between the lead actor and the director. I winked at David as I stepped past him. He grinned back at me.

"How're we doing, Benny?" I asked, stepping up next to him.

"We're done," he said. "Mary Frances will do the new blocking as I've just given it."

"It sucks," Joe said. "If she does all of that, she'll tramp all over my lines. No one is going to hear anything I'm saying."

"My blocking isn't your business," Mary Frances said.

"It is if you're doing it while I'm speaking. Damn it, it's hot under these lights. Do they have to be so bright? They're giving me a headache." Joe looked flushed. The nun's habit was not helping him keep any cooler.

"How about a break? We could all use a little fresh air," I said.

"Thank God," Joe said. "I've drunk half that pot of tea already." He was the first offstage.

After break we tried the tea scene again. This time it was Joe who seemed to be in a daze. The more we repeated the scene, the more he seemed to forget what it was he was supposed to do. The lines eluded him; the blocking went undone. Benny screamed at him. Joe screamed back. The actresses playing the nuns assumed the look of weary secondaries who know that what they think doesn't count, but God, how they'd love to say it aloud. We took an aspirin break. Joe swallowed four of them, washing them down with more tea. We plowed into the tea scene one more time.

She sees the others sitting about the day room. Their faces betray no sense of confusion. Sister Apollonia is devouring a sandwich with a gusto that seems almost gluttonous. Sister James sits with her teacup delicately placed on her lap. The others are talking, their tea getting cold. They are trying to get the measure of the visiting nuns. Company is so rare. Yet each seems content. Even the lieutenant's assistant, who is struggling with his robes, looks more at peace to Klarissa than she herself. She sighs aloud.

The Mother Superior asks her if something is troubling her. What can she say? Nothing? Everything? She pulls at her collar, then takes a tissue from her sleeve. She is feeling flushed. Her face is suddenly awash in perspiration. Frantically, she starts to wipe her forehead as the other nuns, distracted by her increasing agitation, try to listen to Sister Lucretia. But who can concentrate with Klarissa making such a fuss? The Mother Superior reprimands her with a stern gaze. Has it gotten suddenly hot in the room? She could use a strong cup of tea to revive her. She wants air. The window is shut, but she thinks she can open it. She stands and takes a step, then another, staggering. She reaches for the mantel, beckoning to Sister James with outstretched arms. Suddenly, Sister Lucretia drops her teacup and pitches face-forward onto the floor.

"God damn it, Joe. That is not what I asked for." Benny was up and charging down the aisle. "Mary Frances is the one who's supposed to faint. Who the hell told *you* to faint? You're wasting my time and the time of every cast member here. Get up. Do you hear me? Get up!" Benny was heaving himself onto the stage.

"Nicky, you better get down here. I think something is wrong," Patsy said over the headset.

"Rebecca, I want full light onstage. Now." I was out of my seat before the headset hit the table.

As I ran down the aisle, light blasted the stage, pouring stark white over every figure. The tableaux was eerily reminiscent of Sister Sally's death. Joe was a crumpled ball of black cloth on the stage floor. Mary Frances stood clutching the mantel. David was on his knees next to Joe. Benny was just stepping up to them. The Mother Superior and the other nuns were partway out of their chairs.

I pushed my way onstage to the center of the action. David looked up at me. "I can't feel a pulse, Nicky," he said.

"Call an ambulance, Patsy," I said.

Suddenly, there were people everywhere. The children flooded the stage. Ilana and Rebecca were standing next to me, asking what was happening.

"Could we have quiet? Please. Everyone, please stand back." I tried to clear a space around Joe. There was a crash next to me. The teapot was in pieces on the floor. I had no idea who'd knocked it over. Everyone was still in motion.

"Oh shit. That's my grandmother's." Now Marty was shouting.

Finally, with Rebecca's help, we cleared the area. I was able to herd the actors to the edge of the apron. We got the children into the house.

On the set, Joe lay very still on the stage floor. Too still. Tea ran across the floor, puddling at his side, a brown translucent liquid that would certainly stain Ilana's costume. The tea that only Joe had been drinking. Poured from a teapot that went missing for almost an hour. We stood silently over Joe's body.

Looking at the scene in front of me, I felt the beginning of fear, and I knew why. I finally believed that Sister Sally had been murdered.

"Hello, everyone. What's going on?"

We all turned toward the house. There, standing in the left aisle, like ghosts cued into the wrong act of a bad play, were Sister Mary Corinne and Edward Rossoff, clutching overnight bags. She was wearing a floral cotton summer dress completely unlike anything I'd ever seen on a nun. They were both grinning like guilty teenagers.

"We're back," she said.

"And we're married," he added, holding up her left hand in his to display wedding rings.

"Did we miss anything?"

TEN

MOST OF THE POLICE were gone. They'd done all the things I'd missed after Sister Sally's death: photos, prints, questions, measurements. They worked surrounded by the convent scenery, under the glow of Rebecca's lights. Our play about murder now had a very real corpse center stage. I realized that I preferred the police action on television—definitely less disturbing. As the police presence wound down, the paralysis of shock began to settle on the theater company.

Corporal Roberts was not paralyzed. Having your daughter only three feet away from a murder probably does that. He'd dismissed the children almost immediately. After questioning, most of the rest of the cast departed. Now he stood in almost the same spot as the day before, facing the rest of us, the decision makers and shakers of St. Gilbert's Summer Theater Festival. We were loosely grouped in the front rows. Patsy and Mary Frances, who looked like she wanted very much to disappear from Daddy's gaze, clung to each other on my left. Roger and Paolo sat just behind me, one empty seat between them. Benny, Ilana, and Rebecca huddled together on my right. At first they'd been whispering intently, but as the night dragged on they sat listless in their chairs. Edward Rossoff and Mary Corinne held hands two rows back. No one was more stunned than Marty Friedman. He sat alone, unmoving, six rows back. I sat front and center. We focused on the corporal. Even though he held our complete attention, there was nothing "triumphant" about this return to the stage.

"Thank God no one else drank tea," Ilana said.

"Yes, for once, Benny, your shit-ass directing paid off," Edward said.

"Please." Mary Corinne placed a restraining hand on his arm.

"Oh, how I've missed you, Edward. And there is nothing shit-ass about my directing. Everything is character motivated."

"Why do you blame the tea, Ms. Mosca?" Corporal Roberts had his pad in one hand, pen in the other.

"It make sense, yes? Someone poison Sally. Now Joe is only one drinks tea—he dies. It is asking who ate bad seafood at salad bar." Ilana seemed genuinely puzzled at the corporal's question. The corporal seemed genuinely puzzled at Ilana's suddenly thickened accent.

Benny was leaning forward in his seat. "You *are* testing the tea, aren't you, Corporal? I mean, someone obviously tried to get rid of it by knocking it over. You *are* going to check that out?"

"We will check out every avenue of information," the corporal said. "But can you tell me why Mr. Sobieski was the only person in the scene drinking tea? It's supposed to be afternoon tea for the entire convent, right?"

"Are you criticizing Daddy's work?" The voice came pounding out of the back of the house. Olivia. We'd all forgotten about Olivia, always lurking, always listening.

"Who's there?" the corporal called out.

"That would be my daughter, Corporal. She's my biggest fan. Olivia, what are you doing here? I told you to go home with the others."

Olivia came striding down the left aisle. She marched right up to the corporal. The contrast could not have been greater: the short, slender young girl standing up to the towering, nearly stout middle-aged man.

"Daddy is a great director. You leave him alone."

"You must be Olivia Singleton. I'm Corporal Roberts of the Pennsylvania State Police. I don't think we've met." He squatted until he was eye level with her and extended his hand. The corporal could be charming when he wanted to be. From his manner I guessed he was used to getting positive responses. Obviously, he'd never met anyone like Olivia.

"I know who you are. You're the dyke's daddy." She walked over and sat next to her father.

Paolo broke the silence. "I believe dykes have 'mommies.' Boy homos have 'daddies.' "

This comment let loose a torrent of pent-up frustrations and fears. Tension poured out in a free-for-all of shouted recrimination.

Benny led the way. "That is not appropriate conversation for a twelve-year-old. You will be a little more respectful in front of my daughter."

"Jesus fucking Christ, Benny. That kid is so wacko, who cares what she hears?" Edward said.

Mary Corinne pulled at Edward's sleeve as everyone started shouting at once. I couldn't make any sense out of it. Who knows what Corporal Roberts thought of the sudden jumble of name-calling.

"I am not a wacko, you sick fuck."

"Olivia, where did you learn that word?"

"You're a married nun. What do you know?"

"Benny, you must discipline child."

"Please, Edward. Sit down."

"Where the fuck do you get off calling me a dyke?"

"Nicky, stop them."

"He can't even *spell* 'discipline.' Or 'direction.' "

"Dyke. Dyke. Dyke."

"Paolo, that's not nice."

"She's going to make some therapist very happy."

"And the entire show is shit. Hear me?"

"Sit down now, Edward."

"I'm not going to be lectured by a cyberslut."

Corporal Roberts did not intervene. I'd read somewhere that this sort of outburst often revealed crucial information to the police. To me it revealed the miracle that this group could actually produce any piece of theater, even a bad one. They certainly never generated this much heat onstage. Did the corporal register that his daughter had admitted to being a lesbian? I couldn't tell. He was very interested in everything Paolo said. I didn't like that. It all came back to the tea. Marty and Patsy found it on a desk in a classroom. They also found Paolo with it. He said the tea was there when he entered the room. And now, Joe had drunk a pot of it and was dead.

I had the same question as Edward and the corporal. Not that I cared about Benny Singleton's idea of character motivation. For me the question was much more practical. I'd rehearsed this scene with Mary Frances yesterday. I'd specifically given her Benny's detailed instructions on when she was to drink tea, when she was to start for tea but decide not to drink, and when she was to gulp, sip, or spew out tea in surprise. Benny and Sally had created a complete catalogue of tea gestures, each of which I carefully imparted to Mary Frances. But only Joe was dead. Why didn't she drink the tea? Maybe she was just confused, but then I didn't believe that Benny would have sat quietly while Mary Frances ignored his precious tea blocking. Now, he was even defending the scene to Edward.

The shouting finally wore itself out. Everyone sat back, exhausted, their nervous energy spent.

I stood up. "Corporal Roberts. Will you come with me, please? I'd like to show you something."

I turned away without waiting for an answer. As I walked up the aisle I could sense the stunned looks from the others. Without objection the corporal followed me.

At my work table I opened the prompt book to the tea scene and began to scan the blocking. By the time the corporal joined me, I could see that something was very definitely not right.

"What is it, Mr. D'Amico?" he asked.

"This is a prompt book. It's a stage manager's script. I or Patsy mark down every piece of information needed to run this show. See these lists at the start of the scene? That's props and their location, right or left offstage. We keep track of all of it, including the blocking for the actors. Look: *K X DS rTable.* That means Klarissa crosses downstage to the right of the table. And this one: *MS ent. L w/ Lt/Asst.* That means the Mother Superior enters left, followed by the lieutenant and his assistant, in that order. The entire play is mapped out in here. Everything that happens in rehearsal."

"I understand the concept."

"Well, look here: *K gulp.* And here: *K sip.* And here: *L sip.* And here: *MS drink.* These are tea-drinking directions. All of these characters: Klarissa, the lieutenant, the Mother Superior, the assistant, the other nuns. They're all blocked to drink tea."

"But only Sobieski did." The corporal carefully leafed through the scene. "Is it common, this sort of detailed direction about drinking?"

"Depends. If the scene revolves around physical humor, it can get this specific."

"This show a comedy?"

"Yes, and Benny is a little more obsessive than some."

The corporal continued to turn pages. "What's this mark mean?" He pointed to a note in the margin of the dialogue that read *SQ 15*.

"That's sound cue number fifteen. I mark all the light and sound cues too. It's what I use during performance to run the show."

"I see. So why didn't the actors do what they were supposed to do?" He looked directly at me. Despite the differences in our height, with him hunched over the table and me standing, we were nearly touching shoulders. In the light cast upward from my work lamp, deep shadows pooled on the corporal's face.

"I don't know."

The corporal nodded his head.

"Mr. D'Amico, at the moment all we have is what's known as suspicious circumstances. But I'm telling you, with two people dead in three days, they are very suspicious. We need to know everything there is to know about everything that's going on here, including this tea business. Who do you think might have that answer?"

"Benny. Maybe Patsy."

The corporal straightened up to his full height.

"Ms. Malone? Mr. Singleton? Would you join us, please?" And then, as Olivia jumped up, "No, Ms. Singleton. You stay there, please."

Olivia was not pleased. She made as if to follow Benny, but Ilana grabbed her. There was a struggle, with a few four-letter words on both sides. Olivia finally gave up and sat back down.

At the table Corporal Roberts flipped the prompt book around to face Benny and Patsy.

"Mr. D'Amico has been giving me a brief lesson in how a theater operates. As I understand it, the coded markings in this book are a record of what happens onstage. Who moves when and where. When the lights go on and off. That sort of thing. Is that correct?"

151

"Yes. It's supposed to be accurate," Benny said. He emphasized the word "supposed" with just enough of a hint of suspicion that I wanted to belt him.

"Then why does this book say that everyone in the tea scene drinks tea, when in fact only Mr. Sobieski did so?"

Benny shrugged. "As I said. The word is 'supposed.' At last evening's rehearsal, I changed the blocking. You'd have to ask Nicky why his book is not up to speed."

"When last night?" I asked.

"This is my fault, I guess, Nicky," Patsy said. "He did it while you were in the shops. I meant to erase it all later, but I guess I just didn't get to it. I got distracted." She looked extremely embarrassed. I could imagine what kept her from completing the job. Apparently, so could Corporal Roberts, who seemed even less happy with the thought than I.

"I see. And why did you change the blocking, Mr. Singleton?"

"It was no longer working. Without Sister Sally, we just didn't have the time to fully explore all the possibilities that such a complicated sequence of actions offered us." Translation: Your daughter couldn't get it down fast enough, so I cut it.

Poor Corporal Roberts. This could not have been easy on the guy. I was almost feeling sorry for him.

"And who would know about this change?" he asked.

"Anyone who was paying attention," Benny said. His sarcasm was providing me with some very handy cover. Obviously, I didn't know about his change in blocking, so I couldn't have been the one trying to kill Joe.

"Why would anyone murder Sally and Joe? It doesn't make any sense," I said.

"Murder doesn't always make the kind of sense we're used to," the corporal said. "Let's rejoin the others."

Before we moved more than a few steps away from the work table, a uniformed state trooper escorted our set designer, Lee Dexter, down the aisle. Normally, Lee had the ruddy look of a burly, well-fed man. Just then his appearance was anything but healthy. Unshaven, with dark circles under blood-red eyes, he looked like he hadn't slept since the day before. One night of working late couldn't possibly account for his appearance.

"What's this?" the corporal asked.

"Gentleman was trying to enter the building. He refused at first to identify himself. Now he says he works with the theater." The trooper had a tight grip on Lee's left arm, suggesting he hadn't discounted further trouble from the "gentleman."

"That's correct, Corporal. This is Lee Dexter, our set designer," Benny said.

"Good evening, Mr. Dexter." The corporal nodded to him. "What brings you back so late in the evening?"

"I work here," Lee snapped at him.

"Ah-huh." The corporal let silence accumulate, but Lee didn't take the bait. I, however, wasn't so bright.

"That's right," I said. "The scene shop is in the basement. I was down there earlier talking with Lee."

"You weren't at your work table all evening?" The corporal shifted his attention and suspicions to me.

"Ah, yes. For rehearsal. Yes, I spoke to Lee earlier. Right after dinner. About the scenery. It was put onstage late last night and this afternoon."

"Ah-huh. Mr. Dexter, perhaps you and I should talk privately. Why don't the rest of you rejoin the others." The corporal dismissed us with the forced cordiality of a funeral director.

Patsy, Benny, and I returned to our seats. Corporal Roberts and Lee stepped out to the lobby. Of course, Lee could have gone out for any number of reasons: run an errand, get a bite to eat, destroy some evidence. I stopped myself. How fast I'd turned into Roger now that I'd decided we were facing murder. What reason would Lee have to murder anyone? But if not murder, then what was eating at him?

"What's with your set designer?" Roger asked. "He looks like he's on the wrong end of a *Twilight Zone* episode."

"I don't know," I said.

"Well, I don't like it," Roger added.

"In that case I'm sure it means nothing," Paolo mumbled, not bothering to raise his head from the back of the seat in which he was reclining, eyes closed.

After that we waited in silence.

Finally, the corporal returned without Lee. The rest of us were released with the standard admonishments not to leave town without notifying the police (which seemed to me to be directed rather pointedly at Roger, Paolo, and me) and instructions for all of us to stay away from the stage, now considered a crime scene. Corporal Roberts wrapped up for the night. I was to be permitted to use my office to close out the day's paperwork.

As we filed toward the back of the house, the corporal turned toward his daughter.

"I'll take you home, Mary Frances," he said.

"No, thanks," she answered, standing next to Patsy. "I'll be along later."

He eyed Patsy for a very long and uncomfortable moment.

"And what should I tell your mother?" he asked.

"She already knows," Mary Frances said.

For one short theatrical beat, his eyes narrowed. Then he shrugged and walked away, leaving me with the suspicion that this was not the first time his wife and daughter had left him on the outside looking in.

Mary Frances had Patsy hang back, wanting the rest of us to exit first, putting a little more distance between themselves and her father. I could sympathize with that urge, but I would, as always, be the last one out. The others exited in ones and twos. I told Patsy to hold on for me in the office. I waited, just Rebecca and I remaining, as she turned off the lights and shut down her computer console. We used the light spilling from the lobby to guide us toward my office door. The theater was completely dark. I wasn't even allowed onstage to turn on the ghost light.

ELEVEN

CONVENT OF FEAR WAS finished. It's not easy to put the brakes on a show so close to opening. Sometimes, it can cost more to cancel than to open and fail. Some shows open for ego. There are actors and directors who can't imagine that they don't have the magic touch, that no matter how rocky rehearsals have been, opening night will be a marvel of artistic beauty. Working with these people is like being strapped to the front of a roller coaster: you just scream and hope for the best. Whatever form the momentum takes, if someone murders both leading players, that pretty much ends the event.

"Could anyone really hate *Convent of Fear* enough to want to kill?" Rebecca asked. She and I were in my office. "I mean, sure, it's not setting the pace for contemporary theater, but isn't murder a little extreme?"

She was sitting on the love seat, making notations in a three-ring binder. Rebecca off headset was always a surprise. Not because her voice didn't match her physically, but because it did, and that is so rare. She was light: pale skin, blue eyes, blonde hair. Even her clothes were light: cool summer cottons hung on a rail-thin, insubstantial-looking frame.

"You just don't want to have to take all those lights down now that you've put them up," I said.

"That remark is too insensitive for comment. Anyway, I'm not going to be allowed to work in there for days. Do you really think this is about shutting us down?"

I just shook my head. It was late. The police weren't fifteen minutes gone. Joe Jr. was barely five hours dead, Sally only two days. The musical director and a lapsed nun had just eloped. Above my desk some crazy had scribbled a cryptic Bible verse. I was never going to get laid.

"How should I know? We can't even be sure that whoever poisoned the tea wasn't trying to kill everyone."

"Or that Benny didn't restage the scene just to get Joe," Roger Parker said, arriving with his typically suspicious imagination.

"Oh yeah," I said. "That certainly wouldn't draw anyone's attention."

"No less obvious than knocking the teapot over," Roger said. "How childish was that? So you guys are shutting down, right?" He sat down, looking more tired than I felt.

"Yes. But it won't be official until tomorrow. I guess we'll get some command from on high at Old Main. Where's Paolo?" I asked.

"He went home. To your place, not New York. Not yet, anyway." Roger's comment fell into the empty space created by our mounting sense of shock. The three of us sat in silence, settling into some sort of posttraumatic reaction. Too numb to speak, too tired to move.

"This looks about my speed," Patsy said from the door. She made a direct line to the love seat. "Move over, 'Becca. I need a cushion. Mary Frances and Daddy are chatting it up outside. That man makes me nervous." She flopped down on the cushions. "Do you have a bottle of Scotch hidden away in here? Aren't stage managers supposed to hide liquor in their desk drawers?"

"I wouldn't worry about Wally," Rebecca said. "He's a lot more flexible than he lets on when he's working."

"I don't have any Scotch," I said. "Who's Wally?"

"Short for Wallace. Corporal Wallace Roberts," Rebecca answered.

"You know him?" Roger asked.

"He's my cousin," Rebecca said, looking from Roger to me.

"You mean you're Mary Frances's cousin too?" Patsy asked.

"First cousins once removed, but who counts that 'removed' thing?" Then, seeing our reaction, she said, "What? What's the big deal? Don't you people have relatives?"

"Of course we have relatives, Rebecca," I said. "But we keep them at a respectable distance. This entire town is one never-ending family reunion. Patsy, are you sure you're not related to someone here?"

"I'm sure. All my relatives are in Philly. Thank God. Where are yours?"

"Elsewhere," I said. "And may they never move from there."

"If it wasn't Benny, then who was it?" Roger asked no one in particular.

Like a light switch being flipped, the mood in the room dropped back to morose.

"Jesus, Roger. Give it a rest, OK?" I said.

"I can't. He told Paolo and me not to leave town. He practically accused Paolo of poisoning the tea." Roger was getting very upset. His knuckles turned white as he gripped the side of the cushioned armchair.

"I don't believe that. What did he say?" I asked.

"He said, 'Don't leave town, either of you.' "

Rebecca laughed. "He asked all of us not to leave town without checking in," she said.

"Roger," I said, "why would he think Paolo did it? You guys just got here. You don't even know anyone here. There are probably a dozen people with better motives."

"Better? How about any?" he asked. "What does he care? Small town homophobic prick. Everyone else is a fucking relative." Roger was in full swing.

Rebecca tried to reassure him. "Look, cousin Wally may be a tight-ass now and then, but he takes this stuff seriously. He isn't going to pin a murder on someone who's innocent just because they're gay."

"Aren't you the optimistic one?" Mary Frances said, joining the crowd. There were now five of us in an office with a maximum comfortable capacity of three. Why did that keep happening?

"I just had a nasty chat with old Mr. Fair-Minded," Mary Frances told us. "It was not pretty. I didn't even know there were so many ugly words for *lesbian*." She sat next to Patsy, who immediately wrapped both arms around her.

"Are you all right?" Patsy asked.

"Now," Mary Frances said. They kissed.

"Yeah, look at them," Roger said. "No one's accusing them of murder. Why shouldn't she be all right? So her dad hates lesbians. Big fucking deal. Move to the city, buy a cat, grind your own coffee, life goes on. What if they lock Paolo up?" He was really looking stricken.

"Roger," I said. "It's going to be all right."

"You don't know that, Nicky. You're just saying it."

"I thought you guys were on the outs anyway," Rebecca said.

Roger took a deep breath. "You married?" he asked Rebecca.

"No."

"Involved?" he wanted to know.

"Well, no, but—"

"And no fucking wonder. If you think one fight is a reason to turn your lover over to the local gestapo—"

159

"My father, whatever he may be, is not the gestapo," Mary Frances said.

"I never said that, Roger," Rebecca said.

We were about five seconds away from really ugly.

"Enough." I pitched my voice low and raised its volume slightly, my best "stage manager in charge" tone. Everyone went silent.

"We're tired and we're going to start saying things we don't want to," I said. I looked directly at Roger, who shifted his gaze toward the floor. Rebecca sighed but said nothing. "And anyway," I continued, "we just don't know enough about what's going on to know who is or isn't a suspect."

"But we do know some things. Probably more than we realize," Mary Frances said, keeping the conversation going.

"Maybe." Where was *this* going, I wondered.

"Probably," Rebecca said, looking at me.

"I agree with her," Roger said, in what was as close to an apology as we were going to get. Then he looked at me.

"What? Why are you all looking at me?" I asked.

Roger shrugged. "You're the organized one."

Did I want to let curiosity drive me to sit around until the middle of the night with four other tired, shell-shocked people till my mind was completely numb with fatigue trying to figure out who was killing cast members? Or did I want a good night's sleep? Well, there's a reason you never heard of a good night's sleep killing a household pet. It's boring.

"OK," I said. "Let's start at the beginning with what's actually happened." I just managed to avoid picking up a pen and paper to make a list. "On Monday night Sally dies onstage from bug poisoning, which she must have been exposed to for a prolonged time."

"But we don't know how," Patsy said.

"But something odd did happen with the props. Sally's cross disappeared," I said.

"Her cross?" Rebecca asked.

"Yes." I leaned forward to emphasize the only clever idea I'd had all week. "Marty couldn't find it Tuesday morning after she was murdered, but it turned up that night in the costume shop."

"What has that got to do with anything?" Roger asked.

"Corporal Roberts said it took repeated exposure to kill someone with bug poison. She was fingering that cross all the time."

"You think someone poisoned her cross?" Mary Frances used a tone very similar to the one her father had when I'd mentioned the idea to him.

"Well, it's possible . . ."

"So, you think Marty took it and then returned it?" Roger asked. He was not looking very convinced.

"Marty, or someone else," I said.

"Ilana?" Patsy wasn't looking so very impressed either.

"All right, fine. Let's forget about the cross—for now," I said. "What else do we know?"

Rebecca's face lit up. "Oh, we know who was in the theater that night," she said.

Patsy was excited by this. "That's right. Benny, Edward, Mary Corinne, Ilana, Joe, Marty, Nicky, me, the kids . . ."

"And half of the rest of the cast," I said. "That doesn't narrow it down too much."

"No, but it does leave out Rebecca and Mary Frances," Patsy countered.

"And Paolo and me," Roger jumped in.

"OK. That is good." I picked up the narrative again. "Sally dies Monday night. Mary Frances joins us the next morning. Corporal Roberts

161

puts his first appearance in Tuesday about midday, just after Marty tells me the cross is gone."

There was a general round of groaning. Ignoring it, I pushed on. "Roger and Paolo arrive. Later that evening, while I'm at the shops—which is when the cross reappears, and I don't want to hear any noise, thank you—Benny reblocks the tea scene. Overnight, the break-ins, then tonight the tea set goes missing, and bang, Joe's dead. What else?"

Rebecca started to laugh. "Mary Corinne and Edward. And that is hard to forget."

"And the guy on the bicycle. Don't forget the guy on the bicycle," Patsy added.

"And we don't know what killed Joe," Roger said, revved up now. Like the rest of us, exhaustion was lost to the exhilaration of the moment.

"We could find out," Mary Frances said. She raised an eyebrow and grinned at Patsy. "We have ways of making people talk."

"Oh no. That's just evil. I won't do it," Patsy said.

"But Pats, it could have been me drinking tea up there. Don't you want to know what this is about?"

"I can't believe you. You're sending me to seduce information out of another woman?" Patsy unwrapped herself from her girlfriend.

" 'Seduce' is a strong word, Patsy," I said. "I bet your friend at the hospital would respond very nicely to just a friendly phone call."

"Then we'd know if it's the same poison," Roger said. He was hot on the trail now.

"Well, you don't think there are two killers, do you?" Patsy asked. She looked around as if she expected murderers to start lining up in the doorway.

"It doesn't seem likely," I said. "But then, what did Joe and Sally have in common? They were part of this production. That's it. Unless they were related too?"

162

Mary Frances made a face. "That would be creepy, since they dated in high school," she said.

Roger and I were both surprised.

"Joe dated Sally? That sweet woman actually spent time alone with him?" I asked.

"Yes, for two years," Mary Frances told us. "And he was nicer then. You know, it's only been in the last year he's been so, I don't know . . ."

"Offensive?" I volunteered.

"Well, yeah," she said.

"But I thought David Scott said that Marty was in love with Sally?" I asked.

"Oh, he's always had a thing for her, but what are you going to do?" Mary Frances raised her hands, palms up. "It was one way."

"So, unless we're talking revenge for a teenage love triangle," I continued, "it's probably *Convent of Fear* that's the connection. That's pretty narrow for more than one killer."

"Or," Roger said, "nuns in general. Don't forget that bicyclist. Maybe whoever poisoned the tea intended to get everyone onstage. Maybe they didn't know about the blocking change. Couldn't just anyone have come into the building and gotten at the tea set? One of the Friends of Decency people? It doesn't have to be anyone connected to the show or even visiting."

I couldn't bring myself to point out how unlikely it was that a stranger could have snatched the tea from backstage an hour before rehearsal, when the place was overrun with people getting prepared. However, his comments did have a positive effect on Patsy.

"OK," she said. "I'll do it. You're right. Someone has been jerking us around, and I want to know who. I'll call Judy tomorrow. They do all these coroner things at her hospital."

"Great. All right, what else do we know?" I asked.

"What we don't know is, how does it fit together? That's the problem," Rebecca said. "What we know makes no sense. We have protesters camped outside. There's a crazy on a bike. Two people are dead by poison. Your office was broken into. Is any of it connected?"

"Has to be," Roger said. He sounded very definite about this.

"Roger's right," I said. "There's just too much going on. Last night, I walked in on Joe and Marty having a fight in the prop room. Joe was definitely trying to get Marty to do something he didn't want to do."

"Like what?" Rebecca asked. "Poison him?"

"No. But if Marty had enough abuse . . ." I stopped. Marty Friedman, cold-blooded killer? No thanks.

"How about this?" Roger asked. "The Friends of Decency want to shut down *Convent of Fear*. They protest. One of them goes over the edge. He's crazy. He starts running down nuns on the sidewalks. Then he kills Sally. Then he breaks in here, and then he kills Joe—who was wearing a nun's habit when he died. And don't forget the security chief. I still think he's in with the Friends of Decency."

"Could just be a nun hater, I guess," I said. "But what about my computer?"

"What about it?" Mary Frances asked, yawning now. Our group rush was beginning to fade.

"They didn't touch it," I said. "Whoever broke in here had a sudden attack of respect for property when they got to my computer. It doesn't make sense. And that Bible quote. Benny and Stan Sobieski both recognized it, but Sobieski lied about it. Why?"

"Do you think Stan killed his nephew?" Rebecca asked. "Why would he kill Sally?"

"I don't know," I said.

We'd run out of steam. The longer we sat in silence, the more tired I felt. It was now well after one o'clock in the morning.

"Look, it's late. We should all go home. I'm tired. Everyone out. Now." I stood up. "We're done for the night. Whatever else happens, we all need some sleep."

Rebecca stood up. "Fine," she said. "Roger, I really don't think anyone is going to frame Paolo. Good night." She took her three-ring binder full of notes and diagrams and left.

"Come on. You're going home with me," Patsy said, and took Mary Frances by the hand. "Good night, Nicky. Roger, I agree with Rebecca. I really do think it's going to be OK."

"Me too, Roger," Mary Frances said. "You'll see. Dad's a professional, if nothing else. Good night."

I sat down again.

The phone rang. I stared at it. I was not happy. I have always assumed a phone call in the middle of the night is never a good thing. It kept ringing.

"Aren't you going to answer it?" Roger asked.

"No, Rog. I am not going to answer it. If I answer it, it will only be bad news."

It kept ringing. And ringing.

"Damn." I picked up the handset. "Hello." It was far too late for formalities.

"Mr. D'Amico. I hear you've another death on your hands. The situation is getting worse."

I'd only heard it once, but there was no mistaking that smooth, honey-toned voice.

"Good morning, Ms. East," I said.

"Good morning. I should tell you that is not my name."

"And I should tell you that doesn't surprise me. Now go away."

"Wait. Don't hang up. I'm sorry I lied to you. I'm just doing my job. I am a reporter. I write for the *World Weekly Journal*."

That was a levelheaded, impressive-sounding name. It needed to be, the *World Weekly Journal* being one of the trashiest of trash tabloids.

"Is that supposed to make me feel better?" I asked.

"I know what will. I have an offer for you, Mr. D'Amico."

I laughed. "Sorry, but that road is closed."

"I was talking about your wallet. We'll pay."

That stopped me. "Pay for what?"

"The inside story on the curse hovering over your production. The retribution of God for the blasphemy that is *Convent of Fear*." She intoned that last line like she was doing the voice-over for a movie trailer. Worse, I think she was serious.

"You're crazy," I said.

"No. Listen to me. If you can tell me anything now, anything at all about the dead nun, I promise we will pay you for the rest of your story. I'm coming to Huber's Landing tomorrow. I'm leaving New York very early. Mr. D'Amico, I'll be bringing cash. Lots of it. Just give me something to start with tonight."

"I'm hanging up." I pushed a second line button, disconnecting her.

"What was that?" Roger was rubbing his eyes and yawning.

"A reporter from a trash tabloid. She wanted to pay me for an inside story on the murders."

"Wow. How much?"

Hard to imagine I could still be taken by surprise after a night like I'd just had.

"Roger, it doesn't matter how much. I'm not talking to her. Though I'd love to know how she knew Joe was dead. Who's giving her info?"

I leaned an elbow on the table. With my head in my hand, I stared into the empty air above my desk. What a day. Starting at noon with discovering my office burglarized—no, vandalized. No, almost vandalized.

"Roger, did the back door thing arrive?" I asked.

"What?"

"For the computer. You were going to get some back door thing to open the locked file."

"It's probably on my e-mail," he said.

"Good. I really want to know what's in that locked file."

"Yeah. Big deal." Roger's eyes were glazed over with the unfocused look of someone who's left the room ahead of their body.

"Come on, Roger. Let's go home. You can tell him how sorry you are you spent all that time online instead of telling him how much you love him." I was trying to be sincere, but maybe it was the stress or maybe it was the humidity or maybe it was that I suddenly felt very much alone, but my comment came off sounding trite.

Roger's attention snapped back to the here and now. "You think it's funny?" he asked. "If that shit frames him for murder . . ." He started to cry.

After a moment, I went to Roger and knelt in front of him, taking his hands in mine.

"Roger. It's going to be OK. You're just stressed out from fighting with him. You're overtired."

"Yeah. But Nicky, this is serious."

"I know it is, but it's also not a TV movie, so cool out, OK? I meant what I said. Go home and make nice with him. Say you're sorry."

"I think that's really sweet," David Scott said from the doorway. He was standing just outside the office.

The light from the lobby caught the left side of his face, accenting the plane of his cheek. One eye glinted in the full light; the other glimmered in shadow. I could tell from the way his T-shirt was clinging to his torso that the humidity had not yet broken. Framed in that light, he reminded me of my first boyfriend in undergraduate school. An actor too, Marcus was one of those pale-skinned, black-haired, blue-eyed types. When he was onstage under even the slightest blue light, his skin took on the look of marble. An image of Marcus as I saw him once from the wings during a performance of *A Little Night Music* raced through my mind as David smiled.

Now, don't get me wrong. I am not just about getting laid. Sure, I like sex, and yes, I was definitely looking for some antidote to Mr. "I Couldn't Possibly Stay Around for More Than Two Months So Now I Am Leaving Without Warning" back in NYC. Still, I think my reaction had a lot to do with the events of the past forty-eight hours. Honestly, I was more than a little afraid. What's so wrong with seeking a little comfort when you're away from home in a strange town with a serial killer on the loose? As soon as I asked myself the question, I realized there was plenty wrong with it. Particularly if you were seeking comfort with a stranger.

What I said out loud was, "Hey."

"Hey," David repeated. "I guess I'm interrupting, huh?"

"Yes," Roger said, standing. "But we needed interrupting. You're right, Nicky. I'm going home."

Alone at last.

"So, I heard someone broke into your office?" David asked.

"Yes. Just part of the everyday fun around here. This place is a lot more exciting than I expected."

"Sometimes that's a good thing," he said. Then he smiled again. "I know a place that makes a great cup of coffee."

"At this time of night? I thought all of western Pennsylvania closed at eleven."

"Typical New Yorker. I know a place across town. Very cozy. Very home."

I wasn't so tired that I didn't notice I was being invited home. And God knows, I wanted to be invited home. But there was this murder thing.

"You know, David, it seems a little, I don't know, inappropriate just now. I mean with all this . . ." I waved my hand about, trying to physically encompass the chaos in one gesture.

"Yeah," he said, approaching until he stood directly in front of me, chest to chest. I didn't back away. "Inappropriate is a tough one."

He kissed me once on the lips, placing his hands on my shoulders.

"No one wants to be inappropriate," he said. He kissed me again.

I wondered if I would ever grow up enough to say no in a situation like this.

We locked lips.

There was a knock on the frame of my door. I felt him begin to pull away, but I held him tightly to me. I could feel the rise and fall of his ribs. My eyes were shut. I could feel his heart beating.

There was another knock. Didn't that child ever sleep? Without opening my eyes, I shouted, "Go home, Olivia. We're closed for the duration."

"I'm sorry to interrupt. Really, I am." It was not Olivia.

David and I jumped apart as if we'd been hit with a stun gun. Mary Corinne, former nun, stood in the entrance, a shy smile on her lips.

TWELVE

"I'M SORRY I CHASED your friend away."

Mary Corinne used the word "friend" just like my mother, shying away from the more obvious implications of "date," "boyfriend," or "lover."

"It's just as well," I said, "things being what they are."

She had insisted that we speak alone. David suddenly noticed that it was later than he'd thought. It's amazing, the effect even an ex-nun can have on two former Catholic schoolboys caught with their tongues down each other's throats. Not that Mary Corinne would be giving us any lectures on morals, having just recently converted to the ranks of the damned. We said our good-byes to David on the plaza in front of the theater.

Heading across the quad toward the chapel, we passed the newest addition to the St. Gilbert's campus. Stationed on the side of the fountain closest to the theater, not far from where the first nun was decked, three Friends of Decency were holding a candlelight vigil under a clouded moon. Probably in memoriam for Sally, or maybe they were observing some sort of religious victory celebration. After all, they were getting what they wanted, whether or not they'd been responsible. *Convent of Fear* was no more. They sat around three candles. As we passed by, I heard the low sound of the praying of the rosary. In the humid, airless night, I could swear the candles burned extra hot.

The expression on Mary Corinne's face as we stepped wide of the vigil was hard to read. It might have been wistful. Perhaps she was already missing her religious community and its rituals. What could she be thinking, watching them pray, knowing she'd officially cut herself off from her religion? I shook my head slightly. It was the Catholic schoolboy again, this time trying to attach significance to the fallen nun. The adult could see she was just tired.

We came to the chapel door, a simple wooden job set among a lush growth of ivy.

"I suppose, Nicholas, some would say I'd given up my right to seek comfort in a chapel, but I still feel there is much for me here."

"I don't know the rules for your situation, Sister," I said.

She looked pained at my use of the title. In the moonlight, her sharp features now appeared worn and weary.

"Please. I'm just Mary Corinne Rossoff now, plain and simple. No titles. Though I don't feel there's much simplicity in my life." Saying this, she opened the door, leading us into a cool, dimly lit interior.

The chapel was a modest size. I knew there were stained-glass windows on both sides of the nave, but the moonlight wasn't strong enough to illuminate them. Light came from candles burning at various altars: the main altar, of course, but also one to the Virgin, along the wall to our left, and one to St. Gilbert, recessed along our right. The air smelled faintly of incense. Maybe there'd been a service earlier that day.

Mary Corinne shied away from the front altar. She chose a pew near the altar of St. Gilbert. I sat down next to her, leaving space for about two people between us. We said nothing for a few minutes. It took me a while to realize she was praying. I waited, almost patiently. Aside from it being late and me being tired, I was not fond of churches.

"Nicholas, I think I've done a terrible thing," she said.

"Wouldn't it be better to discuss this with a priest or an old friend? There must be someone who can empathize with your situation better than I can."

"No, I don't mean Edward. I have no regrets there. I'm talking about something else. Something I think has resulted in murder."

We sat silently again. There was no sound in the chapel.

Finally, impatiently, I said, "Then you should go to the police. We're involved in something very serious here."

"I understand the gravity of the situation. But, as I said, I only *think* I've caused trouble. Until I'm certain, I don't want to risk involving anyone who is innocent."

"But you barely know me, and I barely know anyone here. Your husband doesn't like me."

"Oh, no, Nicholas, that's not true. Edward thinks very highly of you. We both do. But I've come to you because I think you will understand. We're both outsiders. We've both taken steps that put us beyond convention. And the other people involved, they're your age. You might understand them better than I."

I wasn't sure I was following the logic, but I was interested in knowing where she was headed. Ever since I'd walked into my trashed office, I'd been feeling as if I were out of step, as if whatever was happening at St. Gilbert's was happening right in front of me but somehow I just couldn't get the image in focus.

"Let me tell you a story," she said, turning to face me. We'd been sitting long enough that I could make out the orangish-yellow light of the candles and the bluish tint cast from their holders. I knew the setup. People lit candles in remembrance of the dead or sick or suf-

172

fering or, if they were feeling grateful, as an offering of thanks to their God.

"You probably know some of it. The story of Joe Sr. and I?"

"Some of it."

"I'm sure. Ilana has never been shy about my shortcomings." And then she laughed. "The truth is, I don't like her either. A bitter soul. I don't think she's ever loved anyone, except Benny. Oh yes, she's passionately devoted to him. She's spent most of the last fifteen years helping to raise his children, not much good it's done her. I'm sure she's given you the wrong impression of me."

"I don't think I have an impression."

She laughed again. In the silence of the chapel, the sound made me flinch.

"The young can be so aggressively objective. Of course you have an impression. Everyone has an impression of everything. The only question is, will they admit to it? Ilana has no trouble owning up to her viewpoint. She told you I killed him, didn't she?"

"Well . . ."

"Of course she did. That woman. Well, it's not true. I almost saved him. And I would have, but . . ."

I could see the first traces of tears gleam behind her wire-framed glasses.

"He was your brother-in-law, wasn't he?"

"And I was a nun. Nothing could have been more unfitting. But you'll understand, won't you, when I tell you you can't choose love? And you can't always wait for the world to approve. That's why I want to talk to you.

"I met Joey when my sister first brought him home," she went on. "It was Christmas thirty years ago. We were all home for the holiday. We—Joey and I—we were immediately attracted to each other. But nothing happened. In our defense I can tell you we held out for almost six years. We tried."

Some defense—waiting until after your sister is married to sleep with her man. I didn't say it out loud. Joe Sr. was a growing presence in my summer. I wanted to know the details.

"Really, it's all too banal in most respects, like some bad prime-time soap opera. We snuck around at motels, grabbing time when we could, guilt-ridden. Fighting. Vowing to stop. Making up. Vowing to go on. I wasn't strong enough then to do what I've done with Edward. Leave my order. But I'm not making the same mistake twice.

"Then my sister got pregnant. We didn't know what to do. Involving ourselves, involving her, that was one thing. We were all adults. But now there would be a child. You have to understand, we were very young—well, no offense, but barely older than you. It seems even younger now. And I'm just giving you the barest outline. I could go on for much longer about Joey. I've had plenty of time to think about him.

"We fought more. Long, vicious fights. In the end, Joey was the better of the two of us. I see that now. Then it seemed like a betrayal, if you can call leaving your mistress for your wife betrayal. That's what he did, Nicholas. He cut me off. After Joe Jr. was born, Joey went back to his wife. We never met in private again."

"Your sister never knew?" I asked.

"Of course she knew he was up to something. But she didn't know it was me. After we stopped I rarely went to see them. Then he killed himself. I still don't know why. Not really. I comfort myself by thinking that he did it out of remorse at not choosing me, but that's not really much comfort, is it?"

She fell silent again. I shifted on the hard wooden pew. I waited, but she didn't speak.

"Mary Corinne, I'm not sure exactly why we're here. Not that I'm unsympathetic, but—well . . ."

174

"Yes. It's late. All right. The point. Joey's real business was his accounting firm, but he worked with Benny at the theater's finances. A year after he was dead, it was apparent that the theater was in big financial trouble. Benny'd been department head and running the summer program for several years, maybe five. He'd come right out of graduate school. Got married, had children—Olivia is just the youngest, you know."

"Oh."

"Suddenly, it all started to fall apart around him. Overdrafts, budget deficits, unpaid vendors. That's when he 'discovered' the fake ledgers. The ones everyone claims show how Joey was using the theater to make himself some extra cash on the side."

"Yes, I know this."

"You know Ilana's version. The version where I left Joey. The version where he uses the theater for a cover. That's not the way it was. He was a good man. He went home to his wife. He never stole from anyone."

"But Benny had proof."

"He had nothing. He claimed to have records, but they were fakes made by Benny to cover his own tracks. Benny was robbing this place blind. And who wouldn't believe him over a dead cheating husband? His proof was nothing but people's misperceptions. Nobody really understood what was happening."

"See, I don't understand any of this part. There is nothing here to steal. This place is too poor for embezzlement."

Now she was excited, gesturing in the dim light.

"They said Joey was running money from his own business through the theater's books. Well, Benny could have been doing something just as devious."

"Can you prove this?"

She grew still.

"No. And that's where I made my mistake. I told Joe Jr., but I couldn't prove it."

"Told him what?"

"What I just told you."

"Why would you do that?"

"He was an adult. He had a right to know his father wasn't a crook. He had a right to know that Benny Singleton was no friend."

"When did you tell him?" I didn't like this.

"Several months ago. I knew it was a mistake as soon as I did it. He was consumed with anger. He was going to prove that Benny was guilty. I counseled him to stop, to let it go. I only wanted him to know that his father was a good man. I didn't mean for him to become so bitter."

I didn't like this at all. It showed in my face.

"Yes," said Mary Corinne. "He said he'd find the proof. Now he's dead."

"And you think Benny killed him?"

"I think Benny Singleton is capable of a great many things."

"Including killing Sister Sally?" I shook my head. I could understand how Joe would be angry. The idea that there was some connection, whatever it might be, between the revelation of his father's past and his own murder didn't even seem too bizarre. But Benny Singleton as a double murderer? No.

"I don't know about Sally. But Benny Singleton is an evil man." Her voice began to quiver.

"That is not what most people say about him."

"Of course it isn't," she snapped. "It doesn't always matter how things happened in the past. What counts is how people perceive and remember them. Benny Singleton is a man whose wife left him to raise his children alone. Me? I'm just a nun who can't keep her vows. Well, he's the liar. A thief, a liar, and only half the man Joey ever was."

176

In the shadows I could see her face twisted with hatred. Only for an instant, then she recomposed herself. But that moment revealed enough of Mary Corinne to make me hope that Edward Rossoff was a very strong man. I considered what she told me. I could see she believed what she said. It was consuming her.

"Why are you telling me this?" I asked.

"Joe Jr. is dead," was all she said.

"Yes, but we still have to deal with Sally. She has nothing to do with this business, does she?"

"No, she doesn't. And that's why I'm not certain. But someone other than me has to know the truth, Nicholas."

"It was a long time ago, Mary Corinne. Like you said, perception is so much a part of the truth. What do you expect me to do?"

"I don't know. I'm just frustrated. But you deal with these people every day. Maybe you know what they think. Maybe you know if Joe Jr. found anything. Did he say anything to you? Did you hear him say anything? Anything about Benny?"

I felt for her. Really I did. She'd made a decision to share her anger with Joe Jr., but instead of comforting him, she might have sent him off to his death. Others might have crumbled at that thought, but not Mary Corinne. Here, not a day after renouncing her entire life to get married, she was trying to set her wrongs right. Still, it was murder we were talking about, not shoplifting.

"Mary Corinne, I'm sorry for what's happened. I am. But if I thought I knew anything of real value, I'd have to tell the police."

I watched her closely. Her face took on an expression of supreme disappointment. Her shoulders slumped.

"I was so hoping you would help me sort this out. I was wrong. Always, I'm wrong." Then she whispered, "My spirit is broken. My days are extinct."

I held my breath. Everyone knew the damn thing except me. I considered very carefully what to say next. I didn't want her clamming up on me like Stanley Sobieski. This time I was going to get an answer.

"Job, isn't it?" I asked.

"Yes. Chapter 17, verse 1. It was the closing line of Joey's suicide note. Are you familiar with Job?" She looked so sad.

I guess she hadn't seen the verse written on the wall of my office. I didn't know exactly how it fit in with Joe Jr. and Sally's murders, but at least one part of this mess was clear.

I stood.

"You won't help?" She looked up at me. Her face was composed in a picture of pleading. Yet even in that warm, soft light, her eyes were hard and hateful.

I pitied her. She was in for a lot of sleepless nights. She'd wanted to hurt Benny Singleton. Now she thought she might be responsible for the death of her former lover's child. I wanted to say something reassuring.

"Mary Corinne, I don't believe that telling Joe had anything to do with his death. I think Sister Sally's death makes that impossible. And even though I think that, and even though you probably don't want to, I think you should tell this to Corporal Roberts. It might help him figure out what's happening. Isn't that what you want?"

"I want Benny Singleton to suffer for what he's done."

I had no answer to that.

I left her sitting in the shadows, torn between the comfort of revenge and the comfort of her God.

I sat on the edge of the fountain. Behind me, I heard the faint murmur of the candlelight vigil. The sound of the water was so loud and the sound of the rosary so soft, I'm sure I wouldn't have recognized the prayer if I hadn't already known what it was. Even then, I could just make out the continued intercessions of the Friends of Decency on behalf of the departed Sister Sally. I added to the noise by splashing my hand in the cool water.

Sitting by a fountain on a summer's night, even a humid, sticky one, should be enjoyable. You ought to be able to lean back, look at the stars, breathe in the fresh air, and do all those generally healthy and relaxing things people do when they leave the city.

I love the stars. I grew up with stars, and I missed them in New York. Another part of my week gone wrong. The ever-present haze obscured the night sky.

As I leaned back, looking up at the haze, my hand lapping at the water, I imagined that I was floating along in a canoe—just me and David Scott. Oddly, we were naked in our canoe, the sounds of a reggae band keeping us company. I was stretched out at one end, he at the other. Slowly, he started to make his way toward me. I could see the play of muscles beneath his skin. In the abundant starlight the hair on his crotch was a soft light brown. I focused my attention there as he rose on his knees and tipped forward to reach me. Tipping, tipping . . .

I caught myself a moment before I tumbled backward into the fountain. Really, this whole murder thing had to be sorted out soon, or I was going to hurt myself.

The problem was, there were just too many story lines in the drama of St. Gilbert's Summer Theater Festival. Multiple plot lines are fine for good plays but no fun when people are getting killed.

There was the production of *Convent of Fear* and the turmoil that surrounded it. This included the Friends of Decency, the crazed bicyclist, and the double murders, which were either some assault on the show or on nuns in general. It was at the point of murder that this story line divided in two. Either someone was killing cast members to stop the show—and that seemed way over the top to me—or someone was using the show as a cover for murdering people. I guess that

179

made it possible that two different events were happening side by side. In this story line, one person had deliberately done in both Sally and Joe Jr.

Then there was the business of Joe Sr., Mary Corinne, Benny, and Joe Jr. This plot also included murder, but only one. I couldn't fit Sally into it. Worse, if I could plug in Sally, this version of my summer vacation required that Benny Singleton be a vicious double murderer. I didn't have a really high opinion of Benny's artistic abilities, but that alone wasn't enough to make me think he'd killed Joe Jr., much less a nun.

Of course, the murders could be completely unrelated. It could just be that two different people for two different reasons just happened to have needed to kill off two other people in the exact same physical space within forty-eight hours of each other. It could also be that *Convent of Fear* was an undiscovered American masterpiece. I wasn't betting on either.

Then again, maybe I'd spent too much time studying well-made plays. After all, it wasn't always all about plot. Maybe this time it was about characters, about who's who and how they relate.

I started drawing a diagram in my mind.

I began with the murder victims. Joe Jr. first, since he seemed so much more entangled.

He was the son of Joe Sr., a man who'd once had—to hear her and Ilana tell it—a torrid affair with his sister-in-law, Mary Corinne. Joe Sr. left behind his brother, Stanley Sobieski, and his son, Joe Jr.

OK. This was easy so far. Benny befriends the boy. Depending on whose version you believe, either because he is truly a good-hearted man (Ilana and Patsy) or snakebitten by guilt (Mary Corinne). Either way, he and the kid become fast buds until just recently, and no one is certain why. Except that now I know it has to do with Mary Corinne's revelation to Joe Jr. about the past.

This was going better than I expected. So far I had love, sex, and revenge—almost all the prime motives for murder.

Joe Jr. had another relative, his cousin Marty Friedman, the prop master. This connection led to Sister Sally, Joe Jr.'s high school girlfriend and the object of Marty's never-ending unrequited love. In turn, Sally and Mary Corinne were friends, and who knows what Mary Corinne told the younger nun.

There was still more love to go around. Ilana definitely had it for Benny. According to Mary Corinne she'd even taken an active interest in raising Benny's children, though I had to question just how well that went, considering how much she and Olivia disliked each other. I wondered, too, if Ilana and Benny had ever consummated this passion of hers. Who would know?

I snorted a quick laugh at that thought. In Huber's Landing it was likely everyone knew. I could probably get an answer from the Friends of Decency if I bothered to ask. I put that idea away and went back to my mental diagram.

I had a picture of the major groups. Add in Corporal Roberts, his daughter Mary Frances, and their cousin Rebecca Tipton, and that completed the family circle.

Except for Sally and David Scott, who were cousins.

David. David. David. Ilana loves Benny, Marty loves Sally, Sally loves God, Patsy loves Mary Frances, Edward Rossoff—who isn't related to anyone—loves Mary Corinne, and I lust after David. And who's getting laid?

I realized I'd strayed from my initial purpose, but it didn't matter. Knowing how they were related or who loved who and who slept with who didn't reveal any serious motivations for capital crimes. To me it still seemed as if there had to be more.

Fortunately, there was a connection that would probably explain one or two other parts of the mystery, but I couldn't check that out until I managed to corner Marty Friedman. I splashed water from the fountain on my face. My watch read 2:50 a.m. No wonder I couldn't make sense out of what was happening. I needed sleep. I walked toward my apartment under the starless sky, the overlapping sounds of the fountain and the vigil first blending and then receding behind me.

THIRTEEN

"I think she's full of shit."

"Jesus, Paolo, she's a nun."

We were driving along Market Street, Huber's Landing's main street. The sky was a sheet of light gray. The air, thick and unbreathable. It was almost one in the afternoon.

"God, is it ever going to rain in this town?" I asked.

"She *was* a nun. Now she's an ex-nun with a past," Paolo said.

"But why lie to me?"

Paolo just sighed. "How should I know why she would lie to you? I've only been here two days. You've been with these loonies for weeks. You tell me. All I'm saying is, I know a lie when I hear one."

We'd been at this all morning.

The boys had been asleep when I returned home the night before. Just as well. They would have been very disappointed to hear that instead of having incredible sex with David Scott, I'd been in a chapel with Mary Corinne. They'd made their interest clear in a short, insistent message taped to my pillow. Pointed instructions were written out in Roger's precise printing:

DETAILS. TOMORROW. DO NOT LEAVE FIRST. WAKE US.

I woke them. Apparently all too early for a tale without sex.

"All that wax and no one to drip it on?" was Paolo's first comment after I'd finished.

"Please, it's not even noon," I said.

We were seated at my battered dinette table having coffee. Since it was too hot and humid to wear anything but shorts, we were all leaning forward, elbows resting on the table, trying not to stick to the backs of the vinyl chairs. My oscillating fan, small and overwhelmed, sat on the fourth chair.

"It's never too early for some of us," Roger said.

Paolo didn't respond. He just smiled, not so sweetly, and began asking questions. I took this to mean that despite Roger's resolve of the night before they still hadn't kissed and made up.

"Why do you think she told you?" Paolo asked.

"I think she's desperate," I said.

"She feels guilty," Roger added.

"More likely she's up to something," Paolo said. "I don't like it. I don't like nuns. I don't like this town. I want to go home." Paolo poured out more coffee in my cup and his own. Roger was left to serve himself.

"You can't leave. That will just make Corporal Roberts more suspicious," I said.

"And why is that, anyway?" Paolo asked. "Does he really think I've been secretly hiding in some storage room, coming out at night to poison nuns? How could I have anything to do with this? He hated me the moment we met. Homophobic prick. You see the way he treats Patsy and Mary Frances."

There wasn't much to disagree with in that statement. We were none of us fond of the corporal. There was no end, however, to how much we could argue about Mary Corinne.

Roger finally ended the conversation by declaring that he was now ready.

"Ready for what?" I asked.

"Your locked file. I received the back door last night on my e-mail."

"God," Paolo said, "I am so desperate for air conditioning, even the thought of computer-geeking my way through the afternoon is appealing."

We finished our coffee, put on the least amount of clothing that public decency allowed, and headed for the theater.

Roger insisted it wouldn't take the afternoon. He said it would be a straightforward procedure to break through the password protection. The back door, some piece of software that poked its way into other software and read code, would have us into the locked file with minimal fuss.

The daytime crowd on the plaza was considerably larger than for the late-night vigil. They were seated on the concrete, which must have been like sitting on a hot plate at full power. Either they didn't notice or polyester was better insulation than I'd realized. As we approached I estimated about thirty people in attendance, a few children, but mostly adults. Didn't these people have jobs?

By now, of course, the Friends of Decency knew me as one of the Satan-worshiping participants of *Convent of Fear*. Seeing the hand-held signs and the sullen, angry eyes, I prepared for an ugly scene. Not this time. The Friends stopped praying as we neared them. They were completely silent, completely still. As one, they watched me use my passkey to open the double glass doors. Only when the doors shut behind us did anyone on the plaza move again, and then only to continue counting rosary beads. The effect was unnerving. I preferred the shouting.

Inside, Roger was happy to have a task he could perform with mastery. He quickly slipped into what I call the black hole of computer space. Immediately, he started answering our comments with half-phrases and grunts. His gaze concentrated on the computer screen.

"I know this act," Paolo said. "Until he's done with whatever voodoo he's doing, we won't rate a decent response. Not that he's been responding decently in general lately."

"Damn," Roger mumbled.

"Something wrong?" I asked. I always ask Roger if something is wrong when he is sitting in front of a computer, usually mine, trying to make it go. I never understand the answer, but I figure if a friend is willing to come to your home free of charge and provide you with his high-priced specialty services, you can at least make polite and sympathetic inquiries.

"Gone," he said.

"Gone?" I asked.

"The locked file. Gone."

"How could anyone take it? Wasn't it locked?" I was leaning over his shoulder, looking at the screen. The usually chirpy omnipresent interface full of oddly shaped icons was replaced by a list of text items. I recognized the old DOS operating system in action. Roger was deeper inside the guts of the machine than I had ever ventured.

He twisted his mouth into a tight knot, then said, "Yes. But if you have the right software, you can unlock it. Like I was going to do. Ah . . ."

"Ah? What ah?" Nothing on the screen changed. I had no idea what had caught his attention.

"There is a utility. Where . . . where . . . where . . ."

Roger was typing instructions, and more lists scrolled up the screen.

"See? Now we're in for serious noncommunication," Paolo said.

Roger pulled himself back to reality. "This may take a while longer than I thought, Nicky."

"That's fine. There's someone I want to see," I said. "If you don't need us, Paolo and I can go do that."

He barely acknowledged our departure, once again lost in the computer screen.

I led us out the back of the building, avoiding the eerie silent treatment of the protesters. As we walked I tried to put together a timeline on the locked file. When had we last checked it? I wasn't certain. We hadn't bothered to confirm its presence after the break-in. Everything was moving too fast then. It could have been removed when my office was ransacked, but that left the problem of the untouched computer even more tangled. I was willing to bet someone had returned for it last night or earlier today. That wouldn't fit in so neatly with my theory, but maybe there was still hope.

In the parking lot behind McNally Hall, Paolo and I climbed into the Thing. We weren't really going very far—nothing in Huber's Landing was very far—but Paolo wanted to start the car.

"It's good for it to run," he said as we detached the heavy plastic side windows and began to fold back the roof.

Inside, I surveyed the stripped-down interior. The Thing was in good shape, but that didn't say much for extra comfort. The boxy structure and bright yellow paint made the vehicle look like some oversized child's toy. And like a child's toy, it did not come equipped with much in the way of extras.

"It would be good for it to have air conditioning or even music. I can't believe you guys came all the way from New York in this."

"I know what you mean, but it irritated the hell out of Roger, so it was worth it."

Once we pulled out on Market Street, Paolo started in again on Mary Corinne.

"She's full of shit," he said.

"We'll know soon enough if she's lying." I was tired of the repetitive argument.

Market Street runs the length of Huber's Landing, parallel to St. Gilbert's College. Ernie's Family Restaurant was one block to our left. The rest of the town was laid out in front of us. As we passed the post office/hardware store, I tried switching to domestic matters.

"So, I guess it didn't go so well last night, huh?" I asked.

"What's that?"

"I mean, you didn't seem too happy this morning."

"Oh no. I'm very happy." Paolo shifted gears and smiled as if he and Roger were the poster children of gay coupledom.

"You know what I mean," I said.

"Poor Nicky. Stuck between discretion and curiosity. OK. Everything went very well last night."

"So why isn't everyone happier?"

"I told you. I am happy. And he will be too, as soon as I tell him I forgive him. Let him sit in it for another day." And here Paolo flashed a truly wicked grin.

"Oh, Paolo. That is so childish."

"Are you giving me relationship advice, Nicky?"

He had a point. Measured in just about any terms, including his four-year relationship with Roger, my record was dismal. Still, it seemed insensitive to me. I said so.

"Jesus, Nicky, you are such a stick sometimes. Always with the duty and decency thing. That's why we're out here baking instead of in some nice bar somewhere having a cocktail."

"What is that supposed to mean?"

"Just what I said. You're a sweetheart, but really, if you weren't so strung up about actors dying while you're stage managing, you'd let the police make this little visit, whatever it is, instead of doing it yourself. Then again,"—and here he flashed that wicked smirk one more time—"maybe you're just trying to be a hero to impress Mr. Chorus Boy. God, what won't a man do if he thinks it's foreplay?"

"It's a good thing you aren't a shrink."

"And it's a very good thing that you're not a detective. You're way too sympathetic. You need a harder heart, babe."

We stopped in front of a two-story wood and shingle building. Plato's occupied the entire first floor. This was no neighborhood bar with dark wood, cheap food, and old men with too much time on their hands. Plato's was a college bar: brass, glass, shots, and nobody runs a tab. There were three small apartments above Plato's. Tinier even than mine, each was a studio with a kitchenette and a bathroom economized in size to hold a shower stall, not a tub. These three apartments occupied barely more than half of the space on the second floor. They were inexpensive alternatives for students desperate not to live on campus, or for a staff member of St. Gilbert's Summer Musical Theater Festival trying to save money. Marty Friedman was doing just that in apartment number 2.

Paolo eyed Plato's as we parked. "Ah, we *are* going for a drink."

"No. We're going to see Marty Friedman," I said. Then I explained to him my theory about the connection between Mary Corinne, Joe Sr., and the break-in at the theater.

"You know," Paolo said when I was finished, "maybe I underestimated you. OK. So what's the plan? Nice fag/evil fag? Let me be the evil fag."

Not even I was ever cheap enough to take advantage of a comment like that.

"I don't expect Marty to be much of a challenge. I think he'll fold pretty fast. We can just go straight after him."

"Doesn't sound like much fun. Can't I torment him just a little?"

"No. You're here for moral support only. Behave. Now, follow me."

We entered the door far to the right of the bar.

"Hey. Nicky. Hi," Marty said, swinging his door open without even asking who was knocking. Sometimes it can be refreshing to be out of the city. Then he saw Paolo.

"It's all right," Paolo said, before I could stop him. "I promise I will not critique the decor, such as it may be."

"Hello, Marty." I pushed past him into the room, Paolo right behind me.

I was expecting the worst, considering the state of the prop shop. Surprisingly, Marty was well ordered in his personal habits. A neatly made queen-sized bed occupied more than a third of the room and explained the ongoing popularity of these apartments to privacy-starved undergraduate couples. No dirty dishes, no dirty laundry, magazines and newspapers organized in one corner. A box fan in the window offered a lot more relief in the way of manufactured breeze than the poor fan I was lugging from room to room across town.

"Well, so, come in." Marty rushed to get ahead of the situation. "Good to see you. Want a drink?"

"This isn't really a social call, Marty," I said.

"Not even a Diet Coke, Nicky?" Paolo asked.

"No. Sit." I pointed to a chair. Paolo sat. "Now, Marty, I think you owe me an explanation."

Friedman backed up one step. "What do you mean? What explanation?"

"I had a long talk with Mary Corinne last night," I said.

"So?"

190

Paolo laughed. "Marty, Marty, Marty. You are a very bad liar," he said.

"And that is not a good thing when you are surrounded by very good liars," I added.

"Well, I think you should get out," Marty said. "That's what I think."

"Not much of a thinker either," Paolo said.

"Look," I said. "I know what you and Joe were arguing about in the prop shop. I know what you did to the costume shop and my office. What I want to know is exactly why you did it."

I was counting on Marty to fold. I wasn't disappointed. Like a bad TV-movie actor, he crumpled onto the edge of his bed.

"Oh my God. I knew we'd get caught. I told him. I told him. Jeez. They got fingerprints, don't they? I didn't kill anyone, I swear."

I certainly believed that.

"The police don't know. And they don't have to," I lied.

"Really?" He looked up at me. This was too much.

"Of course they have to know, Marty. Two people are dead."

"I didn't do it. I swear."

"Well, I'm getting something to drink," Paolo said, and he walked over to the fridge. "Anyone else want anything?"

"All right, sure," I said. "Anything with caffeine."

"Marty?"

"Uh, water?"

Pathetic.

"So why did you trash the theater?" I asked.

"I didn't. Joe did. He went crazy. I couldn't stop him."

Paolo was opening cupboards. "Where are the glasses?"

"Left side," Marty said.

"I'm not following you, Marty," I said, trying to ignore Paolo's "I couldn't care less" act.

"He said there was information on Benny that would clear his father. We used my passkey."

"So why the costume shop?" I asked.

"He said we had to make it look like someone was trying to get at the show. To cover up what we were really doing. Anyway, he hates Ilana. He hates anyone he thinks takes Benny's side."

"So you ripped up the costume shop out of spite?" This was weirder than I'd thought.

"I told you," he said, "I didn't do it. I even stopped him from damaging the costumes."

"Great, but you let him into my office? Should I feel special?"

Marty just sat there staring at the floor. I stood a few feet in front of him, the window fan blowing wet air onto my face. Paolo was making noise with ice trays at the sink. The scene was all too B-rate matinee until Marty's next comment.

Without looking up, he said, "Joe said he knew who killed Sally. He said he'd tell me, but only if I let him into the offices." Marty was crying now.

Paolo stopped making noise.

"He never really loved her. Not like I did. I would've saved her. He never really cared."

His emotional response blind-sided me. I had the urge to leave right then. If it were only Marty's tears, I probably would have. I had confirmation of my theory about the break-in. The untouched costumes and untouched computer had made me suspicious that it was someone who didn't really want to hurt the show. The Bible quote clinched the identity of the vandal. But now that I was sure of who and why, how could I leave if Marty knew who killed Sally?

I felt like shit, but I pushed on. "Who killed Sally, Marty?"

"He never said."

"What do you mean, he never said?" I surprised myself with a sudden shout. Immediately, I regretted it. Marty hunched over further, closing himself off physically. I'd seen actors do this in rehearsal while directors were talking to them. They were no longer listening or cooperating.

"Marty, I know you want to know who killed her. You have to tell what happened." I can't say I was proud of myself. Manipulating the grief stricken is not a hobby of mine.

A moment passed—in theater time, a three count—and then: "He said he wouldn't tell me unless I opened more doors. So we went to your office. You have the oldest files and the oldest computer. Joe thought there'd be a good chance of finding something. He said no one used that office much during the year. It was a good place to hide things. But there was nothing in the files, and then the computer had that password protection thing. We couldn't open the file. He really flipped. He ripped that place apart. He almost bashed in the computer, but I told him if we did that, we'd never get the info out of the file. That seemed to calm him down at least some."

"So you didn't touch the computer at all?" I asked.

"Joe fixed it so we could get to the file and no one else could," he said.

"What's that?" Paolo asked, suddenly very attentive. "What did you do to the computer?"

"I didn't do anything. I don't know enough to do that stuff. Joe did it. He did something that he said would 'hide' the file. I don't even know what that means."

"I don't either," Paolo said, pulling out his cell phone, "but Roger will."

While he dialed, I kept after Marty. I had to know.

"But why didn't he tell you who killed Sally?"

"I just wouldn't go on unless he told me. He was crazy. It was frightening. But I refused to open any more offices until I knew."

He was very proud of himself. Just what I admired, a vandal with self-restraint.

"He tried to get me to give in, but I wouldn't. Then he just started laughing at me. He said he didn't know who killed her. Didn't have any idea. He just wanted to get into the files, and if I wasn't going to help, then fuck me."

The way Joe used Marty was appalling, but you had to give him credit for being clever. The Bible quote almost worked. Too bad he wasn't better read; he might have pulled it off.

Paolo handed me a soda. "Good news. Roger already figured out where the file was hidden. He's trying to open it now."

"Paolo, you actually look proud of him," I said.

"I never said he was stupid, just annoying now and then." He turned on Marty. "So where's the petty cash?"

I'd forgotten all about it.

"Joe took it. He said it would make the whole thing look more believable. I don't have it. Honest."

"Very convenient. I couldn't find any water." Paolo sat down.

I shot him a warning glance. Marty was wound pretty tight. Anything more from us seemed pointless if not cruel.

"I didn't want to do it, Nicky. Really. I'm sorry. I kept putting him off, but she was always after him. For months she was on him, pushing him. She kept telling him he had to avenge his father. All this stuff about clearing his name."

And who else could "she" be? I could feel Paolo smirking at me.

"Of course she did," I said. "What did you expect?"

"Expect? I don't know, but she's a nun—was. Shouldn't there be something in there about forgiveness? She hates Benny Singleton. And she pushed Joe to hate him too."

I finally looked at Paolo.

"Well, well," he said. "Mary Corinne lied. What a surprise."

We were back on Market. The street was empty. All the sane people were inside making love to their air conditioners.

I'd told Marty that he needed to call the police and tell them his story. He didn't like that idea. He was afraid someone would kill him too. I didn't have an answer for that, but I did know that you don't keep secrets in a murder investigation. I couldn't force him, but I made it clear that I wouldn't be withholding information from Corporal Roberts, including anything he'd told us.

We left him still sitting on the edge of his bed, still staring at the floor. He neither moved nor spoke as we said good-bye.

As we drove along I could easily picture the scene when, for Joe Jr.'s own good, of course, Mary Corinne laid out how Benny Singleton had smeared Joe's father two decades earlier. The weeping, the sighing, the downcast eyes and averted glances, the self-recrimination—what mask wouldn't she have donned until his hatred matched her own? Hearing Marty's story, I realized what an actress Mary Corinne really was. I'd only had one brief glimpse of her anger. She hated Benny Singleton in the way people hate when they've nursed and tended their anger over a lifetime. Yet she'd taken me in completely. I wondered why she'd been content to make wigs all those years when she was clearly more suited for performance. Maybe she couldn't sing.

She couldn't do anything directly to Benny. She had no proof. And there was Edward. So she'd laid her hate before Joe Jr. in the hopes he'd do what she couldn't. But something went wrong. Joe was dead. Now she needed someone to provide her with information. Someone near the middle of the action. Someone like me. A sucker who'd plow ahead and do the dirty work. Even badgering a man in mourning. The image of Marty sitting in his tiny studio crying pushed its way back into my mind. My next conversation with Mary Corinne would not be so pleasant.

As we approached the post office/hardware store, Lee Dexter came rushing out of the alley next to the building. He dashed into the street without looking. We only avoided running him over by inches. He stopped when he heard the squeal of the tires. Now, if I'd almost been run over (and I've had a few taxis give me a near scare), I'd be agitated or annoyed or something unpleasant. I braced myself for an onslaught of Crazy Dexter. Instead, he just stood there grinning at us.

"Would've been a shame to ruin my paint job on him," Paolo said after we came to a halt.

"Nicky. Hello." Lee was sweating profusely but didn't look as if he minded one bit. In fact, he was more of a physical wreck than the night before, but he was grinning. His work overalls were showing the wear of days of continuous use; he might even have slept in them. He obviously hadn't showered. Yet his grin was getting wider and more expansive every second. He looked ecstatically happy. Nice Dexter was on full display. Pulling his sunglasses up over his forehead to see us clearly, he revealed dark circles under bright red eyes. The man was a mess. He wiped the sweat from his face. Then he started laughing. It was a near-maniacal performance.

"How's it going, huh?" he asked. "Nice car. Haven't seen one of these in years."

"It's Paolo's," I said.

"Oh, hey," Lee said. "Sorry about the other night, guy. Really. Hope there's no hard feelings, huh?" He reached across me to extend his hand toward Paolo. I could smell the alcohol on him.

"No. None at all." Paolo shook hands very quickly.

"Great. Just great. Look, I got to run, guys. See you later." Lee tossed us a brief wave of his hand as he rushed across the street.

"OK, now that was weird," Paolo said.

"Why's he so happy?" I asked.

"Well, there are only so many things that can bring a smile to a man's face in an alley." Paolo put the car in gear and took off.

"Please," I said. "Must it always be sex?"

"Did you ever notice that it's only the people who aren't getting any who keep complaining about innuendo?"

If there'd been a radio, I would have turned it up full.

We pulled into the McNally Hall parking lot. Directly ahead of us, where the sidewalk separated the lot from the building, a security guard stood over someone lying on the cement. Paolo took a sharp left, parking as far from whatever was happening as he could.

"I don't suppose we can enter your office from the roof?" he asked.

"Nope. Whatever is happening back there is between us and the door. The only other choice is through the main lobby."

"Which means more *novenas*." Paolo leaned back in his seat. "Nicky, did you ever wonder if this entire mess is some sort of delayed punishment for the nasty things we did to nuns when we were in grade school?"

"I have no idea what you did in grade school, but I was a saint," I said, opening my door and climbing down over the side panel.

"Why oh why do I believe that?" Paolo joined me. "OK. Lead on, Saint Nicholas."

We weren't even halfway across the parking lot before I could see that the security guard was Harry, the same one who'd been in my office the day before. As for the person on the ground, I assumed she was another nun. It just seemed that kind of week. Probably the crazed bicyclist at work again.

"Hello, Mr. Dimito," Harry said to me as I stepped up to the scene.

"D'Amico," I said.

"Yes, sir. I remember. Too bad about that yesterday. I was thinking how it is these days with people just tearing things down. Always tearing things down. Never building them up. I don't go for tearing down. No, I believe in building."

"Harry, help me up, please," said the woman on the ground.

"Sister, are you sure—"

"Up, Harry," she said.

"Yes, Sister. Here, take my hand."

Harry bent over and extended his hand. She was neither tall nor bulky and sprang to her feet with ease. Once she was standing, I could see the giveaway signs of nunhood. Her silver hair was closely cropped. Her blouse and skirt combination cut straight, severe lines along her body. Of course, there were sensible square-toed shoes. She brushed herself off.

"Sister Grace, are you sure you're OK?" Harry asked. "I can get an ambulance."

"Nonsense. I'm fine." Then, as if realizing her response was too abrupt, she added, "Thank you, Harry. All of you. But, really, I'm perfectly fine." She tried to smile, but I wouldn't say the effort was worth the result.

"What happened?" I asked.

I could feel Paolo tugging on my elbow, hoping to stop me from getting caught up.

"You know who just came barreling out of—" Harry tried to answer my question, but was cut off mid-sentence.

"I'm sure we all have better things to do than to stand here gossiping on the sidewalk in such dreadful weather," Sister Grace said. "Who are you, young man?" She turned a pair of opaque gray eyes directly on me.

"I'm Nicky D'Amico, and this is—"

"Oh yes. The stage manager. There will be time enough for that later. I suggest we all move along. Thank you again, Harry. Good afternoon." Sister Grace turned herself around and walked away.

Time for that later?

"OK, everybody into the AC," Paolo said, and he started for the door.

"Harry, who came barreling out of where?" I asked.

Paolo stopped but didn't bother to turn around.

"The bicyclist, Mr. Daminno. The one in the yellow raincoat. Just came barreling out of nowhere and ran Sister Grace right down. Like I said. Always tearing things down. Never building up. No respect. No long-range view, if you know what I mean. Good thing Mr. Dexter and I were both nearby."

Now Paolo turned around. "Lee Dexter?" he asked.

"Sure. Who else? Your friend's a joker, eh, Mr. Dammanino? I just wish the sister would have waited for him to get back. But you can see how she is. She just does what she wants."

"I can see that. But why did he leave?" I asked.

"He didn't just leave. That's another thing. I don't think people pay attention, do you? My wife, she pays lots of attention, and I think it pays off for her. She's always winning the prize at bingo. I think she hears more numbers than anyone else. Now *that's* paying attention."

"That does makes sense, Harry," I replied. Fortunately, Harry couldn't see the expression on Paolo's face. I prompted him further. "So, Lee didn't just leave?"

"No. He wouldn't just leave Sister Grace like that. Mr. Dexter is a hothead, but he wouldn't leave a nun just lying on the ground. Who'd do that? He chased after the bicycle guy."

"Oh, of course he did," I said. "I see. Lee's a great guy, Harry. A great guy."

"One of the best, Mr. Damneco. One of the best. Well, I have to go. Going to have to make a report, you know. Report everything, that's the rules."

Harry strolled away. I looked at Paolo, who at that moment definitely looked like someone who'd leave a nun lying on the ground.

FOURTEEN

I WAS THIRSTY AND grimy, confused and angry. The layer of sweat on my face thinned and evaporated as we walked past real offices on our way to the windowless box I worked in.

We entered the auditorium. Across the rows of blue seats, the stage looked abandoned. There was no ghost light, only the light spilling from the entrance, casting mostly shadow over the day room setting. The wing spaces would be completely dark. We hadn't received official permission to remove any part of the murder scene.

"There will be other, better shows," Paolo said, putting his arm around me.

"What makes you think that I am not getting all misty-eyed over murder?" I snapped.

"I'm sure you do, but I've heard your whole riff on the promise of empty space. That stage isn't empty—it's deserted. You hate that."

"You're right. Come on."

Roger was waiting for us, four empty cans of Diet Coke lined up on my desk.

"You see, Nicky? We've been hard at work while he's been here guzzling soda and lounging," Paolo said.

"There's a soda machine downstairs," Roger said. "I haven't emptied it yet, so help yourself." He was leafing through one of the magazines that was part of the general wash of clutter in my office/storage space.

"Do you want your messages?" Roger asked.

"You answered the phone?" I couldn't imagine Roger interrupting a computer-induced reverie for something so low-tech as a ringing telephone.

"People kept coming by and bothering me."

"That's the thing about people," Paolo said. "You just can't unplug them."

"First things first, Rog," I said. "What was in the file?"

"Nothing."

"Nothing. What do you mean, nothing? Why would anyone lock an empty file?" I didn't want any more contradictions, just one clear, unambiguous explanation.

"Well, maybe you start to create the file and you figure you're going to put something serious in it, so you password-protect it, but before you actually enter any data, you get interrupted and then you just never get back to it. And there you are—empty locked file." Roger shrugged his shoulders as if this sequence of events were as common as stumbling out of bed in the morning to make coffee.

"This happens a lot?" Paolo asked.

"I've never done it," Roger said. "And I don't think I know anyone who has, but that's one way you could."

"You think that's what happened?" I was standing next to him. The computer screen reflected the disappointment in my face.

"No. There's plenty of data in this file."

I looked to Paolo, a question on my face. He shrugged.

"Roger, honey," I said, trying not to sound impatient. "Start over, OK? You said there was nothing in the file."

"Well, I didn't mean 'nothing' like 'nothing at all.' I meant 'nothing' like 'nothing important.' "

"Let me know when we get to the part that's in English, OK?" Paolo took up his usual spot in the armchair. He began to pull the stuffing out through a hole in the fabric. "Or if you find an interpreter."

"Don't take it out on what's left of the furniture," I said.

"It's just some win/loss figures. Here, look at it. But it's nothing. I mean small change." Roger sounded a bit defensive.

He worked the keyboard and mouse until a record of figures appeared on the screen. Whoever made this document must have decided that the password protection was enough. The information was in easily readable form. Years, divided into wins and losses, were laid out across the top of the screen. Tracking down the left side were dates, each of which represented a different bet. There was no telling what the mystery gambler was betting on, but he certainly wasn't losing any sleep over the venture. The win/loss columns, each automatically tabulated, showed mostly five- and ten-dollar bets, with the very rare twenty. The bottom line indicated a net loss over the last four years of $75.00. The most recent entry was for six weeks prior.

"Seventy-five dollars? The total loss is seventy-five dollars?" I had pinned so much hope on the contents of this document. The detective game wasn't nearly so much fun when you weren't getting answers.

"Why hide that?" Paolo asked. "I could drop more than that on one night out."

"See? Nothing." Roger leaned back and chugged the last of his Diet Coke.

"Yeah, nothing all right," I said. "No info, no motive, no other clues. 'Nothing' is too kind a word for this. Can you at least tell who did this?"

"I don't see anything that identifies the user. Anyone who had access to this machine could do it."

"Where does that leave us?" Paolo asked.

"I have no idea," I said.

"Still thirsty?" Roger asked.

Paolo stood. "OK, OK," he said. "You did such a good job, let me." He headed for the hallway.

"That was a compliment, right?" Roger was beaming.

"Yup," I said. "I think all is forgiven. But you aren't supposed to know that yet. And you will probably have to give up online chatting."

Roger shrugged. "I could live with that."

"How do you put up with him at close quarters?" I asked, settling into the love seat.

"What makes you so sure that Paolo isn't the one doing most of the putting up with? Never thought of that, did you?"

"Not you too. Paolo just lectured me on relationships. When I get back to the city, I'm going to make finding single friends a priority."

Roger just laughed. "So tell what's happening."

I filled him in on our visit and the run-in with Lee Dexter and Sister Grace.

"So you think that Mary Corinne set Joe Jr. up to go after Benny?"

"Looks that way," I said.

"But someone got Joe before he could find any dirt on Benny," Paolo said, returning with Diet Cokes for everyone.

"And if they are cause and effect," Roger said, "Mary Corinne must be pretty afraid that she's next." He popped the tab on his soda can.

"That's how I see it," I said.

"And that points to Benny, doesn't it?" Paolo asked.

"You think, huh?" Roger asked. "I think it's pretty obvious what's going on around here." He smiled at both of us, daring us to give him a cue line.

"Oh, I'll bite, he's my husband," Paolo said. "What is so obvious, Roger?"

"Marty Friedman. He's the murderer."

"Obvious?" I asked. "So this is 'obvious' like the file had 'nothing,' right?"

"Will someone please turn on the closed captioning?" Paolo added.

"Very funny, guys. Yuk, yuk. But listen to this." Roger leaned back in the desk chair and placed his hands together, fingertips to fingertips, a gesture I assume he picked up from a movie. "Here's how I figure it. We don't really know what happened to this office except for what Marty told us, right? He could be making up any story he wanted to about breaking in here. Joe isn't going to drop a dime on him. Say he and Joe have a real thing between them, some big argument. Marty knows Mary Corinne is pushing Joe, so he breaks in here—alone—writes that verse on the wall, kills Joe later, and pushes the blame off on Mary Corinne and Benny. See?"

" 'Drop a dime on him'?" Paolo said. "I really am going to disconnect the cable. No joking." He shook his head and reached for another magazine.

"What about Sister Sally?" I asked.

"Well, maybe they were fighting over her?" Roger suggested. "Why not? They were both in love with her. She was young. We already have one nun stepping out, why not two?"

" 'Stepping out'? You are really frightening me," Paolo said.

"We don't know if Joe loved her or not," I said.

Paolo put his magazine down without opening it. "You know, I don't like the idea of Marty Friedman as a murderer, but Roger does have a point, Nicky. Why should we just assume that Friedman is telling the truth?"

"I guess he could be lying, but I've seen this guy in action for weeks," I said. "I just don't think he'd be that clever or calm enough to make up a story like that and stick to it. The problem is, we have no compelling reason for anyone to actually kill someone. Except . . ."

"Except?" Roger echoed.

"Except Benny," I said.

"That's what I'm thinking," Paolo said. "Joe gets too close. Benny does him in. It's the only motive we have. And if Mary Corinne thinks so too, she's one worried ex-nun."

I had the same old objection. "I agree with that, but what about Sally? We just don't know enough about her."

Roger started to bounce up and down in his chair. "How about this. This is good. It's Benny, but he kills Sally first to confuse everyone. Huh? Pretty good, huh?"

"Roger, there is nothing behind door number three," I said. "Calm down. We have nothing to go on here. So what if Benny cooked the books twenty years ago? Who could prove it now? The entire sequence of events is juvenile. There isn't enough money here to kill for." I spread my arms wide to encompass the idea of St. Gilbert's Summer Theater Festival, including my rundown office.

"Unless it's just a front. What if he were using the theater in some way to funnel other monies?" Paolo asked.

"What, like drug money?" I asked. "Like Benny Singleton is the campus drug lord?" I'd sooner believe Marty Friedman had committed two premeditated murders.

"How would you do that anyway? I mean exactly what goes into laundering money?" Roger asked.

"I have no idea," Paolo said. "OK? It's just a thought. Somebody is killing people. There has to be a reason. Money laundering makes as much sense as anything else."

"It does," I agreed with him. "That's the weird part."

"Wait a minute," Roger said. "How come that nun knew who you were? Who is Sister Grace?"

206

"She's the president of the college, that's who she is," Benny Singleton said as he entered the room.

We each jumped in a different direction. I stood to block the view of the computer. Behind me, I heard Roger tapping on the keyboard, no doubt wiping the screen blank. Paolo swung his legs over the side of the chair, assuming an instant pose of casual boredom. To me, all that activity screamed cover-up, but Benny didn't respond at all. He just stood there, dripping sweat and looking like someone's confused elderly uncle. The problem was behind him. Partially hidden by Benny's bulk, but still visible, Olivia Singleton's eyes searched the room.

"Why do you want to know about Sister Grace?" Benny asked.

Once again, my stage manager's instincts came to the rescue: always tell as much of the truth as you can.

"I met her earlier today, and she seemed to know who I was. I had the impression she was planning to see me again, but I had no idea who she was."

"Well, you will be seeing her again soon," Benny said. "We have another meeting to go to at Old Main. I've been calling your apartment all morning."

"I helped," Olivia said. "I've been looking for you." She smiled at me. How could such a nasty kid look so innocent? She stood next to her father in her T-shirt, baggy shorts, and sneakers. She even had skinned knees.

"And I wanted to give you the information on the viewing," Benny said. "I assume you will be there?"

"Viewing?" I asked.

"Tonight. For Sally. Here." He handed me a typewritten piece of paper. "These are the details."

The phone rang.

Roger back-stepped from my desk, tripping over the chair as he went.

"It's the phone," he said.

"Jesus," Paolo said.

It rang again.

"Why don't you answer it?" Olivia asked, stepping farther into the room.

"Of course I'm going to answer," I said. Reaching for the phone, I remembered Phyllis East, ace reporter. She must be in Huber's Landing by now. I braced myself for another round of cat and mouse.

"Hello, Nicky." Thank God, it was Patsy.

"It's Patsy," I said to everyone in the room.

"Oh. Patsy," Roger said.

"Patsy," Paolo repeated.

"What is going on there?" Patsy asked. "Are you guys drunk?"

"No. Nothing much happening here at all," I answered.

"If you say so. You sound weird to me. Look, I talked to Judy Winiski, at the hospital. I know what killed Joe."

I sat down. Roger, Paolo, Benny, and Olivia were silent, all staring at me.

"There's no reason to come in today," I said. I did not want Benny to know that I was interested in getting that information pre-public-release. Suddenly, forcefully, as if I'd not really considered it before, I took in the existence of a murderer on the loose. Someone who might just train his attention on a too-inquisitive stranger from out of town. Someone who just might be standing five feet from me.

"Who was coming in?" Patsy asked. "Mary Frances and I are going to the lake for the afternoon. Do you want to know what killed Joe or don't you?"

"That sounds great," I said to Patsy. Then, to the people in the room, "Patsy and Mary Frances are going to the lake this afternoon."

"It's a great day for it," Benny said, as if he'd never heard of such an idea. "Maybe Olivia would like to go to the lake too? Huh?" He tussled her hair.

"Oh, Daddy. Stop." Olivia giggled and blushed and for one moment behaved like the twelve-year-old she was, embarrassed at a public display of parental affection.

"Do you want to know or don't you?" Patsy asked. " 'Cause Mary Frances wants to leave soon."

"You know, that's right," I said. "Why don't you give me the list now, and I can check off all that stuff this afternoon before we send it back." I reached for a pen.

"What is going on there? Hello?" Patsy said.

"No, there's time," I said. "Benny's here, and we have to go to a meeting, but we have a few minutes."

I could hear light dawning at the other end of the phone line.

"I get it. You have to talk in code right? Cool. Hey, Mary Frances, come listen to this." Then, back to me, "So I can say anything I want, but you have to go on like we're doing theater business, right?"

"That's right. I'm ready." I felt a slight sense of relief.

"Do you know that Mary Frances has a spot on her inner thigh that drives her wild every time I lick it?" Patsy said.

I am sure Watson never did that to Holmes.

"I think we should stick to the items we mentioned last night, OK?" I said.

"We don't have time for this," Benny said. "Tell her you'll talk to her later. We have to go."

"We're running short of time here, Pats," I said, giving Paolo a look which I hoped conveyed "Help."

"Where do you have to go?" Paolo jumped right in.

"Why do you care?" Olivia asked.

"OK, OK," Patsy said. "How's this." And now she was whispering: "Digoxin."

"Ah-huh." I made a note.

"I'm just curious, sweetheart," Paolo said to Olivia. Then, to Roger, "Isn't that what you call twelve-year-old girls?"

"It's some kind of heart medication," Patsy answered me. "If you've had a heart attack, you take this stuff to keep you going. According to her nurse friends, he had just about enough to kill. Anything less and you'd get sick but you'd probably recover."

I kept scribbling meaningless notes on the pad in front of me, while Paolo's diversionary tactics gained ground.

"I don't like your tone," Benny said to Paolo.

"So, you're saying there couldn't have been, say, ten of them?" I asked Patsy.

"My tone?" Paolo said. "I'm just making polite conversation here. Nice chitchat. Small talk. Roger, defend me."

"Ten what?" Patsy asked. "Oh, I see. No—one person had to drink the entire pot. There was no other way." Patsy sounded very certain of this.

"Yes. Well," Roger fumbled. "Tone is a difficult thing, of course. Difficult."

"But where would I get one of these, Patsy?" I asked. "I don't remember ordering one."

"Some defense, lover," Paolo said.

"I don't think we need to parade your lifestyle in front of my child," Benny said, assuming his most officious style.

"Oh, Daddy. I know what gay is." Olivia shook her head and rolled her eyes so hard I could feel the breeze.

"Remember," Patsy said, "Benny and Edward both had heart attacks about two years ago. One or both of them could be using it. And I think I heard somewhere that Mary Corinne once had one, or maybe

210

she just has heart disease?" She was guessing with the last bit of information. Still, there was Mary Corinne again.

"That is not the point, Olivia," Benny said, frowning at his daughter. "And don't interrupt."

"OK," I said. "I'll take care of this, Patsy. You two have fun."

"You be careful, Nicky," Patsy said. "I'll call you later." Then she was gone. I turned my attention to the argument going on around me. As usual Benny's efforts to discipline his daughter were failing.

"I wasn't interrupting. No one was talking," Olivia said.

"Benny, I thought we didn't have time for this?" I stood.

"And we certainly don't want to be in the way," Paolo said. "Everybody out."

Paolo and I rushed for the exit.

"Wait." We stopped. All eyes turned toward Roger. "Your messages," he said.

"Messages?" I asked. "Oh, right. Messages. Well?"

"Well, some security guy. He wanted to give you the incident report number on the break-in. I wrote it down on your desk pad."

"Perfect," I said. "Thanks. Let's go."

"And—there's more. If I'm going to be your secretary, you can at least listen." I think he was actually enjoying tormenting me.

"Sorry, Roger. What else is there?"

"Phyllis East—"

"Oh Christ," I said. The reporter. I had a picture of her lugging a suitcase filled with unmarked twenties around campus, calling my name.

Roger gave me a look of mock annoyance.

"Phyllis East," he started over, "called. She was very upset not to find you here. You know, I think she may have been drunk, but she has a great voice."

"Who is Phyllis East?" Benny asked.

"The reporter who called yesterday." I answered. "She's from the *World Weekly Journal*. She said she was coming out from New York today."

"That's not good, Nicholas," Benny said. "You know you are not supposed to speak with the press."

"I haven't. Anyway, I guess she's not here. Maybe she's not coming."

"Then if the fun is over, could we go now?" Benny was doing his best impression of an aggrieved adult weary of the antics of the young'uns.

"OK, OK. We're out of here." I started for the door again.

"Excuse me." Roger rapped my desk with his knuckles.

"What is it?" Benny snapped.

"Message number three, Nicky." Roger pointedly addressed himself to me. "Mary Corinne stopped by. She said it was important."

FIFTEEN

He looked like Benny Singleton—wide, balding, and in need of a tailor. He moved like Benny Singleton—great gulping bursts of air blowing in and out of his underexercised body. Ilana Mosca said he had a heart of gold. Edward Rossoff said he was a shit. Mary Corinne said he was as good as a murderer. His daughter adored him. But what did any of that mean? I couldn't make sense of any of it.

Benny and I were on our way to Old Main. At some point the grounds crew had turned on the sprinklers. We walked in and out of fine mists that didn't so much cool you off as remind you that somewhere a cool place must exist. Along the walkways, the spruce trees were holding up well, but in the flowerbeds and along the buildings, the lilies and rhododendron were beginning to show some wear. In that early part of summer, the campus flowers were blooming mostly yellow-orange and rust colors, dotted here and there by the red of geraniums. Once again we walked alone. The few people on campus during the summer were mostly staying out of the afternoon heat.

What could I say to him? "Oh, by the way, Benny, did you kill Joe Sobieski yesterday by dumping your heart medicine in his tea? And while we're at it, how about that Sister Sally? Some laugh, huh?"

I tried to distract myself by imagining what St. Gilbert's must look like in winter. Here in the mountains the snow would probably be up to your hips. I'd be walking across the campus, bundled up beyond recognition. The freezing wind biting at my face, I rush to a nearby dormitory. There, I find a blazing fire and, coincidently, David Scott. I strip out of my heavy winter clothing. The flicking light of the fire plays shadows over us as we stretch out on the plush rug. The bright glow of the flames, the heat on my skin . . . hot.

Too damn hot. Sweat trickled down my cheek as we turned the corner to Old Main. This time, Patsy and Mary Frances were not sitting outside Old Main to greet us.

There were no friendly faces inside either. We were on the second floor again. We passed by the glass and wood cage that was Public Relations. Ahead of us were polished double wooden doors with the title President embossed in gold letters across one panel.

Inside, a secretary sat briskly transcribing from a Dictaphone. We waited a moment until she reached a stopping point.

"Good afternoon, Benny. I'm so sorry about everything." She smiled at us.

"Thank you. That's very kind of you." He did not smile.

"Sister Grace is expecting you. Just take a seat, and I'll tell her you're here."

The waiting room was distinctly different from the one outside the office of the director of public relations. Instead of Danish modern that looked sleek and felt dreadful, the outer room of Sister Grace's suite was designed in warm colors with cushiony chairs. The furniture in my office must have looked like this decades ago.

Almost immediately, the secretary ushered us into a surprisingly modest office, spacious without being cavernous. There was no high-tech gloss of glass or metal. The colors were rich, subdued natural woods, the fabrics on the window and cushions weighty but not ponderous. Three visitors were already present, lined up on either side of the desk along the far wall. The tableaux was perfectly staged. All eyes were inevitably drawn to Sister Grace, sitting bolt upright behind the desk, her silver hair glinting in the sunlight that poured through the window behind her, a sharp contrast to the understated colors surrounding her. She fixed her gray eyes directly on us as we entered. She did not rise.

"Good afternoon, Benny. Mr. D'Amico. Please sit down, gentlemen." She indicated two chairs in the center of the room. When seated, we were facing her. On her left was Oscar Brocket, the public relations director, and on her right were Patricia Madison and Stanley Sobieski. We were definitely in the principal's office.

She skipped the preliminaries. "I am sorry, but *Convent of Fear* is finished. Obviously, as much as we hoped your show would be a vital part of putting a new face on St. Gilbert's, we cannot continue to jeopardize the well-being of the participants. Someone has seen fit to indulge in murder, and we must take the steps necessary to ensure the safety of staff, students, and visitors. We will, of course, make all suitable and legal arrangements with the theater's staff as per their contracts. Patricia will oversee this. You need not worry, Mr. D'Amico, about compensation."

"I wasn't worried, Sister. I—"

"Good. We pride ourselves on being fair, Mr. D'Amico. Now, let me also say that, under the circumstances, it is imperative that no one— and I mean this quite explicitly, Benny—no one speak to the press. I have had a phone call. A reporter named Suzanne West. She seemed to know a great deal more than I would like her to."

"When was this?" Patricia asked. "You never mentioned this."

"Last night. And I'm telling you all now, aren't I?"

Suzanne *West*? Not very creative.

"Did she have a voice like honey?" I asked.

"Really, Mr. D'Amico." If she'd been wearing glasses, Sister Grace would have looked at me over the top of her frames.

"Sorry, Sister. It's just that a reporter named Phyllis East has been calling me. Well, the name . . . and she has a distinctive voice."

"Indeed. As you say, she has a . . . *pleasant* voice. I suppose others might use the word 'honey.' " Others, but not Sister Grace. "What did you tell her?"

"Nothing. I refused to speak to her. She did offer me money."

"This is not good for anyone," Patricia said. Once again, she looked calm and collected in her bright, puffed-up outfit. She and Sister Grace were emotional twins and visual opposites.

"I didn't take it," I said.

"I should hope not." Sister Grace looked at me as if I'd suggested a seance in lieu of Sunday Mass.

"She's supposed to be coming to town, but she hasn't arrived yet," I added. I really did want to be helpful.

"This is just great," Stanley Sobieski said. "Trash tabloid reporters roaming around trying to dig up dirt. This is exactly what I warned against." He pointedly made his last remark to Patricia.

For whatever reason, Oscar decided then was the moment to join the conversation. "You've done just the right thing, Nicky. It's very important to contain the message we present in media outlets that might, in other venues, raise not necessarily doubt, but concerns or questions—"

"Oscar." Sister Grace didn't even bother to look at him.

"Ah, right," Oscar said. "You did the right thing."

"Thank you," I said.

216

"When Ms. West or East—whatever she is calling herself—arrives, Mr. D'Amico, I trust you will say nothing to her, but instead refer her to me?"

"Of course, Sister. I—"

"Very good. Oscar has prepared a statement, with Patricia's help, which will be the official position of the college. No one is to say anything that will add to or alter that statement in any fashion. Are we clear on this?"

Benny and I nodded in agreement.

"Excellent," she said.

"Yes, certainly," Benny said. "I wouldn't—"

"Thank you, Benny. I am very sorry that it must come to this. We had such high hopes for this season. Such an adventurous season at that."

"Too adventurous, if you ask me," Sobieski said.

"Thank you, Stanley, but I'm not asking," Sister Grace said.

Sobieski was not put off by the rebuke. "All I'm saying is that a less 'adventurous' season might not have led to this. But no one asked me, did they?" He didn't exactly look heartbroken to see that we'd ended up with the show closed.

"If I might add something," Oscar said. "Benny, the statement I am giving out is complete in its support of you, your efforts, your talent, your staff, your theater, all the work you've done in the past, the efforts of your students, the fine—"

"Oscar." Sister Grace cut him off again.

"Ah. Right. Supportive. We intend to be supportive, Benny."

"I appreciate that, Oscar," Benny said.

"Then I hope we can put the issue of the press behind us," Sister Grace said. "I also expect that everyone at St. Gilbert's will be fully and thoroughly cooperative with the police."

Benny and I nodded in agreement.

"But, I wonder," Benny said, "have we really explored the possibilities of a postponement instead of a complete shutdown?"

"Out of the question," Patricia Madison said, picking up the conversation. "Benny, do you realize what kind of liability we are open to here? *Convent of Fear* is done. This season is done. Do you understand, Benny? The entire season is shut down. Nothing more this summer."

"I understand that is what *you* intend, Patricia," Benny said.

"It is what *I* intend, Benjamin," Sister Grace said.

And there was no arguing with Sister Grace.

The meeting continued with more of the same. No one looked at me. No one spoke to me. The college officials were barely speaking to Benny. They were making pronouncements, declaring what was to be. Sister Grace and the lawyer were alternating monologues, occasionally punctuated with Oscar's spineless assents, while Stanley Sobieski sat grinning in the corner. I wasn't certain why I was there. Maybe they really did think it was important to have me on board. Maybe they wanted a witness. Mostly I felt like an audience. Problem was, I make a lousy audience.

"I know who broke into the theater," I said.

My statement was met with silence.

"I said I know who broke into the theater."

"We heard you," the security chief snapped.

"Have you informed the police, Mr. D'Amico?" Sister Grace asked.

"Not yet," I said. "I haven't had a chance."

"There has been a murder. What could be more important, young man, than aiding the police in their investigation?" she asked.

"Well, I just found out, and then we had to come here."

"This is ridiculous," Sobieski said. "I don't know why we have to listen to this." He twisted in his seat to speak directly to Sister Grace. "This boy and his friends have been nothing but problems for the police since Sally died. You do know that one of them was found with the poisoned tea that killed my nephew?"

"I've been fully briefed by Corporal Roberts, Stanley. Thank you," she said.

"I just thought you'd want to know that Marty Friedman and Joe Sobieski were the vandals," I said.

"You leave my nephew out of this, you little queer," Sobieski spouted. I wished Paolo were with me. He was much better at handling the Stanley Sobieskis of life.

"Stanley, I think it'd be best to refrain from making this personal," Patricia said, and she placed a restraining hand on the security chief's arm. Count on a lawyer to stop all the fun.

Sister Grace stood. "I think we're done here, gentlemen. I am sorry we've had this little disagreement. I assure you again, Benny, if there had been another way, I would have taken it. As for you, Mr. D'Amico, I suggest you go to the police with whatever it is you know. I assume you have proof?"

"Marty Friedman himself told me they did," I said.

She nodded. "That would seem to be conclusive. Patricia, if this is true, we will have to reconsider the Friedman boy's contract."

Sobieski started to speak. "I didn't mean to—"

Sister Grace silenced him with a simple hand gesture. "I know exactly what you meant to do, Stanley. We will discuss it later. Good day, gentlemen."

"Benny," I said as we made our way toward the main staircase, "what is with Stanley Sobieski?"

"I have no idea, but I agree with Sister Grace. If you think you have something to say, say it to the police."

At the top of the stairs, we were suddenly face to face with Corporal Roberts. "Say what to the police?" he asked. He was just reaching the second floor. He looked annoyed and overheated. His uniform was fast losing whatever crisply pressed shape it may have started out with that morning. A double murder and a newly out lesbian daughter were definitely making for one grumpy, unhappy-looking cop.

"Say that the level of homophobia in Huber's Landing is nearly unbearable," Benny answered.

"What are you talking about?" I asked. I was stunned.

"Admit it, Nicholas. You were admirably restrained in the meeting, but I could see you were highly offended. And why not?"

"Is that so?" Roberts looked even more put out.

"Yes, it is," Benny said. "We've just come from a most blatant display of bigotry. It made me embarrassed to be a heterosexual."

I had no clue as to what game Benny was playing, but I was going to let Corporal Roberts know about Marty and Joe. "Corporal, I—"

He turned on me, rage in his eyes. "I am not responsible for whatever abuse you people bring on yourselves. We were fine until you got here. You did this. She never would have done this on her own." He looked like he wanted to say more, but his face was turning bright red, his voice choking. He towered over me. I felt the full force of his size and bulk. Then the moment passed. With a sound in his throat that was equal parts groan and grunt, he backed away one step. He hurried off toward the president's office.

"That is exactly what I mean," Benny shouted after him, then quickly descended the steps.

It was just me and the paintings of past presidents that lined the walls. I asked them what awful thing I had done as a child to deserve St. Gilbert's Summer Theater Festival. They were as helpful as Sister Grace. I rushed to catch up with Benny.

Exiting Old Main was like being hit in the face with a hot, wet towel. I could feel my energy level drop, but I pressed ahead.

"Benny, what was that about?"

"No need to thank me, Nicky. I abhor bigotry wherever I see it."

"Thanking you wasn't what I had in mind."

"Well, whatever you have in mind, it's going to have to wait. We have company."

Benny was looking in the direction of the theater. I saw Lee Dexter running toward us, waving his arms and shouting.

"Where the hell have you been?" he asked Benny. He was drenched in sweat and out of breath. The good humor he'd shown earlier in the day was gone. Without the grin, he looked dangerous. There was real anger in his voice.

"Closing the coffin on *Convent of Fear*," Benny said. "Why? Did you want to mourn with us?"

"I need to talk to you. Now. Alone."

"We're in the middle of a conversation here," I said.

"I don't care. I need to speak with Benny. Now." We were witnessing Crazy Dexter at full force.

"This is hardly the time or place, Lee," Benny said.

"Now, Benny. Now." Lee was shouting.

I would have been offended if it were anyone else. But taking a Lee Dexter fit personally was pointless.

I spread my hands wide. "OK," I said. "We can talk about this later, Benny."

"Well, if you don't mind, Nicky."

"Yeah. Run along, Nicky," Lee said, mimicking Benny's voice.

I wondered if it was safe to leave Benny. There was a delirious gleam in Lee's eyes that suggested distance was a good option for everyone.

"Maybe we should *all* go back to the theater," I suggested.

"No, it's fine," Benny said. "We'll be all right, Nicky."

"OK. Then I'll see you all later." I wasn't happy, but I couldn't see any other choice. I continued along the walkway. Benny and Lee strolled a few feet in the opposite direction before stopping to talk. I made it as far as a spruce tree before my concern stopped me. I couldn't hear what they were saying. I could see, though. Lee was gesturing wildly. I don't think Edward Rossoff could have kept up that pace. Benny stood quietly, motionlessly listening to whatever Lee was ranting about. Beyond them, and not too surprisingly, Olivia appeared on the other side of the quadrangle, taking up a position opposite me, intently watching her father. I was getting used to that child endlessly roaming the campus. It seemed she was never too far away from Daddy for too long.

"Some sight, huh?"

I jumped. Ilana Mosca had come up behind me. In a concession to the afternoon heat, she'd shed at least two layers of clothing. That left, as far as I could tell, three more.

"If you want to hear, Nicky, you need to move closer," she said.

"I am not eavesdropping," I told her. "I was worried about Benny."

"I think you tell me half truth. Shame on you. And you need better hiding place. Anyway, Lee will not hurt Benny. He never does. He just screams and screams, and then everything is over."

"This happens a lot?"

"With Lee, always."

"What do you think he's yelling about?"

"Why do you ask so many questions, Nicky? Show's over. Go home." Ilana looked tired, worn out. It could have been the heat, but somehow I wasn't so certain. She looked almost relieved, as if whatever was wearing her down was finally over.

"Ilana, what's going on? We're closing. This theater might never reopen. But instead of everyone being upset, you people all look perfectly content. Even Benny doesn't seem to be worked up over this. What is it?"

"You don't understand, Nicky. No one is happy. Who could be happy at death of theater? But some things, they go so long, when they end you are maybe just little relieved. You know this feeling?"

222

She was speaking to me but watching Lee and Benny. What a tableau we made. Ilana, Olivia, and I watching Benny and Lee, watching each other watch. Each of us standing exposed in the middle of campus. We were out in the bright open day but might as well have been sitting in some darkened room.

"There are too many secrets here," I said.

"No, it's exactly opposite problem. In small town, you can never really keep secret."

"Since Monday night, nothing has made much sense around here," I said. "You aren't helping any."

She snorted what might have been almost a laugh.

"Yes. It is like childish nightmare, isn't it? It makes so little sense. And this heat. I hate it. I am going back inside. Don't stand here too long. You will get ill. Whatever Lee is saying is not that interesting. And Benny, you will not hear his answer. You will miss the only thing worth hearing, yes?"

I looked at her face and realized that she was not staring at Lee and Benny, but just at Benny. Ilana was always staring at Benny, the man with the heart of gold. Funny, I'd never really appreciated it before, that look of complete absorption, her patience, her praise. Mary Corinne was right. Ilana had probably been in love with Benny Singleton for more than half as long as I'd been alive. I had no idea what that might feel like.

"Ilana, I'm sorry . . ."

She looked at me for just a moment. "You see? In end there are no secrets. This heat." She left with as little ceremony as she'd arrived.

It was all like some childish dream or fantasy. The images keep sliding around, seemingly unrelated to each other, as if the mind were changing channels every time the body moved in sleep. I looked back at Lee and Benny one more time. Now Benny was getting more agitated. Suddenly, I was overwhelmingly fatigued. All that hate. Mary

Corinne hating Benny. Ilana hating Mary Corinne. Lee hating Benny. Edward hating Benny. Marty hating Joe. Joe hating Benny. Olivia hating everyone but Benny. I wondered, who did Benny hate? Tired of it all, I turned toward the theater, leaving Olivia to stand watch over her father.

Back at my office there wasn't much to do. Still, I was under contract. I busied myself with the only task I could find, the tedious chore of collecting scripts and scores from the cast. The material was supplied by a rental agency in New York that licensed the production around the country. Failure to return a script or score to the agency constituted copyright infringement on the part of the theater. Normally, we would have just asked the actors to turn their books in on closing night. Since you can't have a closing without an opening, I spent the afternoon on the phone leaving messages asking everyone to please bring their copies in so that I could package them for shipping.

When I did leave my office, I was faced once more with the forlorn look of the abandoned scenery onstage. Nothing had been touched since Joe's death. I walked down the side aisle, deep into the darkness, almost halfway into the house. If we'd gone on as scheduled, I would be surrounded by technicians attempting to fine-tune the production instead of standing in an empty theater. In a few hours I would be listening to the musicians tune up. Then, having called the actors to places, I would cue the orchestra, and the downbeat of the overture would mark the first full-scale rehearsal of *Convent of Fear* at St. Gilbert's.

Not today.

Something moved onstage.

The ghost light was not in place. The stage was exceptionally dark. Yet in the slight bit of light spilling from the back of the auditorium, I was sure I saw motion on the stage. No one had any business onstage. Anyway, how could they see what they were doing?

"Hello? Who's there?" I called as I walked farther down the aisle. "Hello?"

There was no answer except the sound of someone running toward the stage left wing. I raced across the front of the house toward the auditorium exit. I banged into the panic bar and emerged into the hallway only a few feet from the stage door.

For a moment I was blinded by the sudden change in light. Then I saw Olivia Singleton sitting on the floor, her back to a wall. In front of her David Scott lay sprawled out in the middle of the hallway.

"Jesus, Olivia," he said, getting to his knees. "You should watch where you're going."

"Me? You ran into me," she said.

"What happened here?" I asked.

"He ran me down."

"The kid's a menace. I'm late already," David said. He was on his feet. "I don't have time for this. Sorry, Nicky."

"Sorry, Nicky," Olivia mocked him. "You gonna kiss him again?"

"Olivia," I started.

"Yeah, yeah, yeah," she said. "I'm out of here." She jumped up and dashed down the hallway to the nearest exit.

"Olivia! Come back here," I shouted.

She was gone.

I turned to David. "Well—"

"Sorry, Nicky. I'm way late now. See you later." He leaned over and gave me a quick peck on the cheek.

"But, I . . . ," was all I managed to say before he disappeared down the hallway.

So who hit who? And who came from the stage? Olivia, who'd probably been doing her usual hanging-out-and-lurking routine? Or David, whom I had never really considered a suspect, but who, when I thought about it, had just as much access as anyone else to either the wooden cross or the teapot. That was a chain of thought I just didn't want to follow.

I entered the stage left wing from the hallway. Without the ghost light it took almost two minutes to feel my way along the wall to the work-light switches. Once I snapped them on, the stage was filled with the flat starkness of fluorescent light.

I stepped into the middle of the day room scenery. Chairs and the love seat were as they'd been when the police had cleared the cast off the stage. The coffee table contained scattered tea items and a tray of lacquered biscuits that were supposed to look to the audience like a tasty afternoon treat. The table was pushed out of its usual position, sitting far upstage in front of the fireplace unit. Probably the police had moved it when they took away the body. The mantel on the fireplace held several empty teacups lined up in a row and a few old athletic trophies Marty had picked up from secondhand stores and refurbished. The rug on the floor was doubled over one edge, rolled back when a cast member tried to revive Joe. The bookcases contained a few real books and panels of painted faux book spines. The set had the same disheveled look and eerie feel you'd find in a room abandoned in a rush by its occupants.

Nothing onstage drew my attention. If the intruder had touched anything, I couldn't see it.

I shivered. Two people had died on this stage within the last seventy-two hours. I pulled the ghost light out of the wings and turned it on. I turned off the overhead work lights and hurried though the wing exit into the hallway, telling myself that I was definitely not going to start believing in theater ghosts.

SIXTEEN

"EXPLAIN THIS TO ME again," Roger said as we reached the first landing of the concrete steps.

"You're telling me you've never been to a viewing?" I asked.

We were thirty minutes south of Huber's Landing, in a town not much larger. Schuman's Funeral Home, a pseudo-Victorian structure, was the most impressive and overdone building on the block. There were three crisply painted white stories behind an expansive, railed front porch. There were smaller porches on either side of the house. The windows on the top two floors each featured a small green awning. The first-floor windows were bay. The steps we trudged up had their own covering, trapping the early evening heat around us. If a single family lived in a house like that, they'd be the richest people in town.

"Certainly not," Roger said. "Do I have to kiss the corpse?"

"Do you get everything you know about the world from television?" Paolo asked. He was right behind us, still trying to find the proper length for his sleeves.

We weren't exactly dressed for mourning. I was a little better off than the boys, having packed black denim and a jacket and tie to wear for openings. They'd arrived with only basic emergency cool weather wear. Both were in jeans and white shirts. Roger wore short-sleeved cotton and Paolo long-sleeved linen, which he was busily adjusting to either roll just above the wrist or just below the elbow.

"Will you stop with the shirt, please?" I said.

"It's bad enough I have to go to this thing without a tie. I can at least get the shirt right. My grandmother would kill me if she knew I was at a viewing without a tie." He settled at just above the wrist.

"This is kind of gross, don't you think?" Roger asked. "Where I come from they just put you in a box and off you go."

"Isn't there a rule about gay men being sensitive?" Mary Frances asked as she and Patsy passed us on their way up the steps.

"Are you guys going to stand out here in the heat all night?" Patsy asked.

"No," I said. "We're right behind you."

The entry room was designed to simulate a large sitting room. Almost before we could notice the red velvet settees and armchairs, David Scott detached himself from a group by the door and came to greet us.

"Thanks for coming, guys," he said.

Did I think he looked great in his T-shirts and shorts? It was nothing compared to the effect a suit one shade lighter than dark blue had on his eyes. They popped out at us, looking almost too delighted for someone in mourning. I remembered that he hadn't been very close to his cousin.

"Hi," was all I managed to say.

Paolo let out an audible sigh. "Come on, Roger, let's get a seat. We'll see you all inside."

"I guess everyone from the theater is here?" I asked after they left. He should only wear blue T-shirts in the summer.

"Pretty much. I'm on official greeter duty. You'd think they'd been the perfect family the way my father and his brothers are behaving now that she's dead. Listen, I'm really glad you came. I mean, I thought maybe I wouldn't get to see you. I mean, you must be leaving soon, right?"

Tight blue T-shirts, the kind that peel off slowly, revealing the tanned skin of his body in a tantalizing, inch-by-inch display of smooth . . .

"Well," I said, "I'm not really sure. But, yeah, probably in a day or two."

Up over his ribcage to the ridge that formed the bottom of his pecs, a hint of the tight, small pink nipples showing under the edge of the fabric as . . .

"Oh," he said. "Well, you know, I will be in New York in the fall. I want to make sure—"

"Excuse me," Marty Friedman said. He was standing at my elbow. I blinked. David was standing in front of me, fully clothed in a tasteful blue suit. Damn.

"Hi, Marty," I said.

He looked like shit. This must have been as hard on him as on anyone.

"I'm sorry to interrupt, but I need to talk to you, Nicky. Can I talk to you? I'm sorry, Dave, but I need to talk to Nicky, OK?"

"Sure, Marty." David was all sympathy. "I'm sorry, you know, really I am. I know this is hard, well, you were closer to her than I was. I'll just see how things are going. Nicky, don't leave without saying good-bye."

"Right," I said. No chance of that.

229

"How are you, Marty?" I asked.

"Not . . . I don't know. Look. Come on." He led the way to a room labeled Meditation Center. Inside, the lighting was appropriately diffuse, the piped-in music aggressively meditative in a New Age way: waterfalls, cymbals, electronic notes stretched to my breaking point.

"So what's up?" I asked.

"It's about the cross. What is this place?" He stared at the light fixtures on the walls, each of which was a flame-shaped sconce.

"What about the cross?" I asked.

"Oh. See, I had eight nuns and eight crosses on Monday afternoon and then eight nuns and seven crosses on Monday night. But I counted again yesterday and, with the new one I bought, I had eight nuns and nine crosses. See?"

He looked so distraught. I don't think he'd been sleeping, and he'd obviously been crying.

"Marty, maybe you just miscounted." I tried to be gentle. "It's been a tough week for you."

"Look. I know you think I'm a loser. Coming back here every year just to be near her. But I am good at this job. I never lose anything. That cross was gone, and then it came back."

"Hey. What are you guys doing?" It was Patsy in the doorway of the meditation center. "Oh my God. What is this place?"

She was looking at the two wing-back chairs sitting in the center of the darkened room. They faced a large display of lilies against a dark stained-glass mosaic of a deer lapping water from a pond in the woods.

"I think it's for being sad," I said.

"Well, it's making me sad," Patsy said. "You'd better get out there, Nicky. I think Paolo's offering a critique to the funeral director on embalming."

230

"He's going to have to wait a minute. Marty and I were just finishing."

Paolo entered the meditation center with his characteristic goodwill. "Jesus. Who designed this? Oh, wait, let me guess. You?" His question was aimed at Marty.

"I have to go," Marty said, and he left the three of us alone.

"God, Paolo, do you have to torment him? He actually is in mourning. And he was just telling me something useful."

"Like why that nun in the box has tangerine lipstick on her mouth?"

"No. Like that there are too many crosses."

"Again with the crosses?" Paolo shook his head. "Could we go in the other room? I'm getting ill in here."

I explained to them what Marty had told me.

"So you think when Ilana said there was never one missing, she was lying?" Paolo asked.

"Possible, or she miscounted. I don't get it. Something is wrong, though," I said.

"Seems pretty clear to me," Patsy said. "So someone miscounted and bought an extra cross. So what?"

"Hey, guys, come on. They're getting ready to start," Roger said, and he wandered into the middle of the room, listening to the New Age funeral jingle. "What's this music they're playing? I like it."

"Am I really married to him?" Paolo asked, heading back to the main viewing room.

"Married?" Roger said. "I like the sound of that." He was smiling.

"Come on," I said. "I don't want them to start without us." I led the way out.

There were still people in the entry room. Several more cast members had arrived. Sister Grace, in a severe black skirt and jacket that made her look like the matron in a prison film, was speaking with

Benny. At the foot of the staircase, Edward Rossoff and Mary Corinne—looking formal enough to greet the queen—stood guard at a potted palm. Several nuns from St. Gilbert's were standing nearby, whispering quietly. Ilana Mosca, in several layers of black gauze, stood alone. Seeing her by herself, I wondered, if she had lied, why, and what had it gotten her?

"Nicholas," Benny called me over. I sent the others ahead.

Benny hadn't worn a tie, but the black linen shirt and charcoal linen pants he wore made me feel even more out of place.

"Hello, Sister Grace. Hello, Olivia," I said, joining them. "Aren't we about to start?"

"Yes," Sister Grace said. "Father Gregory just arrived. But before we go in, I wanted to tell you that I'll be investigating very closely the source of any leaks to the press. Your conversations with that reporter, East, or whatever she's calling herself, have not gone unnoted, young man."

"I see. And did you notice that she seemed to know what was happening here before she spoke to me? Someone absolutely tipped her off about Joe's death."

"Of course I did. That's what I'm speaking of. I'm not your grade school principal, Mr. D'Amico. Whatever you may think of nuns in general, I am not a fool." Sister Grace looked me directly in the eyes.

"Can we see the dead body now?" Olivia asked. "I want a good seat. Close to the front."

"Really, Benny," Sister Grace said. "Do something, won't you?" She tossed a disparaging glance at Olivia, then walked way.

"I don't like her," Olivia said.

Oddly enough, I did. First nun I'd liked since I was six.

"I'm going in," I said.

The only other person left in the sitting room was Ilana, still standing alone.

"Ilana," I said. "Coming in?"

"I wait for Benny, thank you," she answered without actually looking at me.

I shrugged and left her standing there.

As I'd learned to do as a child, I first went and knelt before the open casket. Sister Sally was laid out in full nun regalia and with the brightest orange lips I'd ever seen above 14th Street. This time I agreed with Paolo: whoever had done this job needed help. I remained silently in front of her for a few moments, studying her elaborate rosary beads and the pale pink satin lining of the coffin. I quickly blessed myself, stood, and turned toward the assembled mourners.

All of St. Gilbert's Summer Theater Festival sat in their best dress outfits in six rows of padded folding chairs, trying to look united in their grief for Sally while hiding their dislike of each other. They were the audience from hell, and I was onstage with the corpse.

In front on one side were the nuns of St. Gilbert's accompanied by an elderly priest. Across the open aisle, the family filled two rows. I saw Patsy and Mary Frances behind the nuns. Patsy was already teary eyed. Lee Dexter was at the far end of their row. I couldn't read anything on his expressionless face. Behind Lee, Stanley Sobieski and Patricia Madison sat side by side, pointedly looking anywhere but at each other. Marty sat across from Patsy, silent tears running down his cheeks. Roger and Paolo were in the third row, just behind the family. Rebecca, the light designer, shared that row with them. In the far back corner, Mary Corinne and Edward were seated, holding hands. He looked bored. She looked sad, but whether for the deceased or herself, I couldn't tell.

As I stood, back to the coffin, Benny, Olivia, and Ilana entered. The only three seats left together were just behind Roger and Paolo, in the fourth row. Olivia was not happy.

"We'll never see anything back there," I heard her say. She came to the coffin. "Are you done? I want to see."

"It's called 'paying your respects,' Olivia," I said, heading for a seat.

"We saved you this one," Roger whispered, refusing to move and forcing me to step over him.

"The best we could find," Paolo said on the other side.

I sat down and looked directly at the back of David Scott's head.

"You know, guys, this is a solemn occasion." I tried not to lean forward and sniff him.

At that moment Corporal Roberts entered. For a few seconds all the hushed chatter stopped, but then it picked up again at a quicker tempo. He moved down the center aisle to an empty seat in the back row, nodding as he went to those he knew. He managed to not know his daughter.

"He doesn't look so hot without the uniform," Paolo said.

Benny cleared his throat loudly behind us.

The priest rose slowly to his feet. He positioned himself in front of the casket. In his hands he carried a rosary and a prayer book. There was no introduction, but I assumed he was Father Gregory.

He waited for the talking to stop.

When he spoke his voice was a thin, air-filled sound. "Good evening. Let us begin."

He opened the book and read aloud in a sing-song chant that probably was more effective from the altar than in a mid-sized room.

"Almighty Father, eternal God, hear our prayers for Your daughter Sally, whom You have called from this life to Yourself. Grant her light, happiness and peace. Let her pass—"

"*Whore.*"

Father Gregory looked lost. He glanced up from his prayer book at us. Then he looked upward, as if he thought the word might have been uttered in judgment by the Almighty Himself.

234

In fact, the woman doing the shouting stood in the doorway, listing to one side next to a spray of oversized flowers. She was testing the delicate faux gold urn by leaning heavily on it with her elbow.

"She was a *whore*."

That voice. Laced as it was with alcohol, it still dripped with honey. Phyllis East.

"That's the reporter," I said.

"Don't be silly, Nicholas. That's Evelyn, Lee Dexter's wife," Benny said behind me.

"Evelyn, please." Lee was on his feet and moving toward her.

I twisted around in my seat. "I'm telling you, that's the voice," I said to Benny. "That's the woman who called me."

Everyone remained in their seats. I could see the family in agitated conversation.

Evelyn Dexter must have been in her mid-thirties but looked far more worn than that. The young woman who'd married her high school sweetheart was long gone. Thin, weary, lined, boozy, a fast-fading blonde, she eyed her husband unhappily.

"Don't come near me, you lousy prick. Oh yeah." She turned toward Father Gregory. "Oh yeah, Father. You didn't know that, did you? Ha. That little bitch in the coffin and my husband have been doing it for two years. In my bed. Whores, both of them."

"Oh my God," Stanley Sobieski said. He was white in the second row. "It's her. I was talking to his wife?"

"Oh, for Christ's sake, Stanley. What did you do?" Patricia Madison, losing some of her usual control, snapped at him loudly enough for everyone to hear. Sister Grace pinned Stanley with a look that screamed unemployment.

"Oh my God, oh my God," Mary Corinne repeated to herself several times. I was watching the family, some of whom were on their feet, but I could hear Edward trying to calm her.

"Could we all please show a little respect. Please." Father Gregory looked about at no one in particular and finally settled on Sister Sally's corpse. "There is a body present."

Marty buried his face in his hands. "Stop. Stop. Stop."

Patsy and Mary Frances tried to comfort him.

"Come on, Evelyn," Lee said. He reached out to take her by the arm, but she ducked out of his grasp and lurched forward to the priest and the casket.

"Look at him crying over her. Think he'd cry over me if I were in there? Let's find out, huh?" She started to crawl into the coffin.

"That's enough, Evelyn." Lee Dexter grabbed her by her shoulders. The family rushed the coffin.

She spun around, furiously swinging. Her right hand struck Lee's cheek open palm.

"Don't touch me. Don't. All of you. What are you looking at? This isn't the theater. This isn't some show. It's my life he's fucked. God, I hate all of you."

She left as she came, suddenly, angrily. No one moved except Lee Dexter, who mumbled something that sounded like "Sorry" as he followed her out. You could hear the flowers wilting in the silence that followed his exit.

"Take your seats, please." Sister Grace, on her feet, faced the room.

Father Gregory looked bewildered. "But—"

"Everyone just be seated. We will continue with the service." Sister Grace stood with her arms folded, challenging anyone to disagree. She may have been smarter than my elementary school principal, but they shared the same determination to have order. We sat.

"Very good." She nodded to Father Gregory and sat down. "Continue, please."

"So, then . . . Almighty Father, eternal God, hear our prayers for Your daughter Sally . . ."

I looked at Corporal Roberts, who hadn't moved or said a word during Evelyn Dexter's outburst. He sat, eyebrows slightly raised, but that was it. You'd think this sort of thing happened in funeral homes every day.

"Let her pass in safety through the gates of death and live forever . . ."

Lee Dexter and Sally. Everyone had acted as if it was news to them, but two years was a long time to keep a secret in Huber's Landing. I watched Marty, head in hands, wondering just how surprised he really was.

"Guard her from all harm, and on that great day of resurrection and renewal, raise her up with all . . ."

Two years was a long time no matter where you were. Had Evelyn known the entire time? Posing as Phyllis East, she'd asked me if Sally had said anything before she died. I guess she'd been looking for last words from the nun to her own husband.

"Pardon her sins, and give her eternal life in Your kingdom. We ask this through Christ our Lord. Amen."

We sang out as a group, "Amen."

Olivia started to giggle.

SEVENTEEN

"You should have seen my Great Aunt Isabella's wake. That was a scene."

We were just pulling up to my apartment building.

"Someone tried to crawl into her coffin too?" I asked Paolo. I jumped down from the Thing. A clammy sheen of perspiration was building on me. I'd taken off the jacket and the tie as soon as we'd left the funeral home, but grubby was a perpetual condition in Huber's Landing.

"Better," he said. "Someone tried to stab her."

"Wasn't she already dead?" Roger asked.

"Of course she was dead. And all laid out in black and lace, too. It was my uncle. He was very angry at her. Some old childhood thing."

We laughed as we took the steps to my apartment.

"At least we've found someone with a reason to murder the nun," Paolo said as I flipped the light switch.

"You know, she has a name," Roger said.

"Yes, but not a real nun name," Paolo said. "When I was kid there was Sister James, Sister Mark, Sister Harry."

"You never knew a Sister Harry," I said.

Paolo stopped in the middle of unbuttoning his shirt. "You never met my cousin Harry, did you?" He grinned.

"But it doesn't help," Roger said. "Evelyn Dexter has no reason to murder Joe."

"You have a cousin named Harry?" I was at the fridge, pulling an ice cube from the freezer. I rubbed it over my face.

Roger was still thinking about Sally. "We know lots of people who hate Joe but not Sally. Now we have someone who hates Sally, but does she even know Joe?"

"What we have is an entire theater full of weirdos," Paolo said. "And the weirdest is Olivia. Jealous wives I can understand, but that kid is just creepy."

I told them about the incident onstage that afternoon.

"But what would Olivia be doing onstage?" Roger asked.

"Please. That child is always lurking somewhere," I said.

"Face it, the kid is sick. Very, very sick," Paolo said, and he headed for the refrigerator. He pulled a beer off the shelf and tossed a Diet Coke to Roger.

"You drink too much of that stuff," I said to Roger.

"She's just way too smart for her age group," Roger said, ignoring me. "She'll grow into herself. Anyway, how do you know it wasn't your chorus boy?" He was trying to position the fan so that the air flow would cover as much of the living room as possible.

"She'll grow into an axe murderer," Paolo said. He was stripped down to a pair of running shorts. "*I'll* grow into an axe murderer if this weather doesn't break."

"Don't get too comfy with that fan. I'm taking it into my room."

"What kind of host are you?" Paolo was back in the fridge. "Is there anything to munch on in this place?"

"I thought I saw some olives," Roger said, shirtless now too. He poked his head into the fridge. The two of them were bent over, scrounging for food like a pair of cartoon characters, tossing takeout containers over their shoulders onto the table.

"Do you ever grocery shop?" Paolo came up for air with a plastic container. He lifted the lid and sniffed. "Oh my God. You think too much Diet Coke is bad, *this* will kill you."

"Only if I eat it. Children, children, if you must, there are chips in the cupboard. And would it be asking too much to have some of my own beer?"

"Demanding, isn't he?" Roger was opening the cupboards, searching for a bag of chips.

"Very." Paolo tossed me a can.

Roger was dumping chips into a bowl. "Is there any dip?"

"I can't even begin to see any reason why David would be involved in any of this," I said, thinking about the possibility of it having been him and not Olivia onstage that afternoon. "You know, Rog, I'm surprised you never suggested Olivia as the killer. She's fascinated with this sort of thing," I said.

"Oh, I thought of her."

Paolo stopped a chip in mid-dip. "Please tell me that's not true."

"No, I did. Really. But I eliminated her," Roger said.

"And why did you eliminate her, Inspector?" I asked.

"Come on, guys—she's only twelve." Roger was so absurdly sincere, Paolo and I crumpled with laughter.

"What? What did I say?" he asked.

"Nothing. Nothing at all. I'm going to bed," I said, still laughing.

"What's your rush? It's early," Paolo said. "There isn't any work to do tomorrow, is there?"

I unplugged the fan. The boys grunted protests through their chips and dip.

"No. There really isn't any work to do, but I've had enough fun for one day. Or is that one week?"

"You know," Roger said, swallowing as he spoke, "the message light is lit on your phone machine."

"Erase it." I left the room.

A minute later Roger knocked on my bedroom door.

"Nicky, you better come listen to this."

An hour later I was back on campus at the chapel. It would have been sooner, but the boys insisted that they come along to keep me safe. Which, when I thought about it, made a certain amount of sense. What really put us behind, though, was Paolo. "You cannot just wander into all that candlelight in the wrong outfit. *Trust* me on this," he insisted.

In the end we accumulated almost fifty extra minutes of trust along with baggy shorts, a white muscle T, and a string of small shells around Paolo's neck that were "guaranteed" to reflect well in candlelight. All of which meant that the newlyweds were waiting impatiently for us.

"Why aren't you alone?" Edward Rossoff challenged us as soon as we entered the chapel. He sounded nervous, fretful.

"Because people die at an unnatural rate on this campus, Edward," I said.

"Anyway, she isn't alone, is she?" Paolo challenged Edward right back.

On the way from my apartment, I had tried to impress on the guys that I wanted this encounter to be as nonconfrontational as possible. Apparently, I failed.

"That's enough. All of you." Mary Corinne sat very still. She was in the same pew we'd occupied the night before. Her voice was in sharp contrast to Edward's, resonating with assurance. Neither of them had changed since we'd seen them earlier in the evening. Despite her tone, she looked hot and weary in too much clothing. "Nicholas, sit with me, please. I want to talk with you alone."

"Mary Corinne, we're way past private chitchat," I said. "You want to say something to me, say it in front of all of us. And why do you keep insisting on meeting in this chapel?"

"You have a shitty attitude, D'Amico," Edward said.

"Edward, please. We're in chapel," Mary Corinne reprimanded him.

"You know, I may be the only non-Catholic present," Roger said, "but I don't think that's appropriate language for a church. Anyone mind if I sit down?" He headed for a pew but stopped himself. "Am I supposed to bless myself or something?"

"I doubt God minds too much," Mary Corinne said. "As for being here, I enjoy the peace of the chapel, Nicholas." She reeked of thoughtful earnestness.

I sighed. Did I really have the energy for this? I longed for one of those twelve-hour workdays that technical week usually brings. How simple the endless repetitive effort to make light and sound cues work. Certainly easier than indulging Mary Corinne's highly defined sense of theatrics. Once again, the chapel smelled lightly of incense. I wondered if she'd been burning it herself. The shimmering candlelight, the hard wooden pews, the statuary, the lapsed nun sitting in profile, the protective husband—all so much more interesting a tableau than we'd ever achieved onstage.

"Mary Corinne, I had a nice chat with Marty Friedman this morning," I said. "I know just how much you tried to restrain Joe Jr. Let's get down to the point, OK?"

She turned full face toward me. For a moment her eyes gleamed hard and flat in the flickering candlelight. I was glad that Paolo and Roger were with me.

Edward began, "I'm telling you, stop giving—"

"Edward, sit down," Mary Corinne snapped.

He sat.

"Marty Friedman is a liar. He has always been a liar. Even as a small child," she said.

"We don't believe you," Paolo said.

"Actually, I'm not so sure," Roger said. "I was thinking—"

"Roger, please," Paolo said, intentionally mimicking Mary Corinne.

I stood up. "It's way too late at night for this. I'm leaving."

"All right, then," Mary Corinne said. "So I didn't exactly restrain Joe Jr. Why should I? How was I to know it would turn out like this? I just can't let Benny Singleton get away with murder. I can't let him."

"Are you sure he killed Joe?" I asked.

"Yes."

"Which murder are we talking about here?" Paolo asked.

"Joe Sr.," I answered.

"Both," Mary Corinne said.

"Then I'll tell you the same thing I told Marty. If you have information, go to the police." I was beyond interested by this point. It seemed apparent to me that Mary Corinne had nothing useful or new to tell. She was just fishing for what we might know, looking for yet another avenue of attack on Benny.

"I told you, all I have are my suspicions," she said. "But I believe them. In my heart, in my soul, I believe that Benny Singleton killed those people."

"So do I," Roger piped up from his pew.

"Roger," I said, trying to quiet him.

243

"Sorry, Nicky, but I do. It makes complete sense. It's all about protecting himself."

"That's what I have been saying all along," Mary Corinne said, very excited now. She turned her attention on Roger. "I tried to convince Nicholas last night, but I failed. I'm so glad someone else understands."

"Well, I don't," Paolo said. "Nicky told us your story, and I don't buy this bullshit about the past and these murders being linked." He shook his head and stretched his arms along the back of his pew. "I don't buy the money thing, I don't see the connection to Sister Sally, and I don't see Benny Singleton killing anyone. Anyway, it was all years ago. It's old news."

"Yes," she said. "So long ago. We were barely more than children. 'When I was a child, I spoke like a child, I thought like a child, I reasoned like a child; when I became a man, I gave up childish ways.' That's First Corinthians, chapter 13, verse 11."

"I know the quote, thank you," Paolo sneered at her.

"Though we may have behaved recklessly, like children, we did it for love. Even now, all these years later, I can see that. Do you know what a person might do for love, young man?"

"Oh, now we're going to get all romantic," Paolo snapped back at her. "Yes, I do happen to know, thank you."

"Damn it, that is it," Edward said, on his feet again. "I will not have you treating her that way." He and Paolo started in on each other while Mary Corinne tried to quiet them. Roger looked on with a patience bred from years of watching Paolo fight anyone who condescended to him.

I stopped listening. I was thinking about something I'd heard Roger and Olivia talk about two days earlier. Something about the "penny-drop." They'd described that moment when the clouds clear, the fog lifts, and the detective suddenly understands. Paolo and Edward continued to argue, but all I heard was the sound of pennies dropping.

"Isn't that right? Isn't that right?" Paolo was talking to me. "Are you listening?"

I wasn't. I was thinking about embezzlement, about suicide and Bible quotes, about break-ins and poisons. I was thinking about Lee Dexter and what he saw when he left Sister Grace lying on the ground, about what Ilana Mosca had said to me earlier in the day, standing in the heat and humidity in the middle of campus. I was thinking about what people might do for love. Mostly, though, I was thinking about Sister Sally and why she was dead and how horrifyingly meaningless it all was.

"Let's go," I said.

"What? Where?" Roger asked.

"Just come on. We have to hurry." I stepped into the aisle. Roger and Paolo, confused but willing, moved to follow.

"You can't just go. You can't just leave." Mary Corinne anxiously tugged on my arm. "What's happening? Where are you going? You know something, don't you?"

"We're leaving," I said, pulling away from her. "I've had enough of both of you. Come on."

Roger, Paolo, and I headed out into the muggy night.

"Shit," Edward said.

"Please, Edward," she responded, just loud enough for us to hear as the chapel doors closed behind us.

Outside I hurried us through the soupy night air toward the theater. No one was in sight. The vigil must have been ended, the protesters long gone. With the show closed, why bother? They probably assumed no one would be at the theater so late.

"What is going on?" Paolo wanted to know.

"I think I know what's been happening. I think I know who did it and why. Even Sister Sally," I answered.

"And what, we're going to go make a citizen's arrest?" Paolo asked. "Slow down, Nicky."

Roger was smiling. "This is exciting."

If I didn't think that we were probably already too late, I would have stopped and lectured him on reality versus TV mysteries. Instead I said, "We're going to find the yellow raincoat, if it's not too late."

We were coming up on the fountain in front of McNally Hall. On our side of the water, away from the theater, we were still in darkness. Dim light from the auditorium lobby spilled into the plaza beyond.

Paolo came to a standstill. "That's it. Stop right here," he said. "Where are you taking us?"

"Onstage," I said.

"Watch out," Paolo said. "There's Singleton." He pointed to the far side of the plaza, where Benny Singleton was just coming into view. Instinctively, Paolo and I dropped to our knees behind the skirt of the fountain. I grabbed Roger and pulled him down after us. A rush of adrenaline raced through my body, wrapping me in sweat.

"Shit," I said.

"Edward, please," Paolo said, mimicking Mary Corinne and snickering.

I whacked him on the shoulder.

Roger was bouncing with excitement. "I knew it was him. I just knew it."

Benny looked around as he headed for the lobby doors. He didn't see us. Using his passkey, he entered the building. We could see him cross the partially lit lobby, moving in the general direction of his office. He disappeared from view.

"Come on." I was on my feet and running. If what I was thinking was true, we'd have to stay close to prevent him from destroying an important piece of evidence.

One quick glance through the glass doors assured me that Benny was not in the lobby. I used my passkey. We followed his path, moving cautiously toward the hallway. We passed the theater doors. I carefully inched my way around the wall so that I could just see the length of the long, dark corridor. Light spilled out of the open door of Benny's office. I pulled back and whispered to the boys, "He's in his office."

"Shouldn't we call the police?" Roger asked.

"And tell them what? That Benny Singleton is working late? I don't think that's a crime," I said.

"They haven't seen him direct," Paolo added.

We were scrunched together, front to back. Roger was behind me, his hands on my shoulders. Paolo hunched behind him.

"Sssshhhh," I hissed. "We have to get onstage, and fast. If I'm right, he's not going to find what he's looking for in his office."

"What's he looking for?" Roger asked.

"I told you, the raincoat. Look, Paolo and I will go into the theater. Roger, you stay here and watch Benny. If I'm wrong and he leaves with it, follow him. Don't lose track of it."

"No sweat," Roger said.

"And nothing stupid, OK?" I said.

"I resent that."

"Just pay attention to it. I don't like this," Paolo said. He was looking at Roger with serious concern.

"Paolo, I'm not going to get near him. I promise."

"Come on. Let's go." I led Paolo away from the hallway to the nearest theater entrance. Just before we passed inside, he looked back at Roger, who was crouched down, peering around the corner toward Benny's office.

247

"Wait a minute," Paolo whispered to me, then scurried back across the lobby. I saw him bend over Roger and say something in his lover's ear. Roger looked up and smiled at him. They kissed. Paolo trotted back. "All set."

I was grateful that I'd left the ghost light on earlier in the day. We would never have made it onto the stage in anything under fifteen minutes otherwise. I headed directly for center stage. Standing still, I slowly surveyed the space.

"So what are we supposed to do now?" Paolo asked.

"We're looking for the raincoat."

"Where?"

"Somewhere. It's got to be somewhere around here," I said.

Paolo surveyed the stage setting. "Jesus, Nicky. It's a theater. There are a hundred places to hide something."

He was right. When I'd been onstage earlier, I'd looked to see if anything had been disturbed. The entire set was in disarray. I saw it all again, the furniture tossed around, the coffee table out of place, the teacups. The difference was that this time I was deliberately looking for a hiding place.

"Just start looking," I said. "It could be anywhere."

Paolo shrugged and walked into the wings. I heard him rummaging about. I started with the seat cushions. Nothing underneath any of them. Not much of a hiding place anyway. The bookcases turned up nothing. This could go on till dawn. I leaned against the fireplace unit and tried to think. Where would I go first if I wanted to hide something onstage? The only piece of scenery with any depth was the fireplace. I bent over and tried to reach up into what would have been the flue in a real fireplace. There was none, just a thin piece of wood probably placed there to stabilize the upper part of the unit. Like all scenery, the fireplace looked good from a distance but was nothing more than a fancy mockup. I stood up. The entire day room set was nothing but theatrical sleight of hand. Close up, you could see the glue and staples, the faux texturing, and the stretched canvas.

Paolo came back onstage.

"Nicky, this is ridiculous. This place is chaos. And it's too dark."

Chaos. Chaos meant disorder. But something I'd seen didn't fit that. I turned and looked at the mantle again. Those teacups, all lined up so very neatly. In front of the fireplace was the coffee table. That would make sense too.

"Here, help me," I said as I began to pick up the teacups. "Take these."

We quickly cleared the mantle.

"Now." I reached out and lifted the top off the mantle. It came away easily. Why not? That made sense. It wasn't meant to support much weight or hold up a wall. In the theater you don't waste material nailing down something that never moves.

I reached into the hollow space between the back wall and the front of the fireplace. I pulled out a yellow plastic raincoat. I looked inside. A dark wig sat bunched up in a corner. No doubt it was red in full light.

"Damn. You did it," Paolo said. "So, what? Benny hid it there?"

"Benny? Are you kidding? Look at this thing." I held it up for Paolo to get a clear view.

"Yeah, so?"

"This is pretty." Benny Singleton himself was standing at the edge of the light cast by the ghost. "Are we having a fashion show?" His glasses glinted. Deep shadows on his face made his cheeks and nose stand out, obscuring his expression. We'd been so absorbed, we hadn't heard him enter the wing. Where was Roger? "What are you doing here?" he asked.

Paolo went on the offensive. "Us? What are *you* doing here?"

"Me? I'm saying good-bye to my show. You don't work in the the-ater, but Nicky does. He can tell you how depressing this is. But how odd to find you here with that raincoat. Are we expecting bad weather?"

"It won't work, Benny," I said. For a long moment he and I stood looking eye to eye. There wasn't a sound in the theater. He spoke first.

"What won't work, Nicky? Your alibi? Oh yes. You're going to need one, I think. What won't Corporal Roberts make of this? Especially since your friend is already implicated in the tea poisoning. I think you're in big trouble."

Just then Roger came running down the aisle. "Nicky, he's headed this way—oh." He stopped when he saw Benny.

"Lost me? Am I under surveillance?" Benny asked.

"Sorry, Nicky," Roger said.

"It's OK, Roger. I didn't expect him, either. What tipped you off, Benny? Or are you just guessing?" I said.

"Nice try, but I don't think so." Benny was smirking. "You're in big trouble. All three of you."

I'd underestimated him. It took a cool head to stand there and try to convince us that we were the ones in trouble. I nodded in appreciation.

"No way," I said. "None of us have a motive. Paolo and Roger don't even have means for the first murder. There is no way this can be pinned on us. The show is over, Benny. Face it."

"I'd have to agree, Benny." We turned as one in the direction of the voice coming out of the dark. Corporal Roberts and a trooper stepped into the circle of light. "I'd heard that theater people kept ir-regular hours, but I had no idea how irregular."

Benny opened his mouth as if to speak, then apparently thought better of it.

"What are you doing here?" Paolo asked.

"No, Mr. Suarez. You have it backwards. In murder investigations, it's the police who ask the questions. You didn't think you'd actually get to the solution before us, did you? We've been watching Benny all day. And all of you for the last thirty minutes. You three have some explaining to do." He turned toward Benny. "As for you. Benjamin Singleton, you are under arrest for the murder of Joseph Sobieski Jr. You have the right to remain silent. If . . ."

I couldn't believe it. They had it all wrong. What was I going to do?

Impulsively, in one quick move, I put the raincoat on.

". . . will be appointed for—" Corporal Roberts stopped his recitation of Benny's rights. "What the hell are you doing?"

"Look at me," I said, buttoning up the raincoat. "Does this make any sense to you?"

"Nothing about you makes any sense to me. Get that thing off him," Roberts ordered his trooper.

"Wait. Look at this."

"Really, Nicky, if you need a raincoat . . . ," Paolo said.

"Damn it. This is not funny. I have a thirty-inch waist. This coat barely fits around me. There is no way Benny Singleton ever wore this coat. Why the hell, then, is he here trying to find it?" I was shouting at them.

The corporal looked at me. Then he looked at Benny. Then once more at me.

"I wasn't looking for a raincoat," Benny said.

"Then what are you looking for, Benny? What's in your office that you need so badly you have to come here at midnight?" I kept pushing, one eye on the corporal. I sensed he was hesitating, wondering what I was getting at.

I'll never know in fact what Benny was thinking, but I imagine he too was watching the corporal closely.

"You've arrested me. Let's go. I want to speak to my lawyer," was Benny's response.

"I don't get this, Nicky. Everything points to Benny," Paolo objected. "He was protecting himself."

Just then she appeared stage right. As usual, we'd none of us heard her coming, but there she was, an open can of Diet Coke in her hand. In the half-light she looked either demonic or innocent, depending on what you were expecting. Paolo just stared, his eyes growing wider.

"Oh my God. Protecting Benny," he said.

"Hey. What's everyone doing here?" Olivia asked.

"Livy, honey, go home. Now," Benny said.

"But I want to know what's going on. Anyway, you have to come too, Daddy."

Benny's composure began to crack. "Not just now, Olivia. Go home."

"Is anyone thirsty? I brought some Diet Coke." She held up the open can. "You like Diet Coke, don't you, Roger?"

"Well, yeah." Roger shrugged his shoulders.

"No." Paolo moved swiftly to grab Roger and pull him back. He held his arms around Roger, hugging his lover's back to his chest. "Roger," Paolo whispered in his ear, squeezing him harder.

"Jesus, babe," Roger said over his shoulder. "I wasn't going to drink—" Roger's focus snapped back to Olivia. "Damn."

"I'm thirsty, even if no one else is. I'm not going to waste this." Olivia raised the can to her lips.

I wouldn't have credited Benny with being that fast. Before any of the rest of us could react, he'd knocked the drink from Olivia's hand. Soda flew in all directions as the can spun off toward the front of the house. He engulfed Olivia in his arms, smothering her in his embrace.

"Livy. Livy." He said her name over and over.

"Daddy, not so hard. It was only soda. I'm not stupid."

Benny was crying. Sobbing into his daughter's hair. The rest of us stood immobilized at the sight. Finally, he looked up. His face was contorted with tears and pain. His eyes darted about as if searching for some way out, even as he held his daughter so tightly she could barely move.

"We'll leave," he said. "We'll go away. That's what Dexter wants. No one has to know. She's a child."

"Benny," I said, surprising myself with the gentleness of my tone. "Benny, it's not going to change. It doesn't matter where you go."

He looked at the corporal.

"Couldn't we . . . she's so young . . . just a child." He broke down completely.

EIGHTEEN

"So you're saying there was no crime?" Patsy was carefully spreading apricot jam on a toasted bagel.

"Well, no embezzlement. I guess what Benny did was a crime. I mean, you can't just fake financial records, can you?" I asked, but not of anyone in particular. No one had an answer.

Patsy, Mary Frances, the boys, and I were crowded around the table in my apartment having a late brunch of bagels, juice, and coffee—what Paolo was calling the "first civilized meal I've had all week."

It had been another late night after Olivia's arrest. The three of us hadn't returned to my place until well after five in the morning. I went directly to bed, where I would probably still have been if Patsy and Mary Frances hadn't shown up with bagels and juice. Roger pounded on my door at eleven. Paolo put on the coffee. By the time I made it to the table, they were wide awake and full of questions.

Now I was trying to make a logical narrative out of what was really an intuitive guess.

"You have to admit, though, it was pretty good thinking on Benny's part." I carved a chunk out of the cream cheese and started smearing it on my bagel.

"I am so totally lost here. What exactly did Benny do?" Mary Frances asked.

"Mostly he mismanaged his job," I answered. "He ran the theater and the department into the ground. But he was young, had a family, and panicked at the thought of losing his job."

Paolo finished the thought. "So he took advantage of his business manager's death and blamed the money trouble on Joe Sr."

"That's it. That is the sum total of the crime twenty years ago. And probably would have been the end of the story except for Mary Corinne, a woman with a truly vengeful memory." I sipped my coffee and wondered what would become of her now. She'd committed no crime, but her desire for revenge had been the original impetus in the chain of events resulting in Sister Sally and Joe Jr.'s murders. I wouldn't want to have to sleep with her conscience.

"I still don't see how you got to Olivia," Roger said. Skipping orange juice, he was already at work on the first Diet Coke of the day.

"You know," Mary Frances said, pointing to his soda can, "that stuff will kill you."

"Almost did," Paolo said.

"I wasn't going to drink it. I was just answering her question," Roger said without any trace of annoyance. The reconciliation between him and Paolo was complete; all infidelities—real and imagined—were forgiven. If the two of them tried to get much closer, one of them would have to be on the other's lap. Soon they'd start buttering each other's bagels.

"Now tell me how you knew it was Olivia," Roger insisted.

"I'll try," I said. "You know we were all having trouble fitting the pieces together. It seemed to me there were too many different story lines. The only motive that tied Sister Sally and Joe together would have been trying to sabotage *Convent of Fear*. But that seemed pretty weak to all of us, right?"

Everyone nodded their heads in agreement.

"But then there was the break-in and the bicyclist, which seemed to give that idea more credence."

Again, agreement.

"But when we found out that the break-in had to do with Benny and Joe, everything got turned around. Now it was just as reasonable to assume Joe was killed because of some event twenty years ago as it was to assume that anyone would actually commit murder to shut down a piece of theater."

"I'm glad I brought extra juice," Patsy said, refilling glasses. "This is going to take a while, isn't it?"

"OK, OK," I said. "Nothing made sense, but the strongest possibility was that Benny was doing this to protect himself. Then, in the chapel, Mary Corinne said, 'When I was a child, I thought like a child, I reasoned like a child.' "

"Corinthians," Patsy said.

"Very impressive," Mary Frances said, snuggling her face into Patsy's hair. I was surrounded by partnered bliss.

"Exactly." I ignored them. "Then she said it had all been for love. That's when I remembered what Ilana had said earlier that day, about how it all seemed like a childish nightmare. When she said that, I was watching Olivia watching her father. One thought led to another, and I realized that if I dropped the idea of someone killing people to close the show, which I never liked anyway, then everything had to be about protecting Benny."

"But murder is a lot worse than cooking the books. It doesn't make any sense to trade the one for the other," Mary Frances said.

"Of course not," I said, "unless you were completely immersed in your own fantasies about how the adult world worked. Fantasies you got through too many mysteries. And if you were getting all your info by listening to only half the conversations and making the rest up yourself, like if you were a child eavesdropping.

"Imagine it this way. Mary Corinne puts it into Joe Jr.'s head that Benny needs to be exposed. Joe starts talking to Marty about it. He starts in on Benny about it. Olivia, always hanging around, always listening, overhears all this—or more likely a part of several conversations—and filters it through her overactive imagination. She hasn't got the adult sense to see the risk is all out of proportion. We do—did—and that's what confused us."

"And when you add that to her obsession with Daddy . . . ," Paolo said. He just shuddered and closed the remaining eighth-of-an-inch gap between him and Roger.

"God, how can you do that in this heat?" I asked.

"Oh come, Nicky, not even you can have forgotten why I'd do this?" Paolo laughed, kissing Roger full on the mouth.

"Ignore them, Nicky," Mary Frances said. "You're the hero today. You're allowed to be bitter. Tell the rest of it."

I was not comforted.

"Yeah, OK. So she rides to Daddy's rescue. She used what was readily available. Bug poison, a raincoat and wig, maybe some old Halloween costume, and her father's heart medicine. It was all supposed to look like an attack on *Convent of Fear*. But we were never comfortable with that, because again, it was all out of proportion. Just a kid's fantasy come to life."

"Wait a minute," Paolo said. "She killed Sally just to confuse everyone? That seems like some fairly serious planning for a kid."

"No, she didn't. And that's the worst of it, I think. She didn't plan to kill Sally. Olivia dusted the cross that was backstage. Joe'd been wearing his costume for days. She expected him to use that cross. Instead, Sally decided to start rehearsing in her costume and just picked up the cross before Joe could. Sally's death was never part of the plan."

"Poor Sally. And you thought of all of this sitting in that chapel?" Patsy looked a bit skeptical.

"Well, I thought that maybe Olivia might be an explanation, and then I thought about that incident onstage yesterday afternoon. I couldn't think of any reason for David to be onstage." I must have sighed. Certainly, I thought about that missed opportunity now that there was nothing to keep me in Huber's Landing. How could I forget, with the love quadruplets practically licking cream cheese and jam off each other?

Mary Frances looked very sympathetic. "New York is a big city, Nicky. I wouldn't worry about one that got away," she said.

I had my usual response to the sympathy of the attached toward the single: I ignored it.

"Anyway," I continued, "Lee Dexter chased the bicyclist and saw enough to convince him it was Olivia. That would explain his behavior toward Benny outside Old Main. She must have had her costume someplace where she thought Benny would easily find it if he looked. Lee spooked her into changing hiding places. She chose the stage. Benny did look, but he couldn't find it at home, so he went to the next logical place, McNally Hall."

"OK, wait." This from Roger, who was not going to let go until I had completely proven my case. "This whole business of going overboard to protect Benny. You have to admit, it could just as well have been Ilana Mosca. She's in love with him."

"True, but Ilana never believed that Benny was anything but innocent twenty years ago. As far as she was concerned, it didn't matter where Joe Jr. or anyone else poked around. They were never going to find anything on Benny."

"Sounds like a lot of good guesswork," Roger said.

Patsy decided to defend me. "I like it. It makes sense. And it's right, so who's to argue?"

"You are shameless, lover," Paolo said. "You're just disappointed you didn't figure it out first." He poked Roger in the side, then kissed him again. The kiss extended beyond a momentary lip lock and looked to be headed all the way into really poor table manners.

Patsy interrupted. "OK. It's late. Let's get going." She jumped to her feet.

"Late for what?" I asked.

Roger looked up from Paolo's embrace. "Oh, well, we have a plan," he said.

"Yeah," said Mary Frances. "We're going to the lake for the afternoon. Sort of picnicking, you know."

"Oh. I thought maybe if we got packed right away we could actually be in the city for dinner at LuLu's tonight," I said to the guys.

Paolo was on his feet now as well. "What, and not see any of this beautiful scenery? I've spent four days in a theater. I want to see the countryside before I head back to Manhattan."

"What are you talking about? You hate the countryside," I said.

"Don't be tedious, Nicky," Paolo said. "We're going to the lake. I'm sure you can think of something to busy yourself with."

"You mean I'm not invited?"

"Well, it *is* kind of a couples thing," Mary Frances said. "I mean, you don't want to hang out watching the four of us being all romantic all day, do you?" She made a face to suggest that this was probably the worst way I could spend an afternoon.

All four of them were on their feet and in motion. The guys were searching for their sunglasses. Patsy was tucking the OJ back in her bag.

"You know, in case we get thirsty," she said.

"We'll have to stop and get some munchies. Nicky, do you have a blanket?" Paolo asked.

"I am not lending you—"

"Look, Nicky," Roger said. "You must have something to get done at the theater before you leave. This is your chance, and then tomorrow we can head back to New York, right?" He looked to Paolo.

"Right. I'd say that's a great plan," Paolo agreed.

In five minutes, and despite my protests, they were all gone. So much for being the hero of the moment. I put on some music and started to clean up.

Not more than twenty minutes after they left, there was a knock on my door.

"Go away," I yelled. "I don't care what you forgot, I'm not letting you in. You're evil and I hate you all."

I turned up the music.

After a moment there was another knock. Someone tried to make themselves understood over the sound of my CD player. After more knocking I relented. Turning the sound down, I walked over to the door, but I didn't open it.

"All right. What did you forget? And why should I care?" I asked.

"Nicky? Is that you?" David Scott asked from the outside hallway.

I quickly opened the door.

"Hi," I said.

"Hi. Am I that late?" He was standing in front of me holding a carton of orange juice. He looked confused. It was a good look for him.

"Late?"

260

"Patsy called me this morning and said be here at twelve-thirty for brunch. I'm sorry I'm late."

Patsy Malone was the finest assistant a stage manager ever had. I adored her. I adored them all.

"Come in," I said to him. "Come in. You're not late at all."

ACKNOWLEDGEMENTS

To get the details correct, I had the excellent advice of Dr. Alan Baldridge of St. Christopher's Hospital for Children in Philadelphia and the research skills of D. Seth Cardwell of Legworks, NY. If I'm wrong on the facts, you can be certain the error is mine, not theirs.

My thanks to Rich Newman, Peter Graziola, Steve Monaghan, Warren Mouradian, Leslie Smith, Paul Harris, Stephen Irwin, Chris Strauss, Mike Campbell, and many many Zitos (Tony, Pat, Mark, Karen, and Chris), each of whom offered encouragement along the way. Angela Zito and Maxine Kalkut-Knox were particularly generous in reading every draft. And Todd Lind, computer maven, is just about the best friend a guy could have.

My gratitude to my editors at Midnight Ink, Barbara Moore and Wade Ostrowski, for taking the chance on a first novel, and to my agent, Alison Picard, for ushering Nicky into the daylight.

Read on for an excerpt from the
next Nicky D'Amico Mystery by Chuck Zito

Ice in His Veins

COMING SOON FROM MIDNIGHT INK

SATURDAY EVENING

"The neighbor, Maria Cepedes, also saw ..."

"... the face of ..."

"... John the Baptist ..."

"... in the recently purchased chunk of ..."

"... chunk of bleu cheese."

"Give the words space," the director coached the actors.

The first actor, the one who'd begun the exercise, stretched his neck from side to side and then raised and lowered his shoulders. The other looked at his watch.

"Chunk of bleu cheese."

"Mrs. Hagida is a member of ..."

"... Mary, Queen of the ..."

"Attitude," the director coached.

"... Universe Catholic Church in ..."

"... Kew Gardens, Queens."

"My cheese is very ..."

"... ordinary ..."

"See the cheese, guys. Share the cheese."

". . . said Mrs. Cepedes."

"It makes me . . ."

". . . sad. I never see . . ."

". . . saints."

"Give and take," the director said.

"Church officials would not . . ."

". . . comment . . ."

". . . on the sighting other than to say . . ."

"Color the words." The director spoke quietly as the actors continued.

". . . that . . ."

". . . they were studying the event."

"Share."

Alex Isola, the actor with the stiff neck, tapped his foot rapidly on the stage floor. He picked up the thread of the news article.

"Mrs. Hagida charges one dollar per viewing . . ."

"You know, she could have got a lot more if she'd been smart enough to see Christ himself," his partner interrupted, speaking to the theater house as if it were filled with an opening-night audience.

"Stick to the words, Herb," Marcus patiently urged.

"Of course." Herb sighed. "The text. The holy text."

Alex pushed away from the folding table center stage. "What is the point of doing this with him?"

"The point of the exercise, Alex—," Marcus Bradshaw started to explain.

"Thank you, I know the point of the exercise. I was in class with you when you learned it. But what is the point of doing it with *him*?"

The exercise was over.

Thick black curtains hung along the back and side walls of the claustrophobic stage space, absorbing most of the fluorescent work light and leaving the two seated actors and the director standing next to the curtains in a dingy, brownish yellow glow. Newspaper clippings were scattered across the table. I served as the lone audience member in the theater. The house lights were at half strength. Their diffuse, incandescent glow cast dull shadows over the construction material stored among the empty seats. In the dim light, the red leatherette seat cushions appeared the same dull brown color that washed the stage. The only sound in the entire space was the whirring of the overhead ventilation fans.

I was huddled in the first row, a stage manager waiting to set up rehearsal. As the tension gathered onstage, I deliberately looked away, doing my best impression of professionalism: detached, neither encouraging nor condemning the participants in the exercise. If we'd been in rehearsal, I would have glared back with disapproval. Keeping order was part of my job, but this was a director's exercise, so I gazed meditatively at a shining red exit sign.

We were in a renovated microbrewery on Greene Street in SoHo in New York City. The entire building was known as the Brewery. The Tapestry Playhouse, with its ninety-nine seats and a stage the size of a suburban living room, occupied the first and second floors. The theater itself was on the first floor, a rehearsal space and dressing room on the second. Above the playhouse were three floors of artists' studios. A lobby served as both box office and art gallery. Aside from nearly a dozen visual artists, the Brewery housed four resident theater companies. With only two weeks to go until opening, our group, the Good Company, had exclusive use of the stage for the next fourteen days.

At the moment our use was being derailed by Herbert Wilcox, downtown drag-queen diva, better known to adoring fans in small East Village bars as "Anita Nutha." Today Herb was out of drag but not attitude. He stood six feet three inches, thin in a way that could only be genetic or the result of a lettuce diet. Glaring down at Alex, still seated, Herb gave an exaggerated Delsarte rendition of indignation—head back, one hand on his chest, the other thrust forward.

"Doing it with me? With me? As if I would do *it* with someone like you." He left Alex and Marcus center, crossing downstage to ask me, "How did you do it, Nicky? How did you manage day after day, week after week, month after month, year after year, decade after decade with these people?"

"It was only four years, Herb," I said.

Marcus looked a bit offended. "That's not exactly a positive response."

"Yeah, Nicky. Couldn't you have said something more supportive? Like, 'It was really my pleasure'?" Alex asked.

Herb winked at me and then spun around to confront Alex. "That's all you think about, isn't it, Prep Boy? Your pleasure. Well, I've had enough of trying to please you."

He stepped off the low rise of the stage into the front row of the house, an opening neither deep enough nor wide enough to be called an orchestra pit. "I'll be in the lobby when you're ready to rehearse."

Herb was barely out of the back of the house before Marcus started laughing.

"You only encourage him when you do that," Alex said.

"But he's funny."

"Don't be so earnest, Alex," I added.

"How come he stomps out of here and I am the one at whom fun is being poked?"

"Oh, Alex, Alex," Marcus said. "We promise. Even though you are obsessive about not dangling your prepositions and actually say things like 'at whom fun is being poked,' we will always adore you and always take your side against evil drag queens, no matter how funny they are." Marcus wrapped Alex in one of his trademark all-embracing, heart-thumping hugs, the sort of hug known to make strong men weak and weak boys faint. I should know.

The first time Marcus Bradshaw kissed me was the Friday evening of our first week as drama students at Baldwin University in Philadelphia. We were on a bench slipped into one of the many parklets dotting the campus. This parklet was a sunken flagstone area, tree-lined with a small semicircular fountain at its center. The perimeter was lit with wrought-iron faux streetlamps. Wooden benches sat next to each lamp. It was, in fact, a small, nondescript bit of concrete with some very nice trees around it. To me, eighteen years old and in a large city for the first time, it was a magical space, instilling a combination of newfound urban freedom laced with an old-fashioned hunger that Marcus, with the aid of a bottle of Jack Daniels, was more than happy to fill. He (with my happy acquiescence) had been marching us toward that kiss from the moment we met at convocation the previous Monday.

That day, onstage at a podium surrounded by the faculty of the school, the department chairman greeted the new term. Decades of tradition ordered our place in the auditorium. As first-year students we were sitting down front, eagerly leaning forward, sponging up every detail of the auditorium. The second years were just behind us, excited, talking to each other, loudly wrapped up in their post-summer-break reunion. The third and fourth years filled in behind them, slouching, school-weary and affecting an exquisitely cultivated state of practiced detachment. The details we saw from our seats in the front showed very clearly the effect of years of benign neglect that even a nationally ranked theater conservatory can suffer. The little signs of corner-cutting were all around us: theater seats just a few years past time for replacement; a fresh coat of paint over a wall instead of a real repair job; a floor mopped clean but overdue for refinishing. And that was just my visual impression. I was completely unversed in the technological inadequacies to come. Still, it was my first time away from home and my first day of theater school. It would be months before that first wave of exhilaration ebbed.

The chairman, a towering figure with a booming voice and two Tonys in his past, keenly aware of his school's outstanding reputation as well as its declining physical state, was performing a well-rehearsed dissembling for our benefit.

"Wealth stifles creativity at a young age. We must look toward the creativity of the mind, as it is challenged by the limits of physical space. Your time here at Baldwin will be one free of the constraints of commercialism. Here, let inspiration spread its wings, free of care for the material world."

"Why do I have the feeling we're going to be very 'free' here?"

I jerked in my seat. The voice came from over my left shoulder, whispering directly into my ear. I turned my head, trying not to draw the attention of the chairman three rows away, and slid my eyes tightly to one side. In that way I got my first glimpse of Marcus. After whispering to me he'd settled back in his seat, looking completely relaxed, as if he'd hadn't moved since the speech started. But that was Marcus. He was certain and gregarious. All that I saw of him in that first constrained peek was a swatch of black hair, one blue eye, half a mouth, a great chin, and the collar of what I assumed was a button-down cotton shirt. I happily filled in the missing details. He grinned at me. I sighed. The girl sitting next to me, whom I had not yet met, poked me with her elbow.

"Slut," she said with a dry good humor. I smiled as I blushed.

The opening-day festivities continued with multiple exhortations to creative frenzy by the chair and each of the heads of the acting, directing, and design options. When it was over, my two new acquaintances and I filed out of the auditorium together. She introduced herself as Anna Mikasa, from Long Island. Marcus was from Boston. They spoke with regional accents not yet wiped out by voice and speech training. Anna talked fast: Philadelphia was nice, but not New York, which she casually referred to as "the city." She'd seen almost everything on and off Broadway in the last four seasons. Marcus, strolling easily through the sunny September afternoon, just kept smiling at me. As we headed to a student café in the basement of a building on the quad outside the theater, I listened to Anna as if she were an exotic bird.

Now that he was in full view, I was completely smitten. Marcus was taller than me by about two inches, but that was not unusual: I'm only five foot seven, so most men I meet are taller than me. His skin was pale while mine was a Sicilian olive tone; he was solid where I was slight. But mostly he was beautiful and he seemed interested in me. It was my fourth day away from home. I was from a small town on the Ohio-Pennsylvania border where this sort of thing never happened. Not to me.

We collected our soda, chips, and sandwiches and headed back outside. Sitting at a metal table on a flagstone patio, I focused my attention on the familiar act of eating. I slowly let go of some of the anxiety I'd hauled all the way across the Appalachian Mountains, which separated my hometown from Philadelphia.

Philly in early September can be a wondrous place. After the August heat and humidity have broken, the city seems crisp and breezy. Unfortunately, that particular September was just an extension of August. It was eighty-seven degrees in the shade, and we were nowhere near the shade. We sat looking out on a large rectangular quad of well-tended, vivid green grass overrun by Frisbee players and lounging students. The trees, and there were plenty, were tucked in close to the buildings. None of them bordered the stone terrace.

We ate and sweltered amidst what to me looked to be the most beautiful arrangement of buildings I'd ever seen. It would not be until a few years later that I learned the names of the various architectural details surrounding me. Eventually I would come to identify the large, peaked dormers and the windows with names like oriel as hallmarks of the Tudor style. The campus was a mix of modified Tudor and Gothic Revival. There were ornate sculptural details trimming the stone bay windows, whose boxlike structure was so different from the traditional New England bay window I'd seen attached to any number of suburban houses back home. The occasional mansard roof broke the style, but still, no matter how adventurous the various architects had been, in the end the overall look of the campus was tied together by the countless small panes of glass and thin mullions that fronted every structure.

Marcus contrived an excellent parody of the department chair. "Your time here at Baldwin will be free of constraints. We will not provide you with costumes or scripts. We believe in the imagination. We shall not even give you a stage."

"Please," I said, wiping my forehead with a napkin. "It's too humid to laugh."

"I need something colder to drink," Marcus said.

Anna stood up, fixing her sharp gaze directly on both of us. Physically she was small. Not just thin or short, but small, close to the ground with miniaturized features that seemed to defy function. She was dark, with deep brown hair and eyes and a brooding color to her that accentuated the compactness of her frame. Her physical presence contrasted sharply with what I came to know as an intensely emotional and dynamic persona.

"No, that's not what you need. You know what we really need?" she asked.

"Portable fans?" I answered.

"A party. It's our first week together. We need a party. We need to bond. Friday night."

That was on Monday. On Wednesday Marcus and I had dinner—alone. It was nothing elaborate. We'd neither of us had much cash on hand. He took me to a place he'd heard of just off campus called Lily's, a restaurant with a menu full of brown rice and vegetables and a garden in the back trimmed in white Christmas lights.

Unlike most of the entering class, myself included, Marcus lived off campus with a roommate, another drama student he'd located through Student Services.

"I'm a transfer student. There's about ten of us. The university has a housing shortage anyway, so they let us out of the first-year dorm requirement. Alex is one too. He's a first year like us. An actor. Quiet type. Well, you'll meet him. You'll see."

I was pouring something called ginger-celery dressing on my salad and trying to decide if I really wanted to eat anything so liquidly green. I bit into a leaf.

"Hey, this is good," I said.

Marcus laughed. "What did they feed you at home?"

"Either chicken or things with red sauce on them."

The rest of the meal was more of the same: me oohing at food I'd never eaten, not even realizing I was near the bottom of Philly's culinary ladder, while Marcus and I swapped stories. By the end of the meal I was able to add infatuation to lust.

On Thursday we hooked up for breakfast before our first class.

"So, did you have cows?"

"Cows?" I chewed on my cereal.

"Cows. On the farm. You didn't have cows on the farm?"

Marcus was eating lox on a bagel. I'd heard of both but had never encountered either. The lox were a strange dull shade of orange that Marcus insisted was the proper color. He'd wanted me to try them, but my morning corn flakes offered too much comfort.

"I didn't grow up on a farm. I grew up in the suburbs."

"Mmm. That's not very exciting. Try this: I grew up on a farm that my grandparents passed on to my parents. They've kept it running despite the rising cost of feed and fertilizer, and they want to pass it along to me and my five brothers, but I don't want anything to do with farming, and my disinterest has caused a great deal of family drama."

"My grandparents were Italian immigrants."

Marcus waved his bagel in the air, "What, immigrants don't farm? OK, how's this: My grandparents ran an illegal immigration scam all through the thirties, helping poor, undocumented Italians slip into the U.S. from across the Canadian border, hidden in sausage crates."

I was laughing. Marcus did that to me. Even later, when the fan was splattered by the proverbial shit, he made me laugh.

"Oh, there he is. That's Alex coming down the steps now. My roommate." Marcus waved and got his roommate's attention.

As he came toward us, I could see that he was just about the same size as Marcus.

"Alex, this is Nicky D'Amico. His grandfather was a bootlegger." Marcus tossed this out as if every third grandfather was a bootlegger.

"Actually, one grandfather was a cobbler, the other a steelworker."

Alex was a bit more formal than either of us. He stuck his hand out. "Alex Isola. I'd rather not talk about my grandfather."

"OK," was all the response I could manage to that comment.

And that was all that Alex said in the five minutes until he left, at which point he said, "Later."

"Doesn't say much, does he?" I asked.

"Well, I don't know. We hardly ever talk." Marcus laughed uncontrollably at his joke.

Friday night we met up before going to Anna's party, which she had somehow arranged to host at another classmate's apartment. The humidity had broken midweek. The night was a perfect September evening—warm but not hot. We were sitting on that bench by the semicircular fountain, this time sharing the fifth of Jack Daniels that Marcus was BYOB'ing for the evening. Overhead, coral-colored clouds evidenced the setting sun we could not see beyond the campus skyline. The sunset gave way to what passed for a brilliant city night sky— three stars and no haze.

"Toast," he said, after I do not know how many rounds of slugging it straight from the bottle.

"No toast," I yelled. "Bagels! Bagels from here on out. I'm in the big city now."

"No, no. Not *just* toast. *A* toast. *A* toast." He put his arm around my shoulder, explaining to me the heartfelt and deep, deep distinction between recooked bread and the exchange of civilities over liquor. "Toast is for . . . for breakfast. *A* toast is for . . . forever!"

"Forever!" I tipped the bottle once more.

"A toast." He held the fifth up. I caught sight of the lamplight refracted through the amber liquid, of Marcus momentarily silhouetted against the glimmer of the multipane window of a nearby dorm.

"Toast," I repeated.

"To us." He swigged.

"To us." I swigged.

He kissed me. And again. We were late to the party. We left it early.

Now, seven years later, we were at the Tapestry Theater and Marcus was turning all that charm and energy directly on Alex.

"Marcus, you cannot possibly defend him," Alex said.

"I'm not defending him. I'm just saying he's funny."

I was fairly certain that Alex had never kissed Marcus while we were at school. I couldn't say whether or not he'd wanted to. I can say that Alex didn't pull away from Marcus's embrace. And for just a moment, I thought I caught a vibe that was a bit more than "former roommates and friends." The moment passed. I pushed the thought aside.

They were built to match: solid, lean men, the kind of man whose embrace is strong and secure. Alex had the same black hair and blue eyes as Marcus. If you didn't know them, you might confuse them. If you did, you would never mistake them. Marcus retained the easy, open manner he had on the day I'd met him. Alex, though he'd shed much of his early shyness, was still more reserved, more cautious. In my mind Marcus's image appeared much larger than Alex's, and not just because I knew that Marcus could screw like a bunny in springtime.

"But it's not funny when he ruins rehearsal."

"Alex, Alex. Trust me, OK?" Marcus was smiling again. "He is not going to ruin rehearsal. Anyway, you look great onstage. Doesn't he look great onstage, Nicky?"

"Always has," I said.

"See?" Marcus said to Alex, as if he'd solved everything.

"You're insane. And you're no help," Alex said to me. "You always agree with him."

"Not always," I said. "Coney Island."

Marcus winced. "Oh, God. Not Coney Island again."

Alex sighed. "All right. Please. Even I don't want to hear about Coney Island again. Just don't ask me do that exercise with him. Ever."

"You have my word," Marcus said, holding the hug a moment longer before stepping back.

"You know, guys, there's going to be a rehearsal in here in a few minutes," I said, focusing my attention back on the task at hand. As stage manager I was supposed to be the responsible one. One of my stage-manager jobs was to keep everyone on schedule. That duty, along with setting up the space, prompting actors who forgot their lines in rehearsal, and keeping a record of the blocking, filled my evenings.

"And, as your producer, I would appreciate your concentration." Anna Mikasa announced her arrival from a spot halfway down the side aisle.

"Nominal producer," Marcus said.

"Temporary," Alex added.

"Titular producer?" I turned in my seat to look at Anna. "I think that one's new."

"You all suck. You know that?"

"Thank you," the three of us answered in unison.

"Yeah, yeah, yeah. So what happened? Why is Herb in the lobby swearing that all he ever wanted was a simple frock and garden of his own?"

"We didn't do anything, Anna," Alex said. "He's a pain in the ass."

"There was just a simple disagreement on the usefulness of an acting exercise." Marcus started to collect the newspaper clippings.

She waited, but no one said anything more.

"I see. You want to add anything, Shemp?" she asked me.

"Ah . . . we have ten minutes till rehearsal, and I need the stage now?"

"Guys, you have got to be nicer to him. You know he feels like an outsider with us."

In this context "us" was a very special term. Anna was not just referring to the four of us. It was understood by each of us that she was referring to "the Classmates," a term that had always required a capital letter. The twenty-one of us had spent four years working, playing, eating, and sleeping together seven days a week for ten months (minimum) out of each year. We learned a great deal at school, but at times the entire experience played out like an extended slumber party/summer camp that left us completely interdependent and totally exasperated with each other. After school we'd almost gone our separate ways, making fitful starts at the post-conservatory life. The pull of familiarity had proven too strong for some; twelve of my classmates had formed the Good Company.

I wasn't officially part of the company. Several months after graduation I'd gone to Los Angeles for half a year, but the West Coast didn't settle well with my Northeast sympathies. Back in New York the Good Company was being founded to keep everyone busy. They wanted me to join, but I kept slipping in and out of the city, most recently to work in western Pennsylvania the previous summer. I returned from that adventure with a boyfriend who turned out to be my geographic opposite. After six months in New York he had headed west.

Now it was midwinter—January in New York City—and I was single and between work. This combination of circumstances allowed me to sign on for just one production: an all-male version of Shakespeare's *A Midsummer Night's Dream*.

Don't get me wrong: it wasn't that I disliked my classmates. Exactly the opposite. I knew them all too well and had, over our four years of near-continuous exposure, grown fond of each in one way or another. It was that familiarity, that intense closeness, that even allowed me to finally get over Marcus and forgive him for trashing our relationship. But in the end that exceptional intimacy took its toll. I was always happy to see them, but only in small doses.

Anna, however, had wanted me for this show.

ABOUT THE AUTHOR

Chuck Zito has spent most of his adult life working in theaters. A graduate of Carnegie Mellon University Department of Drama, he recently left his post as executive director of Diversionary Theatre in San Diego. He now lives in New York City. *A Habit for Death* is his first novel, with more Nicky D'Amico mysteries to come.